Forbidden Son

by

Loretta C. Rogers

This is a work of fiction. Names, characters, places, and incidents are either the product of the author's imagination or are used fictitiously, and any resemblance to actual persons living or dead, business establishments, events, or locales, is entirely coincidental.

Forbidden Son

Cover Art by *Rae Monet, Inc. Design*

The Wild Rose Press
PO Box 708
Adams Basin, NY 14410-0708
Visit us at www.thewildrosepress.com

Publishing History
First Vintage Rose Edition, 2012
Print ISBN 978-1-61217-000-8

Published in the United States of America

He towered over her, his stare drilling into her. His eyes seemed to capture her from hair to high-heeled shoes. Clearing her throat, she tried to appear businesslike.

"Have I changed so much that you don't recognize me, Tripp?" This wasn't at all the way she had rehearsed the scene in her head. She didn't blink an eye—afraid any reaction might betray her uncertainty.

"Look, miss, I don't have time for twenty questions. I meet a lot of people, if—"

She wanted him to remember, to remember her, to remember—what? That seventeen years ago she had walked away from him? That she hadn't had the courage to stand up to his father and fight for her position in the life of the man she loved. That for sixteen years she had raised the son he never knew existed. She should never have left Tripp. So much guilt, for so many mistakes. She had no one to blame but herself.

She lifted her eyes to his. "Seventeen years ago, in Charleston, South Carolina, I asked you to take me for a ride in your shiny white BMW."

The silence of the office closed in around her.

Dedication

To all the military men and women—
Those who have sacrificed for my freedom
And those who are still fighting today.
God bless you all.

Chapter One

Washington, D.C.
1980

Dear Senator Hartwell,
Seventeen years ago we—
Honey Belle Garrett crumpled another sheet of hotel stationery, tossed it toward the wastebasket, and missed. The numerous wads of paper scattered over the hotel room's carpet reminded her of giant dustbunnies.

Dear Tripp,
Do you remember when—
She bent over a fresh sheet of paper and scrawled the few words only to abandon the thoughts. Frustrated, she pushed from the chair and padded, stocking-footed, to the bathroom for a temporary escape from the task she dreaded.

She leaned against the sink to look at herself in the mirror, swallowing convulsively as she peered at the pale reflection with its haunted eyes.

Dragging in a deep shuddering breath, Honey Belle wondered how she would explain to a United States senator that seventeen years ago he'd fathered a child.

Her child.

His child.

Now she was in Washington, D.C. with their son, who in two days would be introduced as a junior page in Congress.

In a few short weeks her life had transformed from that of a single mother happily in charge of her

1

own quiet world, teaching rambunctious third graders and cheering at football games for her son and his teammates, to that of a woman who felt as if she were marching toward the gallows. She looked down and saw her hands were shaking. Strange, she was usually a confident, self-assured woman.

"Damn," she whispered, "what am I doing here? I should have stayed in Georgia." And then she reminded herself of the importance of meeting with the senator before he and her son accidentally bumped into each other.

After splashing her face with cold water, she wearily returned to the bedroom.

On the desk lay two pictures. She ran a loving finger across the image of her sixteen-year-old son. The other photo was of his father at the age of twenty-two. The two were twins, seemingly, and this frightened Honey Belle. Neither son nor father knew the other existed.

Picking up the telephone, she dialed the hotel restaurant and ordered a pot of coffee and a peach turnover. She needed something strong and black to clear her head while she searched for the elusive words to pen in the note requesting a meeting with the senator.

While she waited for room service, she paced back and forth, aware she had a hard furrow to hoe.

She answered the rap on the door almost like an automaton. "Who is it?"

"Room service. You ordered a carafe of coffee and a peach popover?"

Honey Belle removed the security chain and opened the door. "Thank you." Handing the room steward a gratuity for his services, she accepted the tray.

She placed the refreshments on a table next to a wingback chair, retrieved a stack of stationery and a pen from the desk, and then, inhaling the rich aroma of the coffee, settled in the chair and poured a cup. As she savored the black liquid, she closed her eyes and tried to arrange her scattered emotions into cohesive thoughts. How could she trust this man not to dupe her?

With a long sigh, Honey Belle opened her eyes and reached for the popover. "When all else fails, eat sweets."

Still restless, she wandered again to the bathroom and turned on the tub's hot and cold water faucets, checking the temperature before she went into the bedroom for her gown and robe. She found her makeup bag, opened it and removed her electric razor, then undressed, tossing her skirt and blouse on the bed.

Taking the razor with her, she returned to the bathroom, turned off the faucets, set a towel where she could reach it, reached down and tested the water, and then stepped in, gingerly.

She liked the way the bath relaxed her, and slid lower into the water. The movement created warm, undulating waves that washed over her body and brought brittle memories of a particular nighttime swim at South Carolina's Folley Beach.

She drew in a deep breath and exhaled slowly as she ran her hands over her naked body. It was almost as good at the age of the age of thirty-five as it had been at nineteen. Her stomach was flat, breasts softly rounded and legs slender. The sensual movement of the water evoked memories of tender caresses by the man she'd loved and thought had loved her, too.

Resting her head on the back of the tub, she closed her eyes, allowing her thoughts to drift back to the year nineteen sixty-four and a sultry June day in Charleston, South Carolina. The day she'd met Tripp Harlan Hartwell III.

Her daydream had rapidly become a nightmare.

She was considered the poor white trash from the wrong side of the tracks—a high school dropout who flipped hamburgers for a living, with no real plans for the future.

Tripp Harlan Hartwell III was the rich college boy destined for greatness. To say it was love at first sight for Honey Belle and Tripp sounded like a tired cliché. The fact remained: they did fall in love, and it was that passion which had set the course for disaster.

She soaked awhile longer in the tub, then turned her attention to shaving her legs. The water grew cold, and she toweled off and slipped into the nightgown and robe. Sitting on the edge of the bed, she checked the time. Almost nine o'clock.

With her son safely housed at the residential hall provided for pages, she had nothing but time on her hands until tomorrow, when she hoped to meet with the senator.

She went to the closet and dug out her suitcase. Unzipping the top, she removed a scrapbook and a large manila envelope—the same envelope Tripp's father had handed her so many years ago—the one that held demeaning pictures of her past. The pictures he'd used to force her to leave South Carolina.

She didn't like having her life turned upside down. Once had been enough. The insecure part of her feared she was about to open Pandora's Box, but the mother part of her was a fierce tigress ready to protect her son against unfathomable hurts.

She removed the robe and climbed into bed. Plumping the pillows with her fists, she propped against the headboard and tucked the quilt around her as if it were a safe cocoon. Then, almost reverently, she opened the scrapbook.

For a while, she stared at the handsome face smiling up at her. The face of the man who'd promised to marry her. The man who'd left her alone and pregnant. Standing next to him was a person she'd hidden from and feared for seventeen years. Finally, she said to herself, "There's no turning back now. This is what it's all about."

She pushed back the damp tendrils of blonde hair as she turned the page and allowed her thoughts to drift backward as she relived all the events that led her to this time and place.

Chapter Two

Charleston, SC
1964

Honey Belle Garrett was born in rural South Carolina, on the wrong side of the tracks. In most social circles that translated into *poor white trash*. She never thought of herself as *trash*, just poor.

Her daddy worked at the pulpwood mill and her mama flipped hamburgers at the Burger Bin. As much as she longed for nice clothes and sweet smelling perfume, Honey Belle knew it took both of her parents' incomes to keep food on the table and pay the rent. Every so often, her mother managed to scrape together enough money to buy a few niceties. All that changed when her daddy had a heart attack. Sick as he was, he still managed to work a couple of days a week.

The rental house Honey Belle shared with her parents was old and musty-smelling. The fans kept the air moving, stirring up dust, and whimsical daydreams.

****

On a sultry March evening in 1964, Honey Belle had barely finished washing the supper dishes when her mama called, "Honey Belle, come sit on the back steps for a spell."

"Just a sec, Mama, I still need to wipe the stove."

When Honey Belle pushed the screened door open, she watched her mother grimace at the door's familiar squeak. Settling on the step, she wrapped her arms around her knees and waited for her mother to speak.

Delilah Garrett mopped the sweat from her forehead with a hankie so threadbare Honey Belle could almost see the moon through the dingy white material. "Lordy, Honey Belle, it's only March and hotter'n Hades. Reckon we're in for a scorcher of a summer."

Even though Honey Belle was an only child, her mother rarely gave her the time of day unless it was *Honey Belle, do this* or *Honey Belle, I need you to—*

This is how she knew something important was about to happen when her mother invited her to sit with her on the backdoor steps.

"Whaz up, Mama?"

Honey Belle's stomach clenched when her mother's mouth tightened and she turned a slit-eyed gazed toward her. "I swannie, Honey Belle. Don't young'uns speak English no more?"

Ignoring the chastisement, Honey Belle concentrated on the stars, and vowed that someday she would leave South Carolina to seek fame and fortune as an actress in Hollywood. Lost in the daydream, she vowed to never again wear hand-me-down clothes or shoes, and she'd have a chauffeur drive her to the ritziest shops.

Her mother's words jolted her back to reality. "Honey Belle, there's an opening at the Burger Bin. I talked to my boss. He said you could start next Monday. It's a full-time job."

It seemed the stars exploded and all Honey Belle's hopes and dreams of a different life shattered into a million pieces. She shifted uncomfortably on the wooden step. "I can't work full time, Mama. There's still two months left of school, and next year I'll be a senior."

"You're sixteen. What with your daddy sick and only working a few days a week, it's high time you

7

started pullin' your weight around here. Why, I've been working since I was fourteen. You ain't no better, little girl."

"But, Mama, if I quit school, I can't go to college. It isn't fair."

Her mother snorted, her voice a sarcastic sneer. "College? Humph. Big plans for a girl who ain't got no money. How do you 'spect to pay for books and such? Besides, it takes brains, which by the grades on your report card, you ain't got."

An awkward silence passed between them. Honey Belle silently admitted she was currently majoring in flirting and boys—especially those on the football team.

She pushed aside the ache building in her chest to plead her case. "Please, Mama. At least let me finish out the year. What difference will two months make?"

Even though it was too dark to see, she knew her mother sat with her legs crossed. She had a habit of jiggling her right foot. The wooden steps vibrated with the rapid movement. "I'll tell you, little girl. It makes the difference between paying the rent and being set out on the street. It makes the difference between puttin' food on the table or starving. It makes the difference in havin' enough money to buy your daddy's medicine. That's what it means."

Honey Belle swiped a finger under her eyes and drew in a deep breath. "What if I worked after school? Wouldn't that be okay, Mama?"

Her mother stood and, in a rare gesture of affection, patted her daughter on the shoulder. "Doctor said your daddy cain't work no more. We're three months behind on the rent, and Mr. Ellerby said he cain't tote us another month."

"I know things are bad, Mama, but with an education I can get a good job and help make life easier for you and daddy. Please, Mama, please don't make me quit school."

The sorrowful sigh her mother heaved pierced Honey Belle's heart. "I had hopes and dreams once upon a time. We all do, Honey Belle. Fact of the matter is, life usually gets in the way."

As much as Honey Belle wanted that intimate moment to last, it passed as quickly as the fluttering wings of a night moth. Her mother's next words brooked no nonsense. "You'll march down to the principal's office tomorrow and withdraw yourself from school, or I'll do it for you. Monday you'll start the wake-up shift. I'll stay with your daddy until you get home at two-thirty."

At that moment Honey Belle wanted to throw up. She didn't bother to hide the groan that rose from the pit of her stomach. The wake-up shift started at five in the morning. Her vision had adjusted to the dark. In the moon's rays, she saw the steel in her mother's eyes, and the iron set of her jaw. When she got that look of absolute stubbornness, Honey Belle knew nothing would change her mother's mind. Not even the devil himself.

****

Time seemed to take wings, and before Honey Belle knew it, three years had raced by. Three years of baking biscuits and flipping hamburgers. Three years of eavesdropping on the conversations of high school kids sitting in the fast food joint's booths, sipping colas and talking about which college they planned to attend, the careers they wanted to pursue. Three years of realizing that dropping out of high school had been a huge mistake.

Never in her wildest imaginings did Honey Belle Garrett dream she was about to make an even bigger mistake, one that would change her life forever.

9

Chapter Three

When Tripp Hartwell III pulled to the Burger Bin's drive-through window in his shiny white BMW convertible, Honey Belle knew he was somebody special. A notorious flirt, she leaned out the window and handed him the order of double cheeseburger, hold the onions, fries, and a cola. She offered him her most seductive smile. "How 'bout a ride in your fancy car?"

She wanted to swim in those blue eyes that reminded her of the ocean on a sunny day. When he smiled, his teeth were perfectly straight and matched the color of his shiny white car. "I don't ride girls in my convertible unless there's a very good reason, darlin'."

She leaned closer to catch the subtle hint of his cologne. Expensive, she guessed, and wanted to snuggle against his chiseled jawline. "Today is my birthday. Is that reason enough?"

He flashed a wink. "Ah, your birthday. I'm not interested in jailbait. What are you, sixteen?"

Still leaning out the window, Honey Belle squeezed her armpits together to accentuate the mounds of her breasts. "When I get home there'll be a birthday cake with nineteen candles on it. I reckon that makes me old enough to ride in your convertible." She returned his wink. "And with the top down, of course."

He arched an eyebrow. It was a simple gesture, but one that pitter-pattered Honey Belle's heart. "In that case, birthday girl, what time is your shift over?"

"First, my name is Honey Belle Garrett. And second, my shift ends at two o'clock. I'll meet you out front, Mr.—"

"Tripp Hartwell the Third."

"My, my. Fancy name to go with your fancy car, Mr. Tripp Hartwell the Third." She smiled pleasantly.

"*Honey Belle*...are you as sweet as your name?" Before popping a French fry in his mouth, he pursed his lips into a kiss. The way he looked at her caused her heart to bang unevenly against her ribcage. She gave herself a little hug when he revved the engine and drove off.

A loud harrumph sounded behind her. She turned to face Carla, a round-faced, red-cheeked girl who worked the counter. "I can see you're busting out all over to say something, Carla. Go ahead, spit it out."

"Hope you ain't countin' on that rich boy to keep his promise."

"You're such a pessimist, Carla. He's a man of his word."

"First, don't be usin' words I don't understand, and second, what makes you so all-fired certain he's *a man of his word*?"

Honey Belle shrugged her shoulders up and down. "I just know."

"Uh-huh. If he does show up, it'll be 'cause he's lookin' to get himself a free piece of tail. And the way you were hanging out that window, you had Fr-e-e-b-i-e written all over your bad self."

A sense of euphoria swept over Honey Belle. "Why Carla Biggers, I do believe you're jealous."

"Jealous? I don't think so."

Honey Belle batted her eyelashes. "Then I'd thank you kindly if you'd mind your own business."

"You know, I read a book once. It was about a girl named Cinderella. You mess with the likes of

Mr. Rich Fancy Car, and you'll find out soon 'nuf he ain't Prince Charmin'. 'Specially when he finds out where you live and meets your wicked mama."

Honey Belle offered an indignant sniff. "I read the same book, Carla. It had a happy ending. And my mother's not wicked, just... Well, she has a lot on her mind."

Carla chuckled as she placed an order on a tray and handed it to a customer. "I'll be the first to say *I told you so* when he doesn't show."

****

No one was more surprised than Honey Belle when Carla whirled into the employee's bathroom. "It's three minutes of two, and you ain't gonna believe it, H.B."

"What on earth are you talking about, Carla? Believe what?"

"Poke your head out the door and take a peek. He's here."

"You mean...*he's* here?" Frantic, Honey Belle snatched several paper towels from the dispenser, ran them under the faucet, squeezed out the excess water and wiped under her armpits. Like Carla, she hadn't truly expected him to show up. "You got any deodorant, Carla? I can't go riding in a convertible smelling like sweaty French fries."

"Nope. Only thing I got in my purse is condoms. Pays to be prepared, you never know when you'll score, girlfriend."

Honey Belle arched an eyebrow and shot her coworker a sarcastic scowl. "A ride in a convertible doesn't mean he or me wants to *score*."

"Hm-huh, I'm just sayin'." Carla shoved the cellophane packet into Honey Belle's apron pocket. "'Sides, I got two young'uns to prove what happens when you don't think you're gonna...*score*."

Honey Belle groaned as she pulled the rubber band from her hair. She raked her fingers through the long blonde strands, gathered the hair, and pulled it into a neat ponytail. She applied a fresh coat of Passion Pink gloss to her lips, and pinched her cheeks to add a little color. "Wish me luck, Carla."

"You're gonna need it, H.B. He's a heartbreaker, for sure."

Honey Belle was fearful Tripp could hear the thrumming of her heart as she approached him. "You're here."

"You didn't expect me to show?"

"Well, I wasn't sure. Some guys like to feed a girl a line of hooey."

"I'm not some guy."

"I know, with a name like Tripp Hartwell the Third, that must make you somebody."

As if wanting to change the subject, he said, "Your chariot awaits, birthday girl."

She'd dated lots of boys. Not one had made her feel giddy. Today, she was giddy. She allowed him to escort her to his car. When she reached for the door handle, Tripp covered her hand with his. "A gentleman always opens the car door for a lady."

"Oh, sure." She cringed inside, fearing her ignorance was showing. It was the first time anyone had ever opened a door for her. She smiled, and as she slid into the seat, the plush fabric felt as if she'd sat in a bucket of downy feathers.

"Ready?"

"Huh?" Honey Belle wondered why she was acting like a dunce. She wondered if he thought she didn't understand English.

He walked around to his side of the car and, in one fluid movement, sat behind the steering wheel. He pulled a pair of sunglasses from his pocket and adjusted them on the bridge of his nose.

Then, as if he'd forgotten something important, he reached behind the seat. With a smile that would light up a cloudy day, he handed her a single red rose. "To the birthday girl."

Wishing she had a pair of sunglasses, she blinked back a rush of tears as she lifted the flower to her nose. No one had ever given her flowers. "It's a wonderful gift. Thank you."

"Want to go watch the submarine races?" A lopsided grin kinked up the corner of his lips.

Filled with hot-cold prickles of irritation, she tossed the rose at him. "I wasn't born yesterday, Mr. Hartwell."

When he raised his eyebrows in mock surprise, Honey Belle balled her hands into fists to keep from slapping him. "For your information, just because I flirted with you doesn't mean I'm easy."

He looked at her as if she'd lost her mind. "I'm sorry, Miss Garrett. I didn't mean to imply—"

"Of course you did. Any idiot knows a guy wants to make out when he drives a girl to the beach to watch the *submarine races*." Her voice increased an octave. She shook with anger. "My friend Carla warned me about the likes of you. I didn't believe her."

"Hey, you've got me all wrong."

"Never mind about riding in your fancy convertible. Besides, it's almost time for my mother's shift to start. I have to get the truck home."

"I'll follow you. You can leave the truck. Accept my apology and allow me to take you to dinner." He grinned. "And no submarine races, I promise."

His smile helped soften her aggravation. "Another time, maybe. My father is sick and requires round-the-clock care."

"If that's a promise, I'll hold you to it, Miss Honey Belle Garrett."

She'd probably never see him again, so where was the harm in agreeing with him? "If you say so."

Eager to make her escape, she ran to the old

pickup truck. Gripping the steering wheel, she allowed her mind to drift, creating a hero of a white knight who would win her love through bravery and integrity, and by the protection of others. Woven in with these traits, he'd have to have the most important quality of all—he'd have to love her unconditionally and forever.

It wasn't until she drove into the driveway of her house and switched off the engine that she realized she'd left the rose on the seat of Tripp's car.

She sighed deeply. Men like her hero existed only in the world of fantasy and imagination. None were flesh and bone. And even if such a man existed, why would he want the likes of her?

Leaning against the seat, she wondered if Tripp meant what he said about meeting again. She'd heard what guys like him wanted from girls like her. Still, her heart warmed toward him. Suddenly, she very much wanted to know him.

"You gonna sit there daydreaming your life away? I gotta go to work."

Sighing, Honey Belle pushed all thoughts of Tripp Hartwell the Third from her mind as she opened the door and relinquished the truck to her mother.

Chapter Four

Sun poured through the Burger Bin's large picture windows. The usual crowd of noisy students gathered in booths while Honey Belle worked in the back, loading the dishwashers. Her job wasn't glamorous, but she enjoyed it—usually. Today, the exhaust fan was broken. Despite a requisition, no one had come around to repair it.

"H.B."

"What, Carla?"

"You ain't gonna believe who just walked in."

"I'm too hot and tired to play twenty questions."

"Then get your bad self up here and take a peek. It's him."

Honey Belle peered around the large industrial refrigerator and spied Tripp standing at the counter. "Holy poop hill, what's he doing here?" He was holding two red roses. A foreboding shiver ran down her spine—one she quickly dismissed.

Her hand automatically touched her sweat-plastered hair. "I can't let him see me like this."

"If he's got any smarts about him, he'll know you can't look like a beauty queen while flippin' hamburgers over a hot round-top all day. If he don't, then he ain't worth your time of day."

Carla made a fluttering motion with her hands as if shooing Honey Belle to the front counter.

Smoothing her trembling fingers down the side of her grease-splattered uniform, Honey Belle scooted around the refrigerator. She longed for a spritz of her mother's treasured eau de cologne water.

She was certain his electric blue eyes were magnets drawing her to him. Her voice seemed to come out in a breathy whisper. "What are you doing here?"

He held out the roses. "One birthday rose for a lovely young lady, and one for a peace offering. I didn't mean to offend you, yesterday, Honey Belle. And if you'd still like to take that ride, my chariot awaits."

She inhaled the faint scent of his cologne, a designer fragrance to match his masculinity. Then she lifted her gaze, fully intending to accept his offer.

"I...I'd love to go for a ride with you." Love to fly to the moon, if he asked, she thought, feeling entirely too giddy for a girl of nineteen.

She returned his smile and could no more have taken back her words than she could have taken away her father's illness. "Can't."

She hadn't meant to cause Tripp to wince, just like she hadn't meant for her voice to sound abrupt.

"I see. Using the father excuse again?"

"It isn't an excuse. Daddy suffers from congestive heart failure. He's in a wheelchair and has to wear an oxygen mask."

She thought his voice sounded contrite. "Once again, I seem to have put my foot where it doesn't belong. At this rate, I'll owe you a dozen roses."

She hugged the flowers to her chest. "Tomorrow is Saturday. I'll ask my cousin to sit with Daddy for a few hours."

"Tell me where you live and I'll pick you up at five."

"I...um...I live at 1423 Barrington Street."

When he turned to leave, she said, "Thank you, again, for the roses."

Carla's voice startled Honey Belle, causing her to jump. "I notice you didn't give him directions to *your* house."

Honey Belle's eyes narrowed to slits. "Mind your own business, Carla."

****

Too embarrassed to have Tripp see the dilapidated rental house where she lived, Honey Belle had given him a false address in the better section of Charleston's upper middle-class neighborhood.

She stood next to an elm tree at the end of a sidewalk, in front of an antebellum home with a sweeping front porch, a neatly trimmed yard, bushes bursting with red azaleas, all surrounded by a white picket fence.

Whatever guilt she felt disappeared when she glimpsed his car driving slowly down the street toward her. She lifted her hand and waved. Then she whispered a little prayer, hoping Tripp knew no one in this neighborhood.

She pressed her hands to her stomach, drew in a deep breath, and blew it out slowly.

Like a proper lady, she waited for him to slow the car to a halt, get out and open the door for her.

"Hi."

"Hi." She smiled.

"You look nice, Honey Belle. I like your hair down." He leaned over and gave her a perfunctory kiss. She felt her cheeks grow warm as he caressed her lips.

"Where are we going?"

"Not the submarine races." He winked and she laughed. "I made reservations for us at the Pirate's Den. I hope you like seafood."

"Love it." She wished the butterflies in her stomach would stop flitting around. Tripp Hartwell was way out of her league. She shouldn't be with him. She didn't know proper table etiquette for an expensive restaurant—or, for that matter, any

18

restaurant. What if she made a fool of herself? What if she didn't know which fork to use? And her seafood experience was limited to fried catfish. She'd always dreamed of lobster. Lobster... No, too expensive.

This was a bad idea. The thought came too late. Tripp guided the convertible into an empty parking space and before she could say *scat* he stood at her door, offering his hand.

With his hand pressed against the small of her back, he guided her toward the restaurant. "I made reservations for the porch. Hope you don't mind."

"Hm. The sound of the waves lapping the shore is soothing. I find it quite relaxing." She hoped she sounded sophisticated.

A hostess greeted them. "Mr. Hartwell, you're at table number twelve."

"Good evening, Jenna, and thank you."

After they were seated, the hostess said, "Your waitress will be right with you."

Honey Belle leaned forward. "She knew you. Do you bring all your dates here?"

Tripp reached across the table and tweaked her nose. "Only the pretty ones."

The waitress came to the table, introduced herself, and poured water into their glasses. "Would you care for a cocktail?"

Honey Belle glanced over the menu at Tripp questioningly.

"Go ahead. You can have anything you want," he said.

"I don't know." She lifted a shoulder into a shrug.

"Do you want a beer, wine, iced tea?"

She met his gaze hesitantly. "Wine, I think?"

"Wine it is." He looked at the waitress who waited patiently. "We'll have the Chardonnay. 1950."

"Bottle or glass?" the young woman asked.

"Just a glass." Honey Belle wrinkled her nose. "First date," she said jokingly. "I wouldn't want to get tipsy and make a fool of myself, would I?" She groaned inside. What a stupid thing to say.

The waitress laughed and walked away to fill their drink order.

Honey Belle glanced across the table at Tripp gazing at her. "I'm sorry. I didn't mean to embarrass you." For the life of her, she couldn't read his thoughts.

"You didn't."

The expression on his face told her she hadn't.

She smiled to herself as she concentrated on placing the red linen napkin across her lap.

"What would you like?"

"Like?" His question puzzled Honey Belle.

He opened the menu and handed it to her. She almost gasped aloud at the prices. Her eyes scanned down both columns. "Holy poop hill, we could buy a week's worth of groceries for the cost of one surf and turf."

She laughed. She wanted to reach up and smack her forehead.

He laughed with her, reaching for his water.

"You must think I have *stupid* engraved across my brow."

"I find you refreshing. I like your wisecracks—especially 'holy poop hill.'" He smiled in a way that made her feel strange.

She had to stop this or he'd guess she didn't live in the fancy house on Barrington Street.

"Thanks. So what shall we have to eat?" She looked back at the menu.

"The scallops in the white wine and garlic is very good." He frowned. "Garlic? Hmm, that leaves kissing you goodnight out."

"Honestly, Tripp, I'm so hungry I could eat a—" She'd almost said *cow*. "Why don't you order for me?"

The waitress returned with their glasses of wine. While Tripp placed their order, Honey Belle savored the first sip. Chardonnay, 1950, certainly tasted better than the cheap wine her mother brought home.

Fussing with the edge of the linen napkin in her lap, Honey Belle searched for something to say. She inwardly cringed when the question popped out. "So, Tripp, do you work?"

He sat the long-stemmed goblet aside. "I work hard at my studies."

"College?"

"Yes. I'm attending Harvard School of Law in September."

Honey Belle pursed her lips. She caught herself before she whistled to indicate she was impressed. "Well, if you don't work at a job, how can you afford such a fancy car?"

"My father is Judge T. Harlan Hartwell. You may have heard of him."

Honey Belle sat a little straighter in her chair. "You mean, as in Judge Hartwell that's always in the newspaper?"

Tripp offered her a smile. "The very same."

Honey Belle's insides quivered. Tripp wasn't merely a rich college guy, he was the son of a judge—a judge with a reputation for not showing mercy to anyone in his courtroom. She needed to break off this budding relationship before it got out of hand.

"What about your mother, what does she do?"

"My mother loves to garden, research her family history, and—"

Honey Belle didn't miss the fleeting shadow of sadness that caused Tripp to stop speaking. "What is it about your mother that makes you sad, Tripp?"

She liked the way his eyes crinkled at the corners when he smiled. "My mother was forty-one years old when I born. She's like a magnolia whose petals are easily bruised, turn brown, then wither away."

For the life of her, Honey Belle didn't know what the analogy meant. "I-I'm not sure I know what you mean, Tripp. Is your mother ill?"

He nodded. "Not in body. It's her mind. It slips away a little more each day."

Honey Belle reached across the table and intertwined her fingers with his. "I'm sorry. It's the same with my daddy. Guess we have something in common, don't we?"

The next hour and a half flew by, and before she knew it, Tripp was paying the tab. "How about a walk on the beach before I take you home?"

As much as she wanted to feel wet sand squishing between her toes and, perhaps, hold hands with the handsome man seated across from her, a little voice inside her head sounded a warning. And as good as the first glass of wine tasted, the second glass had left her feeling all warm and fuzzy inside, and perhaps a little tipsy, too. "It's late. I wouldn't want to worry my parents."

Honey Belle loved her parents. Between work and sitting with her father, she didn't often date. Tonight she felt like Cinderella. But like all good fairy tales, it was time to bring this one to an end.

Sheer and utter dread weighed heavy in the pit of her stomach as Tripp drove toward Barrington Street. What if he insisted on walking her to the front door? What if he asked to meet her parents? What if...what if?

When he pulled to the curb and shut off the engine, relief washed over Honey Belle with a fierce intensity that left her weak in the knees. She said, "The lights are out. I guess my parents went to bed early."

"Too bad, I wanted to meet them."

"My father doesn't respond well to company. The least little thing wears him out."

"Another time, when it's more convenient."

She waited for Tripp to open the car door. A true southern gentleman, she thought. Not like the rednecks she'd dated who reeked of cigarette smoke.

"I'd like to kiss you goodnight, Honey Belle."

She lifted on her toes and ran her hand upward over his chest. Very slowly, never breaking eye contact, she raised her mouth to his. "Hm. Aren't you glad you didn't have the shrimp with garlic sauce?"

He laughed, and so did she. "Good night, Tripp."

She stood next to the elm tree and watched until the taillights on his car were no longer visible.

The sky had grown dark, but the streetlights illuminated the sidewalks and the older homes lining both sides of the street.

She slipped off her high heels and, holding one in each hand, raced the full four blocks to the gas station where she'd left her old pickup truck. Thirty minutes later, she crossed the railroad tracks and rattled down a washboard road that the county refused to maintain. A few minutes later, she pulled into her own driveway. It wasn't a nice place to live.

She grabbed her purse, and dug out her key before she opened the screened door and let herself in the house.

The house was small, with a living room that also served as the dining area, a galley kitchen, two bedrooms, and a bath. Beyond the back steps was a yard littered with old car parts and rusting barrels overflowing with bags of garbage.

She never wanted Tripp Hartwell the Third to know where she lived. If he asked her out for a second date, she'd make certain she met him at the elm tree on Barrington Street.

Chapter Five

Tripp whistled a nameless tune as he let himself into the kitchen of his parent's stately home. What made the house, though, was the back porch, which his grandfather had closed in with glass panels. Even in the middle of winter it was warm and cozy on the sun porch. Between the porch and his mother's green thumb, plants thrived there as if living in a greenhouse. Beyond the porch, in the backyard, was a swimming pool and a well-groomed garden of flowering plants, stone paths, and dribbling water fountains, his mother's pride and joy.

He went to the refrigerator and poured a glass of milk and helped himself to a man-sized scoop of peach cobbler. He could hear the television going and the sound of a familiar newscaster's voice as he reported on the unrest in Southeastern Asia. Specifically a place called Vietnam.

He ambled toward the den and sank deep into the plush leather sofa made of hand-tooled Moroccan leather. "Think there'll be a war?"

Tripp's father cast his son a casual glance. "The way politics are running now, there's no doubt about it. My guess is it'll be a money war."

"What about my draft status, Dad?"

"Nothing to worry about, son. You still have your college eminence. That and my political influence will keep you on the home front. Can't have your mother all upset and worried about her only child going off to war, now can we?"

Tripp didn't think of himself as a coward. He

just didn't see much sense in getting killed for a senseless cause. "No, sir. The last thing I'd want is to cause mother unnecessary upset."

"She's a true southern belle, as delicate as those hothouse flowers she's so fond of."

"Joe Brimley quit college to join the Marines."

The elder Hartwell swiveled around to face his son. "The devil, you say."

Until she spoke, neither son nor father was aware of the delicate-boned woman who stood in the doorway with her hands clutched at her throat. "*La,* Nancy Carol is surely beside herself with grief." She sat on the arm of the sofa and placed her hand on Tripp's arm. "I couldn't bear it if you went off to war. We have a long and esteemed heritage of brave family members who served our country. Some didn't survive. Promise me, son, promise you won't..." A sob tore from her throat.

Tripp's father pushed from the overstuffed chair, made of the same leather as the sofa, and went to the liquor cabinet, where he removed a bottle of amaretto. He filled a snifter and handed it to his wife. "There...there, Mary Alice. No need to fret yourself. Our boy will attend Harvard just as planned."

As he handed his wife the glass, he glanced over her head to his son. "Tripp, why don't you escort your mother upstairs? Tell her about the girl you took to dinner tonight."

Tripp nodded. He lifted his mother's free hand into his. "I met a girl with the most unique name."

"*La,* is that so? What is it?"

"Miss Honey Belle Garrett."

"Garrett. I once knew some Garretts from Tennessee. I believe they were sharecroppers." She wrinkled her nose as if the word *sharecropper* had soured in her mouth.

"She's a true-blood South Carolinian, mother."

"Honey Belle is a sweet name. I'd love to meet her, Tripp. Shall I arrange a small soirée?"

"Not yet, mother. We only met yesterday."

"Where did you meet this young woman?"

"I stopped in for a hamburger. We, ah, bumped into each other." He didn't dare tell his mother that Honey Belle worked at a burger joint. Southern aristocracy frowned upon common laborers. Come to think of it, why would a girl who lived in a beautiful antebellum home on Barrington Street have to flip hamburgers? She did say her father was sick. She did drive a beat-up old truck. With the world getting ready to turn upside down over unrest in Southeastern Asia, and with the drop in the economy, times were hard. Maybe she was earning college tuition. He shoved the thought aside.

At the top of the stairs, Tripp guided his mother to her bedroom suite. He kissed the top of her head. "Goodnight, Mother. Rest well."

When he turned to leave, she said, "I'm not as addle-patted as your father thinks. It's just, sometimes, I seem to have a fog that covers my brain and I forget things."

The doctor had said Tripp's mother suffered from early on-set dementia. Tripp had been a change-of-life baby, born on his mother's forty-first birthday. Now at the age of sixty-three, she was a diminishing shadow of the woman who had loved afternoon tea parties with her lady friends, researching family heritage, and doting on her son and husband. He'd do anything to protect her.

His father, on the other hand, was a hardened criminal attorney, now a judge, who brooked no nonsense for those who broke the law. Even if Tripp hadn't planned to follow in his father's footsteps, it was expected that the day he graduated from Harvard Law School he would join his uncles at Hartwell, Hartwell, and Calhoun, Attorneys at Law.

Walking down the hall to his room, Tripp brushed his teeth, folded his clothes, and put on a fresh pair of boxers before climbing into bed. With his hands cupped behind his head, he replayed the evening with Honey Belle. She reminded him of an unrefined gem who needed a little polishing. He liked this girl and intended to ask her out again.

****

It was late, and Honey Belle knew her mother would be furious. Her mother's philosophy was *as long as you live under my roof, you'll abide by my rules.* And the rule for Honey Belle was, "Home before midnight on the weekends and home straight from work during the weekdays."

She'd often thought about getting an apartment, moving out on her own. Minimum wage didn't bring in much. Between her own and her mother's salaries, together, they managed to keep up with staying one month away from being evicted on the rent, from having the electric shut off, and with paying a little each month on her father's ever-growing mountain of doctor bills.

Moonlight passed through the broken window in her bedroom. With no money to replace it, she'd placed duct tape over the crack to keep the glass from falling in.

Wound up tighter than a corkscrew, Honey Belle knew she needed to sleep fast. She held the clock toward the moonlight. The hands indicated midnight. She set the alarm. Her wake-up time would come before she was ready. Sweat pooled between her breasts and she shucked off her nightgown, pulling the sheet up to cover her nude body. Her mother had once called her a Jezebel when she'd found her daughter sleeping buck naked. Honey Belle had responded with, "At least Jezebel is better than being named after a tangerine."

And then she'd asked, "Why did you name me

27

after a citrus fruit?"

Her mother had heaved a sigh. "It's an elegant name. Be proud of it because it's the only worthwhile thing I'll ever have to give to you."

The remembrance hurt. She wondered why she'd meant so little to her mother.

Honey Belle concentrated on the ceiling fan's whirring noise. She reached up and pulled the chain, turning the fan to a higher speed. A lot of good it did. For all the blades' movement, hot air stifled the room. She'd stake her life that Tripp's entire house was air conditioned. She longed for air conditioning. For her, such a luxury was as far away as the moon.

Drifting off to sleep, her thoughts centered on Tripp, she remembered he was two years older than herself. He had the chiseled features of a movie star. He was observant. His eyes seemed to watch everything. Maybe that's why he decided to become a lawyer. She found it bothersome that he seemed to read her every thought.

He was tall and strong. Not like some of the milksop college guys who patronized the Burger Bin. She liked everything about Tripp Hartwell the Third. Most of all she liked his voice. It was the kind of voice that announced football games, or belonged on the big screen. It was a voice that would make members on a jury sit up and listen.

In her heart she knew he was the kind of man she could trust to share her innermost secrets—her hopes and dreams for the future—and he would listen intently, promising to make them all come true. She hoped.

A cloud drifted in front of the moon, shutting out the light. She listened to the clock's rhythmic tick-tock, and imagined it saying, *He loves me, He loves me not, He loves me.*

Before drifting into sweet oblivion, she thought about how special the day had been, how special he was, and the warm way she had felt when he'd placed his hand on the small of her back and guided her toward the restaurant and her first taste of expensive wine. The way his eyes crinkled at the corners when he smiled. It was all too wonderful.

A shiver rippled through her body. For no good reason, she felt like crying. She pulled the sheet up and tucked it under her chin. Her mother had once said that sooner or later all good things come to an end. Meeting Tripp was a good thing. She hoped her mother was wrong.

It seemed she'd barely closed her eyes when she heard her mother's voice. The shrillness intruded into her dream, and she tried to shut it out. The voice shouted, this time more insistent. Honey Belle groaned. Surely it wasn't time to go to work.

"Honey Belle, help me."

Honey Belle sat up in bed. She blinked, trying to focus her eyes in the darkened room. Remembering she was naked, she groped the end of the bed searching for her nightshirt.

"Honey Belle, wake up. It's your father."

She pulled the nightshirt over her head, struggling to find the armholes. She stubbed her toe on the door jamb and crow-hopped to her parent's bedroom. "What is it, Mama? Another heart attack?"

"I don't know. Get the truck. We've got to get him to the hospital."

Honey Belle raced back to her room, switched on the light. She grabbed a pair of jeans and tugged them on under her nightshirt, then slipped her feet into a pair of sandals.

Slamming the back door behind her, she ran to the neighbor's house and, with both fists, banged on the front door. "Mr. Jimmy, wake up. We need your help."

She continued pounding on the door and calling the man's name until a light switched on and the door opened.

"It's two in the morning, girl. This'd better be important."

Honey Belle stepped back as the towering six-foot-five giant glared down at her. "It's daddy. Help me get him into the truck."

"Heart attack?"

"Maybe. Won't know until we get him to the hospital."

"Damned shame ambulances won't come to Shanty Groves."

Honey Belle ran to keep up with the giant's long strides.

"Couldn't afford one even if they did. Besides, I can get him to the hospital quicker if I drive."

Once they had her father settled on the front seat, Honey Belle thanked her neighbor and promised to bring him a sack of hamburgers with extra pickles as payment for his assistance.

She put the truck into gear and spewed dirt as she spun out of the driveway. The truck bounced and bucked as she tried to ease over the bumps. She spoke through gritted teeth. "Damn these potholes and double damn the county for not fixing them."

"Stop your cussing, girl. Concentrate on gettin' us to the hospital in one piece."

When the wheels hit the asphalt pavement, Honey Belle gunned the accelerator, praying the old motor wouldn't let her down because of the strain.

She heard the warning bells and saw the railroad crossing arm's red flashing lights as she approached the train tracks. She didn't have time to wait on a twenty-car freight train to inch by at a snail's pace. Her daddy's life depended on how fast she could get him to the emergency room.

"Trains comin', Honey Belle. I can see the engine's light."

Ignoring the tension in her mother's voice,

Honey Belle said, "I'm not stopping, Mama."

"The cross arms are comin' down, girl. You can't bust through 'em. The law'll put you in jail."

Honey Belle pressed down on the accelerator, asking the truck for more speed than she knew it had to give. "I'm driving around them, Mama. Hold Daddy tight and hang on."

She touched her father's arm. "I'm sorry, Daddy. I don't mean to hurt you."

The pain in his eyes flashed panic through her. The odometer read 60 miles per hour. Honey Belle had to beat the train to the crossing arms. She needed to get over the track before the arms came completely down. The thrum in her heart matched the pulsating veins in her temples. What if she didn't beat the train? She wiped a sweat-drenched palm down her jeans and then switched hands to dry the other one, too. She gripped the steering wheel.

The train whistle blasted, the engine's light flashed like a one-eyed Cyclops.

Honey Belle pushed for more speed—seventy miles per hour. It was a neck-and-neck race, with the train gaining. Seventy-five miles per hour...eighty. "Hold tight, Mama."

Honey Belle held the steering wheel in a death grip as the truck's tires hit the tracks with a vengeance. She didn't have time to see the terror in her mother's eyes as the truck went airborne.

Sparks flew from the truck's front bumper when it landed with a bounce that nearly jarred Honey Belle from the seat. She managed to glance over her shoulder to see freight cars whizzing down the track. She'd beat the train with only seconds to spare.

Her father moaned again. She listened to him struggling to breathe. "We're almost there, Daddy...you okay, Mama?"

"Besides being scared out of ten years of my life and hitting my head on the ceiling, I'm no worse for wear."

Five miles down the road, Honey Belle guided the truck to a halt under the emergency room's portico. Her legs trembled as she jumped to the ground. She commanded her mother, "Stay here. I'll go get someone to help."

As soon as the ER had admitted her father, Honey Belle's mother said, "You go on to work. Tell the boss man about your daddy."

Her mother's sallow complexion and dark circles under her eyes worried Honey Belle. She chalked it up to stress and exhaustion. "You gonna stay with Daddy, Mama?"

"For a while. Whatever this costs, heaped on top of what we already owe, sometimes I don't think we'll ever have two nickels to rub together. I'll call your cousin Bubba to bring me to work."

"I'll get you some coffee and sweet roll, Mama. Try to rest a little while you're waiting. Okay?"

Honey Belle felt sick to her stomach. She wanted to reach out and hug her mother—to give herself some comfort, too. She didn't, fearing her mother would rebuff the affectionate gesture.

She hadn't noticed how cold the waiting room was until her mother shivered. Honey Belle walked to the nurse's station and asked for a blanket.

"It's for my mama. We're not used to air conditioning." She didn't know why she'd felt it necessary to offer an excuse. Returning to where her mother sat huddled in a chair, Honey Belle draped the blanket over the frail body. "I'll come back and sit with daddy as soon as my shift is over."

"No, you won't. You'll go home and get some proper rest. Can't afford for neither one of us to get sick."

Honey Belle turned with a reluctant shrug. She walked through the hospital's automatic doors and into the darkness.

Chapter Six

"Honey Belle." Her mother's voice was low and harsh.

Honey Belle swiped at the mosquito buzzing around her ear as she opened the screened door and stepped into the kitchen. She swore the temperature was hotter inside the house than the out in the mid-July night, and by the tone of her mother's voice, the climate was about to get hotter.

Still languishing in the memory of Tripp's sensual caresses, she ran her tongue over her lips, recalling the taste of his moist kisses. The sound of her mother's voice came again, this time like cold water being dumped on sizzling coals. She sighed, wondering what she'd done this time to warrant her mother's wrath.

"What is it, Mama?"

"Brought your daddy home from the hospital today. Where you been?"

"You said for me not to worry because Bubba had volunteered to drive you home and help get Daddy settled in bed."

"That ain't what I asked you, girl. I asked...where you been?"

"It's Sunday, and my only day off. I went for a walk on the beach."

Her mother reached out and grabbed her arm. She tapped the watch on Honey Belle's wrist. "Apparently, you cain't tell time."

Oh, here we go again. The words sounded so clear inside her head that Honey Belle feared she'd spoken them out loud. She jerked her arm away.

"Why are you so angry, Mama? I'm only ten minutes late."

"You think, just because I've been spending time at the hospital with your poor sick daddy, that word about you and that rich boy wouldn't get back to me?"

"Tripp and I aren't doing anything wrong, Mama. We're friends. That's all."

"Uh-huh. When mama mouse is away, her little one will get caught by the cat. I'm telling you, cain't no good come of it. He's rich, and like most rich folks he's used to gettin' anything he wants."

"You're wrong, Mama. Tripp isn't like that."

"How come you didn't let me know where you were?"

"I'm nineteen years old. I'm not a child that needs to report in twenty-four hours a day."

"As long as you live under my roof and eat my food, you'll do as I say."

A pause, then her mother continued. "Mark my words, daughter, he'll use you up, and when he's finished gettin' all the goody, he'll throw you away like a piece of cheap trash."

The words caused heat to grow under Honey Belle's scalp. She balled her hands into fists and clenched them until her fingernails dug into the palms of her hands. "You have a dirty mind, Mama. Tripp respects me. Why, he's never even tried to—"

The anger in her mother's watery gray eyes startled Honey Belle. "Ever since you've been going out with that boy, you've picked up some high-toney ways. How come you never invited him to supper? I'll tell you why. 'Cause you're ashamed of where you live, 'fraid your daddy and me will embarrass you."

Honey Belle opened her mouth to defend herself. Her mother's words cut her off. "Let me tell you, Miss High-and-Mighty, in less time than it takes to snap your fingers that boy will sweet talk you into letting him pluck your ripe little blossom. Soon as he's deflowered you, he'll drop you like a hot spud."

At this moment, Honey Belle longed for a best friend, a safe haven to run to, a shoulder to cry on. Although they had no friendship outside of work, there was Carla. One problem: she had no idea where the girl lived.

It crossed her mind to hop into the truck and drive to the nearest pay phone, look up Tripp's address in the phone book, and show up on his doorstep. No, that wouldn't do. How would she explain herself? Besides, what would his parents think?

She pushed around her mother and took a single step toward the bathroom. She squared her shoulders and jutted out her chin as she turned to face her mother's scowling frown. "Like I said, Mama, you have a filthy mind. You're wrong about Tripp. Very wrong."

Heat and anger boiled inside Honey Belle as she locked the bathroom door. She reached down and jammed the rubber plug into the bathtub's drain hole, then turned the cold water faucet to full force. With trembling fingers, she stripped out of her clothes, allowing them to drop to the floor, where she kicked them into a heap.

Settling into the tub, she lay back and closed her eyes, allowing the rising water to cool her body and her temper.

Two loud raps sounded against the closed door. "You get yourself in trouble with that boy, don't expect me to get you out of it. You hear me, Honey Belle?"

Sliding beneath the water, Honey Belle held her breath until she ran out of air. She came up gasping. As much as she tried to be a good daughter, it seemed everything she did angered her mother.

She'd given up her education and gone to work,

she helped with all the expenses, cleaned the house, cooked meals, did the laundry, and tended to her father. She did it all without begrudging either parent. Tears dripping from her chin mingled with the bath water.

Reaching forward, she pulled the plug and watched the water swirling down the drain. At nineteen she saw her future slipping away with it.

That night as she lay in bed, voices kept her from going to sleep. She lay still, concentrating, trying to hear the muffled words coming from her parents' bedroom.

She eased from the bed and pressed her ear against the wall. She sensed the tension in her father's voice. "Why are you so hard on Honey Belle?"

"Because she reminds me of me."

"That's a helluva reason, Delilah."

"Yeah, well, it's true."

"Then I guess you've resented all these years we've been married."

"Listen here, Jack Garrett. I spread my legs for you, didn't I? I can see her travelin' down the same road."

"You keep pushing, and you'll push her right out the door."

"She don't make enough money to strike out on her own. Where'd she go?"

"Use your noggin, woman. It's not where she'd go, it's who she'd run to. You say you're afraid she'll end up like you? Well, keep pushing, and she'll end up in that rich boy's bed."

Her father's spasmodic coughing caused Honey Belle to cringe. There was no debating the fact his illness was the reason she stayed. He'd sheltered her from her mother's attacks. Now diagnosed with congestive heart failure, it was only a matter of time before the sickness took him away. Sadness stabbed her heart at the thought of losing him. She'd stay until that time came. Then, come hell or high water, her mother was on her own.

Honey Belle's fingers knew exactly where the penlight lay tucked in the nightstand's drawer. Flicking it on, the small beam shone on the booklet she pulled from its hiding place. Holding the light in one hand, she used the other to flip through the pages of the vocational school's glossy cover.

She sighed. Getting her general education diploma seemed like an impossible dream. She ran down the list of vocations—secretary, licensed practical nurse, food technician—nothing interested her. Didn't matter. With giving almost every penny of her paycheck to help with bills, her plans for saving money might as well be like trying to reach for the moon.

Then an idea struck.

She'd work two jobs. One to support herself and one to pay for an education.

She drew in a deep breath, exhaled slowly. A smile tugged at the corners of her lips. She had a plan. It was her secret. For the first time in her life, she felt a sense of hope.

****

Tripp whistled as he set the glass of milk aside and concentrated on cutting a generous wedge of pound cake.

"You missed supper, son."

Clad in a gold-striped silk robe, Tripp's father leaned against the kitchen door, his arms crossed over his barrel chest.

Startled, Tripp knocked over the glass, spilling milk across the counter. "Geez, Dad, you scared the piss out of me." He grabbed a dishtowel to mop up the spreading white liquid.

"From the tune you were whistling and the grin on your face, I'd say you have more on your mind than cake. I hope it's about starting law school in September."

Tripp stood over the sink and wrung out the towel. Wetting it, he wiped up the remaining milk from the counter and the splatters on the floor. He ran the cloth under the faucet, wrung out the water, and neatly draped it over the sink.

Back to his fork, he picked it up, shoveled a piece of cake into his mouth, and spoke between mouthfuls. "Well, not exactly about school."

"Then perhaps about a certain young lady you're keeping company with?"

"Yes, sir. Honey Belle is as sweet as her name."

"You like this girl?"

"I do. A lot."

The way the elder Hartwell cleared his throat caused Tripp to set the plate aside. "I can tell by the look on your face, Dad, you have something on your mind."

"About this young woman...what do you know about her?"

"Mm, not much. Her father is sick. Instead of going to college, she works to help with medical expenses." Tripp braced his hands against the counter and leaned forward. "Honey Belle is a good girl. She's funny and honest. She lives on Barrington Street, and I like her."

"How much do you like her?"

Tripp rubbed his face and tried to think where this conversation was going. He laughed without humor. "If it's law school you're worried about, don't. Wild horses couldn't keep me from Harvard, and I haven't given up my dream of pursuing a seat in the Senate."

He'd said the right words. The words his father needed to hear. Visible relief replaced Judge Hartwell's furrowed brow.

"It's late, and high time I put these old bones of

mine to bed. 'Night, son."

"Rest well, Dad."

The Hartwells were one of the most powerful and influential families in South Carolina. Tobacco, cotton, politics. Tripp knew his father had an eye for the governor's seat. It was a given fact that any girl he chose to marry would need a pedigree to match that of his mother. He was a little surprised by his father's concerns over Honey Belle. It wasn't like him to pass judgment on someone he hadn't met.

Honey Belle was his friend. Yet, he had to admit, there was something special about her, something that made him want her as more than a girl to hold hands with while walking barefoot on the beach. When she smiled up at him, he wanted to drown in her eyes—eyes the color of the lilacs in his mother's garden.

Honey Belle stirred emotions in him that no other woman had. He could smell her as if she stood next to him—clean, familiar, distinctive.

Thoughts of her caused his groin to swell to a throbbing ache. What was it his grandfather used to say when he told of stories about sleeping in foxholes during the war—something about using Minnie and her four daughters to relieve himself when a woman wasn't around?

Tripp held up his right hand and flexed the fingers. *Well, Minnie, it's just you and me and the girls, tonight.*

Chapter Seven

The sultry Sunday afternoon weather was perfect for the yellow sundress Honey Belle wore. One of the straps slipped down over her shoulder and she adjusted it.

While she waited for Tripp in her usual place under the elm tree, an old saying popped into her head. *Time flies when you're having fun.* And she was having fun. More than she'd ever had in her life.

Before she'd realized it, June had sped forward to the dog days of August. She tried to shake the strange melancholy that had persisted for several days. September was a few short weeks away, and soon Tripp would leave for Harvard.

She knew when the time came to say goodbye, he would promise to write, to telephone, to come home on the holidays. At least that's what the guys in soap operas always did. And like those actors, eventually the phone calls would stop, the letters would grow less and less, and when holidays came, Tripp would come up with excuses as to why it was important for him to remain on campus.

She had tried to guard her heart, but it seemed her heart had a mind of its own. Against her will, she'd fallen in love—a forbidden love. It was common knowledge that the rich didn't associate with the poor—at least not knowingly.

She vowed to savor each precious hour they spent together, and when the time came for him to leave, she'd bite back the tears and with a smile on her face would let him go.

The neighborhood was quiet now, with little

outdoor activity, and it was apparently too hot for even the songbirds to muster a warble.

She pulled a clean hankie from her purse and dabbed at the perspiration collecting on her top lip. The high-heeled sandals she wore hurt her feet. She glanced at her watch.

A few minutes later she recognized the familiar sound of the BMW's engine. The car came into view with Tripp behind the wheel, easing down the street toward her.

She gave a little wave as he expertly maneuvered the sports car against the curb. In these few short weeks they'd been together, she'd learned he had a voice that teased, and hands that held hers tight when they walked on the beach. There was a scar on his chin from a childhood accident on the monkey bars. She wanted him to be the person she could confide in and share her secrets with.

She smiled as he climbed out of the car and slammed the door.

"Hello, good-looking. Going my way?" Tripp laughed as he placed his hands around her waist and pulled her against his chest.

"I'm waiting for my boyfriend."

Tripp glanced over his shoulder as if searching for someone. "I think he's stood you up."

She turned a little and they were face to face, practically nose to nose. He smelled of soap and aftershave. Her voice was a breathy whisper. "I could use a ride to the beach, if you're going that way."

She liked this flirtatious game they were playing.

Tripp sprinted to the car's passenger side, opened the door, and bowed deeply from the waist. "My chariot awaits, madam."

She laughed, but deep inside she wondered what she was to him. What would he say if she asked? She shoved the thought aside and stepped into the car. "You are very gallant, kind sir. I accept your offer."

****

Tripp watched the changing expressions on Honey Belle's face. He wondered if she was thinking of the summer evenings they'd spent together. There was so much he wanted to say to her, but everything that came into his head seemed inappropriate, somehow lacking. He felt something twitch inside him, something deep and old. He sucked in a deep breath and exhaled slowly.

Like a blazing ball of fire, the sun hung just above the horizon as Tripp pulled into a parking space and shut off the car's engine.

The gentle sounds of waves lapping the shore, then receding into the ocean, greeted them. A sea breeze caused Honey Belle to shiver. She ran her hands up and down her arms. "The sun looks as if it's sliding between earth and sea."

Tripp felt her closeness, her warmth as he spoke. "I know. Take your shoes off and let's go. I have a surprise for you."

He grabbed a blanket from the back seat and handed it to Honey Belle. Walking to the rear of the car, he opened the trunk and pulled out a cooler.

At their favorite spot, she spread the blanket over the sand while he opened the ice chest. He handed Honey Belle two chilled, long-stemmed, fluted glasses. Usually they drank beer, but not tonight. Tonight he'd brought champagne.

He paused a moment before filling their glasses.

****

Honey Belle enjoyed the way the bubbles tickled her nose. Holding the glass out for a refill, she wondered why he'd brought champagne.

"Are we celebrating something special, Tripp?" Her eyes were on a level with strong masculine thighs clad in denim. A tapered waist flared to a broad chest, every muscle and sinew clearly delineated by a simple white T-shirt.

"You and me, Honey Belle, we're celebrating—us." A breeze lifted Tripp's hair off his forehead, and suddenly he spread his arms wide. "Honey Belle Garrett, I've fallen hopelessly and madly in love with you."

He'd spoken the words she'd imagined in her head since the first time they had kissed. But—had he really said *I love you?* Perhaps along with the third glass of bubbly, she had only imagined hearing the words.

"Tripp, if you just said what I think I just heard...oh, my gosh." Skepticism kicked her in the chest. "You're not trash talking, are you?"

He lowered to his knees, lifted the glass from her hands and set it in the sand, then brought both of her hands to his lips. His gaze was commanding enough that it sent little chills skittering through the pit of her stomach. "I mean it, Honey Belle. I'd never joke about loving you."

Her heart skipped a beat when he opened his arms and invited her in. For the first time in her life, she felt a measure of security. She pressed her body to his, yearning to garner all his strength, his body warmth, his love—in the event she woke up and found it was all a dream.

He drew back a little, and with his thumb under her chin he lifted her face. Her lips met his. On a scale of one to ten, in the kissing department, tonight Honey Belle scored him a twenty.

At first the kiss was a soft touching of lips—a nuzzling. Then it deepened, became demanding, and left Honey Belle breathless. Tripp was the first to pull away.

The champagne made her feel bold. She took his hands in hers. She felt the warmth in his hands. Although they'd never had sex, they had participated in some serious foreplay. When he unbuttoned her blouse, she didn't resist. He kissed the tip of her nose, her chin, her cheeks, and went back to linger over her mouth.

Between the champagne and the kissing, Honey Belle's body hummed with desire. Just thinking about the way he touched her took her breath away. She felt her nipples begin to tingle, and warmth spread between her legs.

"I want you." His impatient hands caressed every inch of her body. He made the words sound almost like an oath as he bent his head and kissed her breasts.

All Honey Belle's fantasies rose up to haunt her as her mother's warnings buzzed around in her head like an annoying mosquito. *He'll pluck your blossom, and when he's deflowered you, he'll toss you away like cheap trash.*

"Tripp," Honey Belle's voice was a cracked whisper. "I-I'm not ready. Please, we should cool off." She pulled her blouse together and fumbled with the buttons.

His blue eyes bored into hers as if guessing the reason for her hesitation. Piercing her with a molten smile, he lifted her hand to his chest. Feeling the heat of his flesh through his shirt, she was conscious of his virile physique and knew she was a prisoner of her own desire.

In a husky drawl, he said, "Yeah. Let's go for a swim. We both need to cool off." He stood and offered his hand to pull her to her feet.

"Not here."

"Why not? Just look at that full moon beckoning us."

"Sharks. I guess, being away at college for four years, you've forgotten this place isn't called Shark Alley for nothing. When the fishermen clean their fish, they toss the heads and entrails off the pier and into the water. This section of the beach draws sharks, even at night. Believe me, it isn't safe to swim anywhere near this stretch of shoreline."

Tripp chuckled and tweaked her nose. "Okay, so we won't swim. What if we settle for holding hands and wading in the surf?"

How could she resist his lopsided grin? She couldn't. Like warm tongues, the waves lapped their ankles as they walked in the opposite direction from the fishing pier.

Without warning, the atmosphere seemed to fill with heavy tension. Aware of his arm around her waist, Honey Belle felt his fingers flex against her midriff. He turned her in his arms. She lifted her lips. To her surprise the kiss didn't come.

"Are you disappointed in me, Tripp?"

He stepped back. "Honey Belle Garrett, marry me." It was a simple statement—not a question.

Standing in the warm surf and bathed in moonlight, she searched his eyes, afraid this entire night was a figment of her imagination. Had she heard him correctly? Had Tripp Hartwell the Third really asked her to marry him?

"Honey Belle?"

She placed her arms around his neck and squealed as she rained kisses all over his face. "Yes...yes...yes." Without warning the practical side of her brain kicked in. "What will your parents say, where will we live, and what about law school?"

He met her concerns with a chuckle. "My parents will adore you. Besides don't worry about them. I'll enter law school as planned. In a few years, I'll pass the bar and work at the family law firm.

"School starts in three weeks. Next Friday, I'm flying to Massachusetts to take care of a registration glitch. While I'm there, I'll check out of the dorm and look for an apartment near campus. Does that answer all your questions?"

She cupped her hands on either side of his face. "Then I'll enroll in college, too. I'll learn how to walk and talk and dress properly. Oh, Tripp, I never want you to be ashamed of me."

In all these many weeks, she'd never told Tripp she hadn't finished high school. Unsure of their future together, she'd thought it unimportant—until now. She had to admit there was a secret part of her that was afraid of losing him if he thought she wasn't smart.

He pulled her against his chest. "I've never been ashamed of you, Honey Belle. Not now—not ever."

The scent of ocean salt filled the air, and while the night seemed to stretch on forever, the sky was littered with thousands of winking stars. Without quite realizing it, Honey Belle and Tripp had waded hip-deep into the water.

Her breath felt lodged in her throat as his dark eyes travelled from her hair, to her face, and lower to linger on her cleavage.

"You are as enticing as a moon goddess. I need you, Honey Belle. I need you in the worst way."

Perhaps it was the way he looked at her with those electric-blue eyes of his, or perhaps it was the way the warm waves caressed her thighs, or maybe it was how the rise and fall of the surf matched the beating of her heart. Whatever it was, she knew neither Tripp nor herself were able to resist the tidal wave of desire washing over them.

No longer rigid in his encircling arms, she leaned against his broad chest, her body gently trembling, allowing him to bear her weight.

Her breasts seemed to blossom and flower at his touch, the nipples ready and eager for his fluttering fingers against their hardening peaks. All thoughts of resistance ebbed away.

"Don't be afraid, Honey Belle."

"I'm not afraid. I need you, too, Tripp."

His one hand supported her back while he used his other hand to move slowly down, smoothing its way over the curve of her hip, leaving her on the knife-edge of need. Her body felt hot and fluid in anticipation of his exploring touch.

Her nipples ached, on fire with pleasure. She wanted him to kiss them, to experience the balm of his tongue.

Parting her thighs for his exploration, she whispered his name as he lifted her skirt and slid her cotton undies down her hips and tossed them toward the shore. "Tripp?"

"Shh. Trust me." He let her go long enough to yank at his denims and briefs as if desperate to be rid of them. She drew her dress over her head, standing bathed in moonlight and passion.

"Put your legs around my waist, Honey Belle."

"Our clothes. They'll wash away."

She didn't know if he chuckled or snorted in aggravation when he gathered their floating garments into a dripping ball and sailed them to the wet sand. "Now, put your legs around me."

Buoyed by the water, unbelievable sensations arrowed through her body as Tripp suckled one breast before he turned his attention to the other dusky peak.

He didn't hurry. He suckled and licked and at the same time his searching fingers found the hot wet center of her feminine cortex.

She gripped his broad shoulders with both hands, loving the feel of the corded muscles in his neck. She heard the sharp intake of his breath as she moved her hand down between them. She trailed her fingers down the hard length of his erection, curling her slender fingers around him.

"No." His hoarsely spoken command and his hand capturing hers stopped the investigation.

"Did I do something wrong?" She tried to keep the worry from her voice. More than anything, she wanted to please him.

He moved away an inch, his face close to hers. His voice rasped, "I'm hotter than a forty-dollar pistol, honey girl. I don't want to shoot off before we're both ready, and I don't want you to have any regrets afterward."

Hugging his shoulders, she held him tight. "Hold me."

She heard the sharp intake of his breath as he lifted her to mount his pulsating hardness. She looked into his hot blue eyes as he slid his hand around her bottom and savagely joined them together in one swift thrust.

With each moan, their writhing bodies cried out for more. They moved as one, clutching, grinding, panting. Time was lost. There was only the rhythm of the surf undulating around them. With each deep thrust Honey Belle moaned with pleasure, until she felt him explode deep inside of her.

After a long shuddering breath, and with their bodies locked together, Tripp carried her to the blanket they had abandoned on the beach.

Chapter Eight

Moisture pooled in Honey Belle's eyes as Tripp gently laid her on the blanket. "You're beautiful, Honey Belle."

"So are you."

"Did I hurt you?"

She traced the furrowed lines that formed concern in his face. "I've had wasp's stings that were worse."

"More?"

She drew a deep contented breath and ran her fingers through his thick blond hair. She had never imagined, never guessed the depths of emotion that could exist between two people.

"Yes, more."

Tripp leaned up on one elbow. "I'm not too heavy for you?"

"No, you're perfect. We fit together like two spoons."

She saw the gleam of satisfaction in his eyes, and the hint of a smug smile. He trailed his hand down her stomach. "I intend to explore every inch of your exquisite body."

Color surged in her face and warmed her cheeks. She was glad it was dark so Tripp couldn't see her blushing.

To her surprise her body stirred in response to his touch. He gathered her in his arms, merging their bodies into one and moving inside her.

She answered his moan with her own as he thrust deeper within her. Her loins, abdomen, thighs were the center of a passionate white flame. And

Tripp was the fire, burning inside her, over and over, crying out above her as he seemed to revel in the same exquisite torture.

She snuggled up against him, her head resting on his shoulder, not speaking, rubbing her hand across his chest, and whispered in his ear, "Tripp, I want you to know something."

His voice was very tender. "What is it?"

"There's never been another. You're the only man I've ever been with. I don't expect you to say the same thing, but I wanted you to know."

Tripp was silent as he held her closer. She pressed against him, felt his arm tighten around her. Her body trembled in anticipation. He kissed her softly on the lips, and she kissed him back. He kissed her neck, her cheek, her eyelids, and she felt the moisture of his mouth linger wherever his lips had touched.

She took his hand and led it to her breast, and a whimper rose in her throat. It felt so right to be here, under a blanket of stars, with the man she loved.

****

The time was well past midnight when Tripp drove toward the Barrington Street address and parked in front of Honey Belle's pretend two-story house with its wide wrap around veranda decorated with urns of bird's-nest fern and a porch swing.

"No light. I guess your parents got tired of waiting up for you." Tripp leaned over and feathered kisses on her lips.

She rested against the BMW's leather seat. She didn't mean to sound indignant, but it came out that way. "I'm nineteen and not a child whose parents should wait for her to come home from a date."

Her eyes took in the shape of his nose, the fullness of his lips, the square jaw-handsomeness.

Running a finger down her cheek, he said,

50

"Woman or not, you'd better go in before your father wakes up and comes after me with a shotgun. At least let me walk you to the door."

Giving Tripp a bright smile and a quick peck on the lips, she opened the car door and scooted from the seat. "I'm a big girl, remember."

"Now that we're engaged, I'd like to meet your parents, and formally ask your father's permission to marry you."

Standing on the sidewalk in the shadows of the street light, her heart plummeted to her stomach. *I've really stepped in it now.* Pretending to live in a nice house with a manicured yard in an upscale neighborhood was one thing. What was she going to do? She certainly couldn't go out and rent a set of parents that would measure up to the standards of Judge and Mrs. Hartwell.

Like Scarlett O'Hara, Honey Belle decided to think about it later.

"Goodnight, Tripp."

The BMW's engine revved and Tripp leaned toward the window and waved. "Sweet dreams, Honey Belle. I love you."

Still feeling the roll of emotion within her and wondering if it showed on her face, she waited until he was out of sight before heading in the direction of the gas station where she'd parked the truck.

Tripp Hartwell the Third loved her. Her feet felt as if they'd sprouted wings as she skipped down the sidewalk.

By the time she arrived home, her clothes had dried stiff from the salt water. Gathering her sandals in her hands, she stood on the back steps and brushed the dirt from her feet. She eased the door open and tiptoed into the living room.

Moonlight lit the small area, making it possible to get to her bedroom without turning on a lamp. Now if she could only avoid the squeaky board in the center of the living room floor...

There was no need to worry about waking her parents. The moment she stepped into the darkened space, a voice stopped her cold. Lamp light filled the room.

Her mother sat on the sofa with her arms crossed over her chest. She didn't say a word. All the while her gaze burned into Honey Belle. Her silence was like an itch that wouldn't go away. When she didn't speak, Honey Belle said, "'Night, Mama."

She could almost see her mother's chest heave with the heavy breath she drew in. The air seemed to squeeze through her mother's nostrils. Her pursed lips looked as if she'd been sucking lemons, and her eyes were narrow, angry slits. "I told you, didn't I...didn't I?"

Honey Belle knew the storm was coming, she just didn't know what kind of storm to expect. Would it be the kind where the sun shone through the rain, doing little damage, or would it be a full-blown hurricane?

She had a feeling it was the hurricane. Her mother had gone from looking sad to looking furious. Her gray eyes were as cold as a December morning.

Honey Belle knew what her mother was referring to. Refusing to cower to intimidation, she lifted her chin to show her defiance. "You tell me lots of things, Mama. Which would you be referring to?"

Her mother pushed from the sagging sofa. She stood in front of Honey Belle. "That boy has done had you. It's written all over your face." She poked a finger against Honey Belle's chest. "And now that he's had you, all the dogs in the neighborhood will come around sniffin'. Even I can smell the musky scent of sex on you."

"You have a cruel and filthy mouth, Mama." Honey Belle tried to turn aside. At that moment, all she wanted was to get away from her mother's accusing scowl.

Her mother reached out and grabbed her arm with such force it felt as if her fingers had bruised the skin. "You're ruined, girl. No decent man will want you. Not now. Not ever."

She sank to the sofa and buried her face in to her dishwater-reddened hand. "I was sixteen when you were born. Your life won't be much better than mine. Always workin' and never getting' nowhere." Tears spilled down her cheeks.

For a moment, Honey Belle felt no compassion for her mother. Unable to hide her resentment, she wanted to lash out with all the bitterness welling inside her, against the shabbiness of the house, the couch with its sagging springs, and the death odors from her dying father.

She parroted her mother's words. *"Always working and getting nowhere? My life won't be much better than yours?* Who was it, Mama, that forced me to quit school and give up my future? Don't sit there sobbing and feeling sorry for yourself and laying blame on me for the way your life turned out."

Her mother's face crumpled into more tears. "I'm sorry. I was wrong to make you quit school. I've known it all along, just didn't know how to take it back."

Coming from her mother, it was a gracious apology, and Honey Belle accepted it. She knelt and lifted her mother's chafed and work-worn hands into hers. "Don't cry, Mama. I know your life has been hard, and you've had your share of disappointments. But I'm not one of them. Why, just tonight, Tripp asked me to marry him. And I said yes. You'll see, Mama. Everything is going to be okay."

With a heavy sigh, her mother lifted the corner of her threadbare nightgown and dried her eyes. She rose and patted Honey Belle's cheek. "You always did believe in fairy tales." She hunched her shoulders, and her feet shuffled toward the bedroom she shared with her husband. It seemed to Honey Belle that her mother was much older than her thirty-five years.

At the door, Delilah Garrett turned and stood staring, her face a mixture of anger and melancholy. "That boy will never marry you, and you're a fool to think otherwise, Honey Belle."

Honey Belle turned out the lamp. Inside the bathroom, she ran a tub of cold water and soaked her hot body. She shampooed the salt and sand from her hair. Rinsing off, she stepped from the tub. Wrapped in a towel, she tiptoed to her bedroom.

Her body no longer hummed with desire. She tried to conjure up the elation she'd felt when Tripp had asked her to marry him, but the attempt failed. She didn't want to think about her mother's harsh accusations.

Outside, the rain frogs croaked for rain. As she lay in bed, their song echoed inside Honey Belle's head—*that boy will never marry you.*

A moment of *déjà vu* washed over her. What if her mother and the frogs were right?

****

Monday morning Tripp stood at the top of the staircase, fighting a case of nerves that matched any he'd met on college exam days. Dressed in a pair of crisp white slacks and a blue golfing shirt that accentuated the color of his eyes, he folded his hands together and stretched them forward cracking his knuckles. He shook off the nerves as he descended the stairs.

Placing his hands inside his pants pockets, he whistled a tune as he strolled into the large airy dining room. "Good morning, Mother." He bent and kissed her on the cheek.

The maid hustled over to fill his coffee cup. "How would you like your eggs this morning, Mr.

Tripp?"

"Sunnyside up, and load the grits with butter."

The woman offered him a wide grin. "Just the way you like 'em, Mr. Tripp."

"Oh, and Pearlie Mae, is that hot biscuits I smell?"

"I 's'pose you want 'em loaded with butter, too?"

"Yes, ma'am, and dripping with honey."

Tripp's father folded the newspaper and laid it next to his plate. "Pearlie Mae, you do spoil us with your cooking." He patted his stomach.

With a giggle, the maid bounced off toward the kitchen.

"She's a jewel, that Pearlie Mae. Don't know what I'd do without her." Tripp's mother flashed a smile across the table toward her son.

Tripp stirred sugar into his coffee. The spoon clattered against the sides of the cup. His throat felt as if it were stuffed with cotton. Without waiting for the coffee to cool, he gulped a large sip, not expecting to scorch the back of his throat. He grabbed the white linen napkin and pressed it to his mouth to keep from spewing hot liquid across the table.

Stricken with a coughing spasm, Tripp's eyes dripped with tears and his face suffused red as his father pounded him on the back. Between sputters, Tripp managed to say, "Now I know what a piece of bacon must feel like when it hits the frying pan."

His mother fussed and fidgeted. "Merciful heaven, Pearlie Mae, bring a glass of cold buttermilk, and be quick about your slow self."

The maid bustled in as fast as her short fat legs would carry her. "Lawsy sakes, Mr. Tripp, maybe I'd better make you a bowl of oatmeal with honey, 'stead of grits and eggs."

Tripp accepted the glass of milk, and allowed the cold liquid to slide down his aching throat. The words came out disjointed when he attempted to speak. "Thank you."

"He'll need more than oatmeal to shore him up if he expects to beat me at golf this morning."

Tripp cleared his throat and gave his father a half-hearted laugh. "Bring on the eggs and grits, biscuits and bacon, Pearlie Mae. I have a golf game to win."

Tripp smiled to himself. At least he'd gotten over his case of nerves. He downed the rest of the buttermilk, allowing his mother to reach over and wipe away the white mustache above his top lip as if he were still her little boy.

He focused his attention on her, knowing his father would be the one to reckon with. "Mother, how would you like to put together a little party? Nothing fancy, just family and a few of our closest friends."

She pulled her overly painted lips into a pout, reminding him of an unhappy clown. "*La*, I simply refuse to give you a going-away party. Why, you've only been home from college a few weeks, and here you are, off again to hide yourself away in a stuffy old library filled with dust-laden law books. It just breaks my heart."

Tripp leaned forward on his elbows. "It isn't a going-away party, Mother." He cut his eyes toward his father. "Remember the young woman I told you about, the one with the sweet name?"

He watched his mother's shoulders stiffen. "Yes, I do. Garrett, and I recalled how the Garretts were sharecroppers from Tennessee."

Tripp held her gaze as he reached out and removed the cup from a hand that reminded him of tissue paper, fragile. "Honey Belle and her parents live on Barrington Street, Mother. They've never lived in Tennessee."

She seemed to brighten. "Well, in that case, is it her birthday, is that why you want me to host a party?"

"No, it's—" He took a fortifying breath and started again. What did he know about Honey Belle, what could he tell his parents about her? He could pacify his mother; his father would have questions. "It's to announce my engagement. I've asked Honey Belle to be my wife."

In an instant, his father's face reminded him of a puffed-up toad with a bad case of constipation. "The hell, you say. I won't have you throwing away law school for some cheap skirt wanting to latch on to the Hartwell fortune."

Tripp threw his father an irritated glance and enunciated clearly, "My plans haven't changed, Dad. I'm merely adding a wife to the mix. And, so you know, Honey Belle isn't cheap, nor is she after money."

His father leaned back and gripped the chair's arms. "This girl in the family way?"

It was like his father not to mince words—to get straight to the point. "No, sir." At least Tripp hoped there wasn't a baby in the oven from their first time making love, and the many times that had followed the same night. Thinking about how her blonde hair had shimmered in the moonlight, and the touch of her silken skin caused him to readjust his position in the chair.

His father's face never got beet red unless his anger was near erupting. "If the girl isn't in the family way, then why the rush to get married, and what do you know about this girl, *and* her family?"

"I'm not rushing, Dad. We haven't discussed a date. Not yet." Squaring his shoulders, Tripp added, "I think Honey Belle would make a beautiful Christmas bride." He decided to shift the focus from his father. "What do you think, Mother—a Christmas wedding?"

His mother's eyes took on a dreamy glow. Like a

cloud blotted out by the sun, she shifted from a sensible, intelligent woman who ran an efficient home and chaired the local women's historical society to an angelic child reaching out to catch imaginary butterflies. He hated the dementia stealing her away piece by piece like a thief.

His father bellowed, "Pearlie Mae, fetch Mrs. Hartwell's tonic." He cut a mean eye toward his son. "Your mother is in no condition to plan a party or a wedding. I'm afraid this announcement of yours might be the boulder that pushes her over the edge."

"I'm sorry. I never meant to—" Tossing the linen napkin to the table, Tripp pushed from the chair. "Under the circumstances, perhaps we should cancel our golf game."

Likewise, his father tossed his napkin to the table. "I'll call the doctor." As he left the room, he glanced over his shoulder. "We'll save this discussion until later."

"No we won't, Dad. There's nothing to discuss. I fully intend to marry Honey Belle Garrett."

Neither one of them moved as they faced each other. Tripp's muscles seemed frozen. Logic told him it wasn't anything he'd said that had caused his mother to drift away. Nonetheless, guilt flooded over him. "I'll help Mother to her room and sit with her until Dr. Weston arrives."

For a long time all they could do was stare at each other, until his father relinquished. Tripp denied an inner stab of pain. "I didn't create this situation, Dad. We have to both come to terms with the facts...we're losing Mother."

The Judge scrubbed a hand across his face. The deep furrowed frown on his brow suddenly ironed out. He drew a shuddering breath that seemed to come from hidden depths. "We'll deal with all these issues next week, when you return home from Massachusetts. I'll drive you to the airport."

"No, Dad, you're the standing judge in the Ferrell murder case. The trial starts the same day I leave."

The Judge's eyes grew shadowed. "Then we'll agree to disagree."

Obviously unaware of the tension between father and son, the maid said, "Sorry to interrupt, Mr. Tripp, but I need help with your mama."

The Judge waved Tripp toward the landing. "Go. I'll call the doctor."

And Tripp took the stairs.

Two by two.

Chapter Nine

Over the next few days, Honey Belle managed to tuck away the doubts her mother had heaped on her. She decided not to tell Tripp about her mother's nasty accusations. Doing so might prompt questions she wasn't ready to answer.

On Sunday, she dressed with care. Without a word to her mother, she left the house and drove to the gas station. She pulled behind the station's garage and parked in the usual place. She'd allowed herself enough time to walk the two miles without working up a sweat.

In front of the Barrington Street house, she stood under the elm tree and waited.

****

Tripp had misgivings as he pointed the car down Barrington Street. He wanted to hope and believe in happy endings. Since meeting Honey Belle, his life had become a series of emotional highs and lows. His entire life had been shaped and molded by family tradition. In college, he'd played the field, never allowing any one woman to get close to him. Now he'd fallen in love. Sure, he'd been intimate, more than once, but he knew the difference between infatuation and the real thing.

Now he needed to steer a straight course in between foolish passion and love, reminding himself that a little distance for a short period of time would do them both good.

He pulled alongside the curb and, leaving the engine running, he shifted the gear stick into park. He opened the door and stepped out. "I believe I owe you dinner."

"I'd like that," Honey Belle said. And then there was his mouth searching for hers.

At last he drew a breath. "Shall we go?" he said, burning her with a hot glance.

His eyes promised more than dinner.

****

"Will you excuse me, Tripp? I need to powder my nose."

"Shall I order you a glass of wine?"

Honey Belle sent him a dazzling smile. "Yes."

Moments later, he was lifting the glass of chardonnay to his mouth when his eyes caught a movement. He lowered the glass slowly. He'd never seen Honey Belle look so out-and-out sexy. The word exquisite came to mind.

She smiled as she made her way across the crowded restaurant. He could see the avid expression on the other men's faces—which she ignored. No doubt about it, Honey Belle was a knockout. She had no conceit, no concept of her own perfection. Perhaps that's what drew him to her. She was beyond the perfect alignment of facial features, the graceful lines and generous curves of her body. She was Honey Belle.

Their eyes met and held in the reflection of the glass, and she blushed—her composure obviously shaken by the warmth of his gaze.

She slid into the chair across the table from him.

Tripp leaned close and murmured, "You know, it's occurred to me I want to feed you and then take you to bed."

Her answer nearly knocked him off the chair. "I want you to."

He laughed. "You are most unique, Honey Belle Garrett."

There was live entertainment—a bluesy singer at a piano. A warm breeze and the cadence of the waves kissing the shoreline seemed to match the rhythm of the music. It was an intimate setting for lovers.

They ordered dinner, a cup of New England clam chowder, almond fried grouper, parsley potatoes, and sautéed mushrooms. A dish of chocolate ice cream completed the delicious meal, washed down by a fine vintage wine.

The orchestra was playing a slow piece. "Do you think we can dance to this?" Tripp asked, impatient to hold Honey Belle in his arms.

"We can try." She wore heels, which brought her almost up to his height. When they danced, she couldn't avoid his eyes. Eyes that seemed to drink her up, swallowing her whole. Their bodies fit, moving slowly to the music, a prelude to another dance. When his hand slipped to the small of her back and drew her closer, a small gasp escaped her. She couldn't contain a shudder of pleasure.

Tripp nuzzled her ear and felt the heat in her face as she flushed deliciously. "This feels nice," he said, his voice husky, not making any effort to hide the effect she had on him. It was too late for pretence now, far too late. "How about a walk on the beach—I brought the blanket."

"Mmm." Honey Belle pulled him close. "Then I think we should leave, now."

When he raised his head to look into her eyes, he saw naked hunger there and knew his eyes must betray the same dazed expression.

****

Honey Belle and Tripp walked hand in hand down the long stretch of beach, far away from the restaurant, until reaching their special place. Lightning cut across the sky, promising an August storm.

An ominous feeling loomed over Honey Belle when Tripp said, "It's too bad you can't get off work tomorrow. I'd like for you to see me off at the airport."

"I wish you didn't have to go, Tripp."

"Don't worry," he chided. "I'll be back before you have time to miss me."

"How long will you be gone?"

"A week. Maybe longer, if I can't find an apartment right away."

A painful lump formed in her throat. "A week seems like forever, Tripp."

He hugged her close. "I told my parents about us—our engagement. When I get home, we'll shop for the perfect ring to place on your long slender finger."

A little gasp slipped out. She whispered, "What did your parents say?"

"The usual concerns. Mostly afraid I won't finish law school."

"What did you say?"

"I assured them there is nothing to worry about."

"Tripp, what if your parents don't like me? I mean, it isn't as if we're both from the same social circles." Honey Belle knew truer words had never been spoken. His parents would never accept a girl from the wrong side of the tracks. How would Tripp react when he found out?

Humor laced his face as he lifted her hands to his lips. "I love you, and that's all that matters."

She wanted to latch onto him and never let go. No matter how hard she tried, she couldn't shake her mother's words. *He'll never marry you.*

"Hold me, Tripp."

She didn't realize she was crying until he thumbed a tear from her cheek. "Hey, why the tears? Meeting my parents is no big deal."

No matter how hard she tried, she couldn't conjure up a smile. Yet the feeling went on, despite herself. "I'm being silly." She patted his chest. "I hope you find a nice apartment with a yard. I'd love to have a puppy to keep me company while you're attending class."

"You won't have time for a dog, Honey Belle."

"Oh, why's that?"

"You're going to school, too, remember? Studying doesn't leave much time for a pet."

Without another word they came together. Entwining his muscular legs around her body, he held her captive. "Besides, I plan to keep you plenty busy."

She surrendered peacefully, and snuggled close to him. She teased, "Keep me busy doing what?"

"Doing—this."

His mouth sought hers as if it were the most natural thing in the world, and he put his arms around her, drawing her close. She leaned against him, allowing all her tension to ebb away. She needed his reassurances.

He slowly undid the buttons on her blouse, ran his fingers across her bare shoulders. "Every time I touch you my world lights up."

"Mama always said I should save myself for the right man. You are perfect for me." Old doubts crept in. A marriage built on a lie was a sham. She needed to tell him she wasn't who he thought she was—that she was an imposter.

Not tonight. Tonight was special.

He leaned over and kissed the tender place where her throat curved into her shoulder. She didn't want their love to be an empty wasteland of sex.

The moon broke through the clouds and cast its light over Tripp's face, outlining the chiseled features of his cheekbones.

"Hmm," he hummed, sending vibrations streaming through her. "You feel incredible." His voice was muffled by the fact that his mouth pressed against her neck.

A sense of euphoria swept over her, and all thoughts of a confession flew from her mind. "You do, too." She tried to gather her wits while at the same time feeling like a feline in heat.

"Tripp, will you have tons of homework at law school?"

He moved away an inch, his face close to hers. "I suppose so. There'll be cases to research and long nights at the law library."

"It sounds like after we're married you'll not have time for—"

He pressed her back against the blanket and slid inside her. "For this?"

Shivering, her heartbeat quickened and her breath grew heavy. His lips were like moist drops of dew caressing her skin. Her body flamed and her flesh ached. "Yes, Tripp, for this."

A little voice inside her head chided her that she shouldn't be here like this, with him. A proper young lady waited until her wedding night to surrender her virginity. But she had already surrendered that sacred part of her. She hoped she wouldn't live to regret giving in to her impetuous desire.

Tripp's passion stole the breath from her throat. Loving him and wanting him, she clung to his shoulders, matching his thrusts and yielding to the desire that flamed inside her.

His lips grew more demanding, his kisses more intense. She nipped the column of his neck. "You taste good."

He groaned deep inside his throat. "So do you."

She shivered as a warm sea breeze wafted over her sweat-drenched body, and allowed desire to pool within her.

Their loving slowed to a gentler pace, laced with unfurling desire, then grew and grew, then turned to pleasure—more intense than ever before.

They made love, giving and taking, expressing what they felt while the words remained unspoken, locked in their hearts.

She wasn't worthy enough to be his wife, yet she loved Tripp Hartwell the Third with all her heart and soul.

Her mother had a saying, *Out of sight, out of mind*. What if Tripp decided to stay in Massachusetts and never return to South Carolina?

Honey Belle's head spun. Her mind went blank. She was lost in a crescendo of confusion.

Chapter Ten

The day after Tripp left for Harvard, Honey Belle received an unexpected visit from the most unlikely person. A visit that made her feel as if she'd died and gone to Hell.

The morning was insufferably hot. Honey Belle was sure if there was a thermometer inside the house the temperature would register at a hundred degrees. The ceiling fan circulated dust, and the floor fans circulated hot air.

"Honey Belle, the heat has got to me. Go next door and use the phone. Tell the boss man I'm too sick to come in today."

The sickly yellow tinge to her mother's skin worried Honey Belle. "Let me take you to the health department, Mama. When was the last time you had a physical examination?"

"There's nothing wrong with me, except this blasted heat. Come November, when it cools down, I'll be right as rain." Almost as an afterthought, she added, "Besides we ain't made of money."

Honey Belle's morning shower had left her feeling sticky and uncomfortable. "The heat is taking a toll on both you and Daddy. We're not behind on the rent. If we ask, maybe Mr. Ellerby will put in an air conditioner for us."

Her mother harrumphed. "That old skinflint isn't interested in fixin' up anything for the likes of us. All he's concerned with is if he's gonna get the next month's rent."

The words "slum lord" came to mind as Honey Belle ran two clean dishrags under the faucet. She wrung out the excess water, filled both cloths with ice cubes from the freezer, and handed them to her mother. "Maybe this will help cool you and Daddy off."

"It's too hot to cook, Honey Belle. Run to town and pick up some chicken tenders and fries. Your daddy might like some ice cream, too."

"Cherry vanilla for Daddy, chocolate for you and me."

Her mother offered a haggard smile and trod toward the bedroom, an ice pack in each hand.

A wave of heat shimmered toward the road when Honey Belle stepped out the front door. At first she thought she was seeing a mirage. She blinked to clear her eyes. The mirage didn't go away. A sleek black limousine sat parked at the edge of the dirt road in front of the house.

She became painfully aware of the front yard—a sandy, sandspur-filled weed patch in dire need of mowing. Plastic flowerpots, cracked and faded from the sun, the plants long dead and gone, bordered the edges of the house. The mailbox, rusted and battered from multiple hits from baseball bats, sat askew on its post.

The contrast between the expensive vehicle and her surroundings made her uncomfortable. Who in their right mind, she wondered, would risk a carjacking to drive through Shanty Groves in broad daylight?

She lifted her hand to shade her eyes from the sun. Hesitant, she walked toward the vehicle. Raising her voice, she called toward the dark-tinted windows. "Are you lost...can I help you?"

A man dressed in a black uniform opened the limo's door and stepped toward her. "Is this the residence of Miss Honey Belle Garrett?"

In spite of the heat, a chill prickled her arms. "Yes, who are you?"

"Judge Hartwell wishes to speak with you."

Unease twisted the pit of her stomach. Why did Tripp's father wish to speak to her? Better, yet, how did he find where she lived? The wheels of her brain rotated in overtime. Had she slipped up and given Tripp clues to where she lived?

No!

Perhaps Tripp had asked Carla.

No, again. Carla, whose circumstances matched her own, wouldn't betray her address to Tripp. Then how did Judge Hartwell find her?

Honey Belle's heart did a little leap. Perhaps Tripp had changed his mind and asked his father to take her shopping for an engagement ring.

No, that still didn't answer the question of how the Judge had located her and his reason for being here.

The uniformed driver opened the limousine's door and, with a sweep of his hand, indicated she should get in.

She smoothed down the green peddle-pushers she wore. The fabric felt fragile from the many washings it had endured. She gave the driver a questioning glance as she slid inside the car and settled on the plush black leather seat and drank in the air-conditioned coolness. Sitting across from her was a distinguished-looking man with features much like Tripp's, but not the same. Though he was sitting, she figured he must be about the same height as Tripp's six-foot stature. He wore a double-breasted navy blue suit. The diamond-studded cufflinks could more than pay for an air conditioner for her parents.

Wordlessly they stared at each other. The silence made her uncomfortable. She waited for him to speak. He didn't. It took a moment for her to find her voice. "This is an unexpected and a pleasant surprise, Judge Hartwell. It's nice to meet you."

Extending her hand forward, she felt awkward and embarrassed when he rebuffed the gesture. Not schooled in etiquette, she feared she'd made a social blunder, and eased her hands together, settling them on her lap. She swallowed, unable to subdue a clamoring pulse.

"H-has something happened to Tripp...is he okay?"

The elder Hartwell reminded Honey Belle of a vulture sizing up his prey when he reached inside his suit coat and withdrew a white envelope. He offered it to her. Apparently, it was the puzzled look on her face that caused him to speak.

Sarcasm laced his voice. "Open it, Miss Garrett."

Once she'd pulled the check from the envelope, she didn't say a word. Lightheaded, she tried to concentrate on all the zeros in the total amount, her heart racing ahead of her brain. She tried to speak. The words stuck inside her throat.

Evidently Judge Hartwell mistook her silence as a demand for more money. "If ten thousand isn't enough, Miss Garrett, name your price." The sardonic smile he offered twisted his handsome features into an ugly snarl.

"This is a wonderful gift, Judge Hartwell. Tripp will be as pleased as I."

His laughter mocked her. "I'm afraid you misunderstand, young woman. I have no intention of allowing my son to marry the likes of you."

How silly of me, to think the money was a wedding gift.

"I may not be a brilliant person, Judge, but I am smart enough to know an insult when I hear one. Perhaps you'd better explain what you mean by 'the likes of me.'"

His angry tone startled Honey Belle. "You are the kind of woman who brings an intelligent man down to her level. I have plans for my son's career."

The man reminded her of a puff adder ready to strike when he leaned forward. "Let me be perfectly clear, *Miss Garrett,* these plans *do not* include you."

A thick fury rose inside Honey Belle, threatening to shut off her air. She tossed the check toward Tripp's father. "Tripp loves me, and we will be married, whether you like it or not, Judge Hartwell."

"Don't press me, young woman. I'm a powerful man."

"I'm not afraid of you."

He settled back against the seat. His eyes locked with hers, his voice even and deadly. "You should be. You see, with one phone call, I can arrange for you and your mother to lose your jobs at the Burger Bin." He accentuated the name of her workplace as if reassuring her he knew where she worked. His hand swept toward the tinted window. "And this pigsty you call home? I can arrange for the landlord to kick you out. I can arrange it to where any hovel you try to rent will be beyond your affordability. And don't begin to think your parents will get new jobs. I know about your father's failing health, your mother's lack of skills, that you're a high school dropout... Need I say more?"

Honey Belle sighed heavily. She blinked back the tears gathering behind her eyelids.

"Ah, my dear, don't look so surprised. I know quite a bit about you and your parents."

Mustering as much courage as possible, she repeated herself. "You don't scare me. After Tripp and I are married and settled in Massachusetts, I'll get a job and send money to my parents. I'm sure Tripp will help out, too."

The Judge roared with raucous laughter, and then a mean sneer draped over his face. "Obviously, you don't know my son very well. When it comes down to who controls the purse strings, coupled with my son's drive to become a high-ranking politician, I can assure you, Miss Garrett, money and power will win out over lust and surviving on baloney sandwiches."

When she opened her mouth to protest, he lifted a large brown envelope from the seat and shoved it toward her. "If you need more convincing, imagine my son's reaction when he sees these photographs. You've misled him, haven't you, Miss Garrett?"

"No. I never have."

"Take a very good look at them. Perhaps you'll change your response."

Not knowing what to expect, her hands trembled as she removed the pictures from the envelope and, one by one, looked at black-and-white images of her backyard, strewn with a sundry of car parts, an old washing machine, a broken toilet, stacks of rotting lumber from a project her father had never gotten around to building, and rusting barrels overflowing with black plastic garbage bags.

There were pictures of her mother wearing a slip while she hung clothes on the clothesline, another of her father and his cronies seated on cinder blocks drinking beer, and shots of various angles of the house with its peeling paint, broken steps, and windows whose cracks were repaired with gray duct tape. The worst picture of all was of her sitting in a man's lap. She held a beer can in one hand and with the other was making an obscene gesture at someone out of camera view. As bad as it was, the last and most incriminating were the scenes of her standing under the elm tree in front of the two-storied house where she always met Tripp, of her walking toward the front door of her pretend home, and then others of her walking away from the house as soon as Tripp had pulled away from the curb.

She turned one particular picture toward Tripp's

father. "This is my cousin. Bubba and I were just having fun."

"Photographs speak louder than words, young woman. They prove an important fact about you. Are you interested in knowing?"

Sitting up a little straighter, and feeling as if she already knew the answer, there was a perverse need to hear someone other than herself speak the words. "By all means, Judge Hartwell, enlighten me."

A scornful smile stiffened his face. "Simply put, Miss Garrett, it proves you are a liar."

It was true. All of it. She was a liar. She had deceived Tripp about everything except the fact that she truly loved him.

In a rush of anger, she ripped the pictures into shreds and threw the pieces at the impeccably dressed man seated across from her. "You are a mean, despicable man, Judge Hartwell. I hate you." She didn't try to control the shriek in her voice.

"Hate me all you please, Miss Garrett. The fact remains that my son's future is at stake. Whatever it takes, I will go to any measure to see he reaches his fullest potential."

Tripp's father slipped a smaller envelope of pictures from a briefcase, and held them for her to see.

"This is blackmail." Consumed with humiliation, she reached to snatch the photographs from his hand.

He laughed and held them out of reach. "Call it what you will, young woman. As a judge, I'd say it's evidence against a conniving little gold-digger."

She wanted to slap the smirk off his face when he held up the image of her mother dressed in a slip thin enough for the sun to outline her nude body, and then the one of herself straddling her cousin's lap, and another of her father in the backyard, asleep on an old divan, a beer can dangling from his hand.

"You've probably heard the old saying, 'You can't make a silk purse out of a sow's ear.' Do you know what it means, Miss Garrett?"

She hated the way he enunciated her name. She let her gaze wander over his shoulder to peer through the tinted window at a dust bowl coming down the dirt road. A pickup truck roared past, shrouding the limousine with dust.

Honey Belle had lost, and she knew it. "I'm sure you're itching to tell me."

"In all honesty, Miss Garret, can you imagine you or your parents at the governor's ball, hobnobbing with political royalty?"

When she didn't answer, he added, "If you care for my son, care enough to step out of his life."

He offered the check, again. "Take it. Ten thousand is enough money to buy you and your family a new start...in a new state." He leaned forward as if drilling his next point home. "I want you gone. Tomorrow."

His narrowed eyes and cold scowl told Honey Belle that Tripp's father was a heartless man with enough power to squash people's lives without remorse.

Beyond lovemaking on the beach, what did she really know about Tripp? What if he shared the same cold and calculating traits as his father? Did she want to spend the rest of her life with a man she might later come to hate?

"How did you find where I live, Judge Hartwell?"

He cocked an eyebrow. "Simple. I hired a private investigator."

She allowed her shoulders to slump. As if the photographs weren't belittling enough, the Judge continued debasing her. "Everything about you is cheap, Miss Garrett, including your name."

She closed her eyes and rubbed them with her fingers. Her bones felt as if they were slowly dissolving. Opening her eyes, she said, "What's wrong with my name?"

The way his gaze drifted over her body caused a convulsive shiver to riffle over her.

"Honey Belle...has the definite ring of a fifty-dollar hooker."

She shook her head in shocked disbelief. She lashed out. Before her hand found its target, he grabbed her wrist.

"I am not naïve enough to believe you and my son haven't cohabitated." He pointed a long slender finger toward Honey Belle. "Heed my warning, young woman, and heed it well. If there is a seed growing inside you, make certain my son never knows about it. Take care of it—quietly." He arched an eyebrow. "Surely you are smart enough to discern my meaning."

Feeling the edges of her temper growing dangerously frayed, she refrained from pressing her hands against her abdomen. Getting pregnant had never entered her mind. She should have listened to Carla—should have used the condom the girl had offered. Should have asked Tripp to use protection. She forced back the groan building in her throat.

"Your meaning is quite clear, Judge Hartwell."

"Good. Then we are in agreement that you are not worthy of my son?"

"No, we are not in agreement." She forced the quiver from her voice. "What you're doing is wrong. *You're* the one not worthy of your son."

Hartwell's face looked so stricken she was afraid he might strike her. "I assure you it isn't my character flaws that will concern my son, not when he sees the pictures. Not when he learns you've duped him. He'll know you for the bloodsucking opportunist your really are."

He shoved the envelope containing the check toward her. Honey Belle thought she'd outsmart the despicable elder Hartwell. She waved the envelope in the air. "What bank in Charleston will cash a check for this amount of money, and especially for someone who doesn't have a checking account?"

"Ah, my dear, I thought you smarter than this. Haven't you figured out by now I know everything about you? At best, the funds are meager. However, we both know you have a checking account. Alas, you are correct. The bank might question whether or not the check is forged if you try to draw funds from it."

He scratched his chin as if contemplating. "Reaching into his coat pocket, he withdrew a monogrammed gold clip with more money than Honey Belle had ever seen in her lifetime. He peeled off several bills and stuffed them inside the envelope. "Five hundred dollars, Miss Garrett...enough to buy you and your parents passage far, far away from South Carolina, and a check for ten thousand as payment for your promise to never, for the rest of your lifetime, contact my son."

A nasty grin twisted his face. "I'm a man of my word, young woman. I have eyes and ears everywhere. Don't think to cross me."

He pressed a button, and the uniformed driver opened the limousine's door. Honey Belle had barely stepped out when the door slammed and the sleek black car roared away, leaving her standing with a white envelope in her hand and a crushing pain in her heart.

Chapter Eleven

Wrapping her arms around her waist, Honey
Belle watched the black car bounce down the dirt
road, trying to avoid the potholes.

As she trudged back to the house, her entire
body trembled as much from fright as from anger. So
Tripp's father had hired a detective to find her. She
should have known all good things really do come to
an end.

Stuffing the cash and the white envelope
containing the check inside the pocket of her peddle-
pushers, she lifted a hand against the white heat of
August. Her mother stood on the porch stoop. "Who
was in that fancy car, and why were you sittin' in
it?"

Fighting the bleakness threatening to consume
her, Honey Belle said, "Let's go inside, Mama."

She walked to the kitchen, filled two glasses
with ice cubes, then added sweet tea and handed one
to her mother. Her insides churned with worry.
Pushing her own glass aside, she crossed her arms
on the table, lowered her head, and buried her face,
setting free the soul-wracking tears she'd forced
back during her confrontation with Tripp's father.

Her mother's tender touches were rare. Honey
Belle cherished the gentle pats to her shoulder. "It
cain't be all that bad, can it?"

"Oh, but it is, Mama... It really is worse than
you can ever imagine." Honey Belle told her about
the photographs and how Judge Hartwell had
threatened to send them to Tripp. Between sobs, she
said, "The Judge said if we don't leave South

Carolina our life will be worse off than it all ready is. He wants us gone tomorrow."

Her mother kept a deceptively straight face while she listened to Honey Belle relate all Judge Hartwell had said. Before she opened her mouth, Honey Belle pleaded, "Please, Mama, don't say 'I told you so.'"

Delilah Garrett raked boney hands through her sweat-drenched hair. "Tomorrow. How...where are we supposed to get the money?"

"He gave me five hundred dollars." She pulled the cash from her pocket and laid it on the table. A little voice inside her head cautioned to not mention the check.

"Whew, Honey Belle, I ain't never in the whole of my life seen that much money at one time."

"What should we do, Mama? Where will we go?"

She harrumphed. "Ain't nothing holdin' us here. Your daddy cain't work no more, and my health ain't good." She tapped fingers against her temple as if thinking of a plan. "We'll go to my sister's."

"Do you think the truck will make it all the way to Georgia?"

"That old truck don't have too many more miles left in it. Bubba offered me fifty dollars for it. While I stay here and pack, you drive to the bus station and buy the tickets. In the morning, we'll pick Bubba up on the way to the depot. He'll have himself a truck and I'll have money to buy your daddy a new canister of oxygen. 'Sides, riding in an air-conditioned bus with reclining seats will be a lot easier on him than the three of us crowded into the front seat of a hot truck."

"Shouldn't we call Aunt Tess? Since the two of you haven't spoken for a few years, she might take exception to us showing up on her doorstep unannounced."

"Don't matter," her mother offered. "Tess won't

turn away family."

"I can't believe this is happening, Mama. It's like a bad dream."

"Then you'd better wake up and get on about the business of buying those bus tickets."

As Honey Belle drove, she mentally compared the lives of her mother and her aunt. The two sisters were as different as night and day. Delilah had run away at fourteen, married at fifteen, birthed a child at sixteen, and generally made a mess of her life.

The obligatory Christmas card once a year with a short note inquiring about the family's health was the sum total of what Honey Belle knew about her aunt.

Once, in a rare reminiscent mood, her mother had dug out an old picture album and talked about her sister. Tess, five years older, had never married, attended nursing school, and lived in a fine antebellum home in Valdosta, Georgia.

Honey Belle had watched Delilah trace a finger over the image of a woman dressed in a nurse's uniform. Even now she recalled her mother's words. "Tess is a little on the hoity-toity side, but if push ever came to shove, blood is still thicker than water."

At the bus station, no parking places were available. Honey Belle circled the block. The day had grown hotter, and she didn't feel much like walking. She drove around the block until she spotted a car leaving the depot. Honey Belle claimed the parking space.

Before purchasing the tickets, she used the pay phone to call her aunt, pouring out all the details of her predicament. Tess listened, giving only an occasional comment to let her niece know she was listening.

Honey Belle twisted and untwisted the telephone cord around her fingers while she waited for her aunt's decision. She feared the worst when silence filled her ear. "Aunt Tess, are you there?"

A heavy sigh echoed through the line. "That's quite a mess you've gotten yourself into, Honey Belle."

"I'm sorry, Aunt Tess. I'll understand if you say no."

Silence.

"Aunt Tess, are you there?"

"It's my house, Honey Belle. There'll be rules to follow, and that includes your mama and daddy, too. Church on Sunday, and no smoking or drinking."

Honey Belle's knees buckled with relief. She leaned against the glass pane in the phone booth to keep from collapsing. "Thank you, Aunt Tess. I promise we'll only stay until we can find a place of our own."

"You've just said your daddy is dying and you're worried about your mama's health. My sister always was bullheaded. We'll get her to a doctor. In the meantime, don't worry about finding a rental house. There are times when this old mausoleum I live in gets a little lonely."

"Mama will be pleased when I tell her."

"Call me when you get to the bus station. I'll come get y'all."

Honey Belle purchased three bus tickets to Valdosta, Georgia. For a moment she felt like a child off on a big expedition, unafraid, seeking adventure. Then she thought of Judge Hartwell. She no longer felt childlike.

****

Three suitcases sat in the middle of the living room floor. The sum total of their lives stuffed into three suitcases. Honey Belle pulled out a chair and joined her parents at the kitchen table.

Breakfast was strained. The scrambled eggs turned cold, the toast dried, and the coffee was bitter. No one seemed to notice.

Confusion, anger and disappointment gnawed at Honey Belle. There was no denying that never seeing Tripp again left an aching emptiness in her heart.

Delilah Garrett broke the silence. "What's the matter, daughter?"

Visibly startled by her mother's voice, Honey Belle's gaze flashed to her. "I don't know...everything."

Surprisingly, her mother had an answer for both. "I guess it's come as a shock to you, knowing I was right about that boy never marrying you. Once we get settled at my sister's, you'll forget all about him."

Honey Belle felt as if her blood pressure had risen several notches above normal.

"Delilah," Jack Garrett wheezed, "you're always pickin'. Pick...pick...pick. For once, leave Honey Belle alone." Honey Belle rose from her chair and gathered the plates.

A touch of sarcasm crept into Delilah's voice. "Dump the scraps out the back door. Let the neighborhood cats feast. And never mind about washing the dishes. Old man Ellerby never done us no favors. He can pay someone to clean this dump."

It was time to go. Time to say goodbye to the only home Honey Belle had ever known. She'd had the same bed, the same quilt, the same pictures on the wall, for as long as she could remember.

She managed to smile. It was hard to smile when she knew she'd never see Tripp again. She wouldn't let herself think about him. She closed her eyes and breathed deep, fighting the sting behind her eyelids as tears threatened to push through. She couldn't cry.

"Come on, Daddy. Let me help you to the truck."

He touched her arm and smiled in a way that said he understood the depth of her emotions.

Chapter Twelve

Change was in the air. August drifted into September. Indian summer set in. A week after Honey Belle's hasty departure from South Carolina, Tripp's plane touched down at Charleston's airport.

A white-hot need rose like an electrical storm inside the apex of Tripp's groin. It didn't matter that he was the son of a prominent judge with influential friends and important political connections. Tripp was anxious to hold the woman he loved in his arms. A week away from Honey Belle seemed like an eternity.

While in Massachusetts, the thought occurred to him that he didn't know her phone number.

Eager to talk to her, he'd dialed information. The operator said, "What city are you calling?"

"Charleston, South Carolina, a listing for Garret at 1423 Barrington Street."

"One moment please."

Tripp had pen and paper ready to scribble down the phone number.

"I'm sorry, sir. There is no listing for a Garrett at that address."

"Are you sure?" What about—" He'd never asked Honey Belle the names of her mother or father. "Never mind, Operator."

He thought it odd that an upper middle class family had no phone listing. He knew her father was very ill. The idea of Honey Belle not having a telephone bothered him. He wondered what she'd do in case she had to contact the doctor or call for an ambulance. Doubt crept in. He'd shoved the thought aside. After all, some folks preferred private telephone numbers. His family did.

Tomorrow, he'd take her shopping for an engagement ring. Depending on his mother's state of mind, he'd ask her to plan an intimate dinner party for Honey Belle and her parents. Then he'd formally ask permission for her hand in marriage.

Tripp knew the Judge would object to his marrying before graduating from law school. He'd cross that bridge when the subject presented itself.

Tonight, Tripp planned to drive Honey Belle to their favorite place on the beach, drink champagne and make wild passionate love to her. He'd tell her about the furnished cottage he'd rented within walking distance of the university, and the beauty of the changing leaves. He hoped she had a warm coat for the cold Massachusetts winters. It didn't matter. He'd buy her a new one.

As he rode the elevator up to the airport's VIP parking garage, he envisioned Honey Belle's velvety lavender eyes glittering with tears of happiness, throwing her arms around his neck and showering him with hot, moist kisses.

He presented the claim ticket to the parking valet, and eagerly waited while the attendant returned with the BMW.

Speeding down Route One, his first stop was at a florist shop, where he purchased a dozen long-stemmed red roses.

Fighting cross-town traffic, an hour later he parked in front of Honey Belle's house. He smoothed his windblown hair, gathered the box of roses in his arms, calmed his pattering heart and, with a jaunty step, strode up the sidewalk.

Standing on the porch, he again ran a hand over his hair to smooth down the wind-blown wispy ends. He rang the doorbell and waited.

"Yes, may I help you?"

He stared at the elderly woman standing behind the screened door. Surely this wasn't Honey Belle's mother. Though she rarely spoke of her mother and had never described her, Tripp tried to hide some of his dismay. Perhaps this woman, with hair the color of snow, was possibly the grandmother.

His cleared his throat. "Is Honey Belle home?"

"I'm sorry. No one by that name lives here."

"Are you sure?" Tripp felt almost as inadequate as the question he ask.

"Young man, seventy years ago, I was born in this house. Fifty years ago, my husband and I were wedded in the back yard. I would certainly know who lives in my house, and I assure you the only Honey Belle I'm familiar with is the tangerine."

Tripp shifted the box of roses from one arm to the other. "Forgive me, ma'am. I don't mean to be insistent. You see, for the past two months I've dated a young woman named Honey Belle Garrett. I picked her up at this address and brought her back home to this address."

"Oh, that young woman, the one who stood under the elm tree?"

He glanced off in the direction of the tree, trying to make sense of the woman's words. "Yes, ma'am. She said she lived here, in this house."

"You seem like an honest young man. What is your name?"

"Tripp Hartwell."

"I knew a T. Harlan Hartwell. He handled the legal affairs for my late husband. Might you be related?"

A mixture of impatience and irritated confusion consumed Tripp. He wanted to find out about Honey Belle, not discuss his father. "Possibly my father. He's a judge now."

Her eyes widened with discernment. "I declare. Isn't this a fine howdy-do? Meeting Harlan's son.

My-my."

"Ma'am, my girlfriend said her father suffered from a serious heart condition. Maybe she was afraid our dating might upset him, and decided to meet me here instead of at her house." Tripp glanced over his shoulder at the neatly trimmed yards bursting with colorful azaleas. "Do you know which house belongs to the Garretts?"

As if trusting Tripp, the elderly woman opened the screened door and stepped onto the veranda. "Do you know the history of Barrington Street, young Mr. Hartwell?"

In some ways the woman reminded him of his mother: hair neatly coiffed, a single strand of pearls around her neck, the blue floral dress with a white circular collar seeming out of place for a casual day at home.

To hide his growing impatience, Tripp placed his free hand inside a pants pocket and fiddled with the loose change. "I'm afraid I must plead ignorance, ma'am."

She swept her hand toward the porch swing at the end of the veranda. "Shall we sit?"

Tripp inwardly groaned. "Ma'am, I'd like to—"

The woman offered him a crinkled smile and walked to the swing. She patted the seat. "Of course you'd like to hear. It's warm outside. Shall I call for the maid to pour us some lemonade?"

He reminded himself a southern gentleman didn't hurt old ladies' feelings. In a rush he sat beside her, refusing the refreshment. "Another time, ma'am. I'm recently home from registering at Harvard. My parents are expecting me. I wouldn't want to worry my mother."

"Well, then, I'll give you the shortened version. You see, the homes on Barrington Street managed to survive the ravages of the Civil War. Most who live here are descendants of those who fought and died with the great southern generals. Folks on Barrington Street have known each other since we were children. The Garden Club ladies work diligently to preserve the charm and dignity that has survived for over a hundred years."

Tripp's fingers worried the red bow adorning the flower carton. He had a bad feeling. "What about the Garretts?"

She touched his arm. "I'm sorry to say, as long as I've lived here I've never known of any Garretts."

Tripp felt like laughing and cursing at the same time. "I don't understand. Why would Honey Belle lie to me?"

The elderly woman turned a sympathetic smile toward him. "Your mother is Mary Alice Hartwell, is she not?"

"Yes. You know her?"

"Not directly. Like myself, your mother is from a long line of South Carolinian bluebloods." A laugh escaped her. "That sounded perfectly snobbish, didn't it?"

Tripp responded with a lift of an eyebrow. "What does this have to do with my girl friend?"

"Does this young woman fully understand who you are?"

"I'm not certain I follow you."

"Of course you do, young Mr. Hartwell. You've been raised in the South. Even in this modern day and time, family name and accomplishments are often the most important considerations in marriage. In some cases, they are the only consideration."

Some bright gold leaves fluttered and fell to the ground, indicating the approach of Indian summer. Tripp's heart fluttered and felt as if it were falling, too. "A person should be judged on their merits, not which side of the fence they were born on."

"If your young lady preferred to stand under the elm tree until you arrived, never introduced you to her parents, used my house as her decoy, and never invited you to sit on the porch swing to do a little sparking..." She drew a deep breath as if allowing Tripp to absorb her words.

Tripp's throat tightened, his stomach clenched. "Honey Belle didn't have to lie. She could have trusted our love. Trusted me."

The woman said nothing else right away. After a few moments, she comforted, "As idealistic as it sounds, the affairs of the heart are never easy, young Mr. Hartwell." She rose from the swing. "If you'll excuse me, I don't tolerate the heat as well as I did when I was young."

Tripp stood, too. "Thank you for your time, ma'am."

He walked down the steps toward the convertible, his thoughts troubled more than he could admit. He pulled the car door open and got in, tossing the box of roses to the back seat.

****

Tripp needed answers. Why had Honey Belle misled him?

Thirty minutes later he pulled into the Burger Bin's parking lot. This time he didn't bother with his wind-mussed hair.

The blast of cold air from the restaurant's interior sent a momentary chill through his sweat-soaked shirt. He removed his sunglasses. Carla stood behind the counter.

"Well, as I live and breathe, if it isn't the college boy returned home. What can I getcha?"

"I need to speak to Honey Belle."

With a shrug of her shoulders, Carla offered a whimsical smile. "Don't we all? The day after you left, she called in saying her mama was sick. H.B. came in 'bout an hour later to pick up an order of chicken fingers and fries. Haven't seen hide nor hair of her since."

"Why do you call her H.B.?"

"Guess you didn't know Honey Belle hated her name. Said 'Honey' sounded cheap, and 'Belle' sounded old. 'Round here, we all called her H.B."

"Can you take a break, Carla? I'm confused as hell."

Without hesitation, the stout waitress called over her shoulder, "Leanne, take the counter. I'm gonna have a smoke." She looked at Tripp. "Want a cola?" Without waiting for an answer, she filled two cups with ice and cola, then walked around the counter. She indicated with a nod. "We'll sit in the booth by the window."

Tripp followed the girl and slid in opposite her. After a healthy swallow of the cold drink, he set the cup aside, then explained about driving to the house on Barrington Street.

"I don't understand why she lied, Carla."

The waitress chided Tripp. "For a college boy, you ain't as smart as I thought you were." She giggled. "Uh-oh, by the expression on your face, I've upset you. Sorry."

Heat grew under Tripp's collar. Heat that had nothing to do with the weather. He worked to squelch the insults forming deep in his throat. "Maybe you'd better enlighten me."

"Okay. First, didn't you ever put two and two together about H.B. driving a twenty-year-old beat-up truck? And second, did you ever ask yourself why a girl who was supposed to live in a fancy neighborhood was flippin' hamburgers in a joint like this?"

He opened his mouth to speak. Carla held up her hand. She placed her lips around the straw and drew deeply. "I told her sooner or later you'd find out. Now that you have, how does it feel to be made a fool of?"

He swallowed against the pressure squeezing

his chest. Blood pounded in his temples.

He shrugged his shoulders, dismissing Carla's snide remark. "I tried to call Honey Belle from Massachusetts. There was no listing."

"Nah, they don't have a phone; always had to use a neighbor's."

"Maybe she had to put her father in the hospital. You said her mother called in sick. Maybe she's in the hospital, too." He reached across the table and clasped Carla's hand. "Look, I don't care where Honey Belle lives. Give me the address and I'll drive out to check on her."

Carla withdrew her hand from his. "The reason H.B. never wanted you to know where she lived is because it's in the worst section of all Charleston. You ever heard of Shanty Groves?"

"No, I haven't."

"It's not a safe place for rich folks in fancy cars. Besides, I drove out to check on her. She ain't there. Neighbor said they were gone. Loaded up the truck with a coupla suitcases and left."

"Did he say where they went?"

"Nope, just that they were always behind on the rent. He figured the landlord gave 'em the boot."

"Even if that were the case, Honey Belle and her mother still had their jobs. Maybe they went to a temporary shelter."

"Listen, Tripp, I ain't the brightest cookie in the jar, but I've been around the block a time or two. You're rich, H.B. is dirt poor. You're on your way to becoming an even richer somebody. She quit school when she was sixteen to help support her folks. She's never gonna have two nickels to rub together. H.B. is who she is and you're who you are. You think your high-falutin' society parents would ever accept a girl from the wrong side of the tracks?"

As if to cool her throat from her long dissertation, Carla drew a generous sip of cola through the straw. "I don't know why she left. Wherever she and her folks went, it's my guess they ain't comin' back. For the both of you, take my advice and leave it be. Go get your lawyer's degree. Marry a rich girl, raise yourself a couple of spoiled young'uns, and forget about Honey Belle Garrett."

With his heart racing and bile rising in his throat, he pushed from the booth. Deep in his heart, he knew everything Carla had stated was true.

"I'll deal with my parents, Carla. Once they meet Honey Belle and get to know her, they'll come to love her as I do."

"Um-huh. If that's what you want to believe to make yourself feel better," Carla shrugged a shoulder, "you keep right on believing it."

As much as he hated to admit it, she was correct in her assumption. He'd been raised in the caste system of the South, where family name and accomplishments were often the most important consideration in marriage. As far as his parents and South Carolina's social registry were concerned, it was the only consideration. Until meeting Honey Belle, he'd never rebelled against this system of antiquated social snobbery.

Tripp pulled a pen from his pocket and scribbled his phone number on a napkin. "If Honey Belle contacts you, please give her my number. Tell her it's important, that no matter what, I love her."

Carla puffed her stout cheeks and blew a breathy, "Sure."

An uneasy feeling twisted Tripp's gut. He held little hope of ever hearing from the woman who had stolen his heart.

Chapter Thirteen

A few minutes later Tripp sat behind the wheel of his car, easing into traffic and then turning on the street leading out of the city limits.

Half an hour later he pulled his convertible up the oak-lined driveway to his house. As he parked, the front door opened and his mother stepped out, a vision in her green gardening slacks and floppy straw hat. She waved a glove-covered hand, a galvanized tin watering can in the other.

He got out of his car and walked toward her for a hug.

"Welcome home, son. I've missed you."

"You are pretty as a picture, Mother."

She gave a playful slap to his shoulder. "In my gardening clothes? You are a dear boy."

"Is Dad home?"

"In his study."

Tripp kissed his mother's cheek. "Excuse me, Mother. I need to speak with him."

"If it's about the engagement party, I've given it a lot of thought. Perhaps you should bring the young lady to meet us before we go forth with plans."

He touched her cheek, happy his mother's mental faculties had returned. He drew a deep breath. "We'll discuss it later, Mother. Right now, I have business with Dad." And then he smiled.

"Of course, you do, dear." She tipped the watering can toward a pot of colorful flowers adorning the porch.

As an afterthought, he cast his mother an impish smile and sang, "Mary Alice, Mary Alice, how does your garden grow? With kitten tails and puppydog tails all wagging in a row."

His mother giggled and clapped her hands like a happy child. "I thank you for the rhyme, but I do believe your version is quite different from the original."

"Mine put a smile on your face, and that's all that matters, 'Mary, Mary, quite contrary—'"

The aroma of frying chicken greeted him, and something baked with nutmeg, as he opened the front door. The thought of approaching his father settled in the pit of his stomach like soured buttermilk.

Long strides carried him down the hall. He stopped at the massive oaken door to his father's study, raised a fist, and rapped once.

"Enter." Judge Hartwell looked up from the folder that lay in front of him. He rose with an outstretched hand. "Tripp, my boy, how was Massachusetts? Get the registration glitch taken care of?"

Tripp pushed the greeting aside. He didn't hide the allegation in his voice. "Honey Belle and her family left town. What do you know about it?"

The Judge spoke sharply. "If you're making an accusation, it's damn well not appreciated."

Tripp answered in a tight voice. "I've had a bellyful of lies, Dad. You made it quite clear how you felt about Honey Belle and my marriage proposal to her."

Without going into detail about his visit with the owner of the house on Barrington Street, Tripp simply stated he'd visited Honey Belle's workplace only to discover she had quit without notice, and a neighbor had witnessed her and her parents leaving with suitcases.

His father tossed the folder aside. "I don't expect you to believe me when I say I know nothing of this young woman or her family leaving town. Granted, I'm not in favor of a union with a girl we've never met and know nothing about, but I'm hurt to the bone that you'd think I was in any way involved."

Hearing that admission, Tripp looked into his father's eyes and thought he saw remorse. Doubt dragged Tripp down. He sighed.

His father walked around the desk and draped an around Tripp's shoulder, hugging him close. "Disappointment and confusion is written all over your face. We're all susceptible to bad judgment calls, son. Like I said, I don't know where Miss Garrett and her family went. And that's the God's honest truth."

Though Tripp had his misgivings, his father had never given him reason to believe he'd stoop to shady, covert dealings. And yet he still wanted to believe in Honey Belle. He moved away from his father's embrace.

"Tripp, son, listen to me, right now you feel as if your world has fallen apart. At some point, you have to move beyond the hurts, or anger and bitterness will keep you from accomplishing your goals in life."

Tripp slumped into a leather chair. He sighed heavily. His "Yeah, sure," didn't sound convincing.

When he rose to leave, his father said, "This past week your mother has been her old self. Let's keep it that way."

"I know. She greeted me, saying we needed to discuss the engagement party. After her last episode, I didn't think she'd remember."

The Judge frowned. "Nor I. We'll not upset her with this nonsense about Miss Garrett. Discreetly explain to your mother you've decided to put marriage on hold until after graduation. Tell her you'd prefer an old-fashioned barbeque with all the trimmings because you'll miss Pearlie Mae's home cooking once you're at Harvard. I believe that will sufficiently pacify your mother."

"What if she asks about Honey Belle?"

The Judge cast his son a wink. "You're almost a lawyer. You'll figure it out."

Over the next few days, Tripp packed books, clothing, ski poles, skis, snow boots, and other personal belongings. Deciding to leave the convertible in South Carolina, he loaded one of the spare station wagons with his gear.

He planned to submerse himself in his studies, and hoped to erase Honey Belle Garrett from his heart.

Chapter Fourteen

Valdosta, Georgia

On a sweltering September afternoon, Honey Belle sat under a canopy listening to a minister speak words over her father's grave. Her mama's ragged sobs tore at her heart. She reached over and clasped the blue-veined, bony hand.

"Don't be sad, Mama. He's in a better place."

"Your daddy weren't much. Dang it, he was all I had."

You have me, Mama. Don't I matter to you? Honey Belle nearly choked on the words stuck in her throat. It seemed even in grief her mother bore no kind thoughts toward her daughter.

Three weeks after arriving in Valdosta, Jack Garrett's health had turned for the worse. He'd passed quietly in his sleep the day after he was admitted to the hospital.

A week after her father's funeral, Honey Belle sat on the bathroom floor, hugging the commode. Regular as clockwork, when she'd skipped her monthly, she hoped, then prayed she wasn't pregnant. As she hung her head over the toilet bowl and wearily mopped her face with a damp cloth, beads of sweat lined her top lip.

Her stomach continued to heave. She tried to spit out the taste of bile as it clawed her throat.

Lying with her head against the cool porcelain tube, she didn't bother to look up when the bathroom door opened.

Sarcasm laced Delilah's voice. "I knowed it. I

knowed it all along. You've got the look about you."

Honey Belle kept her eyes closed. Hoping to settle her stomach, she drew several deep breaths. "What is it you know, Mama?"

"You're green as a gourd. Don't take no rocket scientist to figure out you done got yourself knocked-up."

Honey Belle opened her eyes and shifted around to turn on the faucet. She ran cold water over the cloth, rung it out and wiped her face again.

"We've just buried daddy. I didn't even get a chance to tell him about the baby. For once, Mama, please this one time, can't you be happy for me? It's your grandchild."

"No, it ain't. It's your bastard."

The bite in her mother's voice caused Honey Belle to look up. Her jaw firmed as she spoke. "Leave me be, Mama. I'm too sick to argue."

With each passing day, Honey Belle watched her mother grow frailer. "What can I do, Aunt Tess, short of forcing her to get in the car and driving her to the doctor? She refuses to go for a checkup. I'm worried about her."

"Delilah always was as hardheaded as a stubborn mule. If I have to pitch a hissy-fit to get her to the doctor, then that's what I'll do."

A few days later, true to her word, Honey Belle's Aunt Tess pitched an old-fashioned, Southern hissy-fit and said she'd drag Delilah by the head of the hair to the doctor, if she had to. Honey Belle had never seen her mother back down to anyone, but back down she did.

The diagnosis was bad. Stage four breast cancer had spread throughout her mother's skeletal system.

"What can we do, Doctor?" Honey Belle dreaded his answer.

"Along with chemotherapy and radiation, we can pray for a miracle."

Though the prescribed treatments amassed a wad of doctor bills, in the end, the treatments didn't save Delilah. Honey Belle thought her mother was too tired and worn out to fight for her life.

Five months later, on a frigid January morning, Delilah Garrett closed her eyes and passed from this world without a kind word to her daughter or for the grandchild she'd never know.

Part of Honey Belle felt as if the world had crashed down around her. She wondered if it was wrong for the other part of her to feel relief.

A few days after her mother's funeral, Honey Belle and her Aunt Tess were in the parlor. January had brought a rainy winter, and Honey Belle sat in front of the fireplace sipping hot cocoa and enjoying the warmth. Her aunt's home was everything she'd dreamed of, with its sprawling front porch supported by huge columns, a porch swing, and a neatly groomed yard surrounded by a white picket fence.

"Honey Belle, it's time you and I had a serious woman-to-woman talk."

Honey Belle nibbled on crackers topped with peanut butter. "Whatta you want to talk about, Aunt Tess?"

Her aunt pointed at the little mound beneath Honey Belle's shirt. "You have some important decisions to make."

"Like?"

"Marrying your daddy was the death of anything good for my sister, and I don't mind saying so. You know it as well as me. Not even forty years old, she was used up and wrung out like an old dishrag."

Though Honey Belle's parents had shown little affection toward her, she'd loved them. "Mama was always telling me she'd made a mess of her life. The thing she never told me was why she chose to marry my daddy at such a young age."

Tess's voice took on a hard edge. "Delilah had a

wild streak in her. She was always in a hurry to grow up. Our mother constantly warned Delilah about sashaying her behind like an open invitation to the boys. Said she'd get caught. Delilah ran away. Mama called the law. Cops caught up with her and brought her home. Delilah hated mother after that. She skipped school, started smoking, drinking, staying out all night. She was the bane of our mother's existence.

"And Delilah did get caught—with you. Jack Garrett was a sweet-talking, handsome good-for-nothing. He promised my sister the moon. All she got was pregnant. Barely sixteen when you were born, she suffered in hard labor for three days. The doctor said you were too big and she was too small. After you came a string of miscarriages, until the doctor said she needed a hysterectomy. That was a blessing in disguise."

"Why didn't you ever marry, Aunt Tess?"

Her aunt moistened her throat with a sip of coffee. "Who says I never married?" As if wanting to change the subject, Tess hastened on. "That's neither here nor there. As I was saying, you have some important decisions to make, Honey Belle. You can choose to educate yourself and raise this child proper, or you can follow in your mama's footsteps, scrimping and pinching and always dreaming about what you'll never have."

Honey Belle caressed the small protrusion beneath her shirt. Inside her womb grew a baby whose life she was responsible for. The decision was an easy one. "After I quit school, it was difficult listening to the kids at the Burger Bin talk about what colleges they planned to attend, their future careers. I always planned to get my GED. But both mine and mama's paychecks were needed to keep us going, especially after daddy got sick and couldn't work anymore. After awhile, time slipped away, and the GED never happened."

Aunt Tess stretched her feet toward the fire, her voice matter-of-fact. "After the baby is born, if you choose to get your diploma, and perhaps attend college, I'll help you with the finances, and this will be your home for as long as you care to stay. If you choose not to get an education," she shrugged her shoulders, "you'll have to find your own place, and take care of the baby as best you can."

Honey Belle choked on the cracker that seemed to grow inside her throat. She'd used a good deal of the blackmail money from Tripp's father to pay for her parent's medical and funeral costs. Funny how, at the time, she'd thought ten thousand dollars would last a lifetime, when in fact it disappeared almost as quickly as water down a drain.

"I don't want my child growing up poor and illiterate, Aunt Tess." She heaved a sigh. "Living in South Carolina, the way we did, I didn't see much wrong with my life."

Honey Belle glanced around the cozy room with wall-to-wall carpeting and not a speck of dust anywhere. "If you'll drive me to the vocational school, I'll start working toward my GED next week. Maybe I can get finished before the baby is born."

Aunt Tess clapped her hands together. "That's the spirit." Then she turned serious. "You've never spoken of the baby's father. Is there a reason?"

"If there were, I wouldn't care to discuss it."

Honey Belle knew she could never divulge Tripp's identity, for more than one reason. First, there were those horrid blackmail photographs to contend with, and, most importantly, she feared what Judge Hartwell would do once he found out she'd had a baby and decided to keep the child.

Her aunt's voice interrupted her thoughts. "Don't you think the father has a right to know? At least notify him so he can pay child support."

"Let me repeat, Aunt Tess, I don't care to discuss it."

"You don't think this man or boy has a moral obligation to you and the child?"

"Aunt Tess, I respect you with all my heart, and I'm forever grateful you're providing me with a home, and the opportunity to get an education." She stared down at the cup in her hand. "Trust me when I say the baby's father couldn't care one way or the other. He's not someone I want in our lives."

With the damning evidence his father possessed, Honey Belle had convinced herself there was no way Tripp Hartwell the Third would want his name connected to her or to a bastard child.

"So be it, Honey Belle. I'll ask no more questions."

Honey Belle stretched and yawned. "I think I'll call it a night, Aunt Tess."

With a quick peck to her aunt's cheek, Honey Belle climbed the stairs to her bedroom. It had become a nightly habit to sit in the rocker and stare out the window at Orion and the Big Dipper, twinkling in the winter sky. Settling in the chair, she cradled the small mound of her belly. She rocked back and forth, picturing herself in maternity clothes, with swollen ankles, needing help to get out of a chair.

She managed to forget, for a few minutes, how drastically her life would change in the spring. When she thought about it, and about raising a child alone, her heart didn't know how to react. Then she reminded herself she wasn't alone. She had Aunt Tess.

By habit she looked upward. "Look, baby, a shooting star."

It was as if the unborn child had heard her voice and rewarded Honey Belle with a fluttering kick. She hadn't expected it, that jolt of excitement, that maternal surge of protectiveness.

She gently caressed the little lump poking her in the side. "Your daddy taught me the names of the stars. When you're born, I'll teach them to you."

She brushed back the rush of tears and fought the melancholy threatening to engulf her as she sat alone in the darkened room.

Her mind drifted to the night on the beach when Tripp had pledged his love to her. She'd made a wish on a shooting star that night, too. It had come true—Tripp had asked her to marry him.

She bent her head toward her stomach and whispered, "I wish upon this shooting star that someday you'll get to know your daddy."

Wiping a tear from her cheek, she was lost in thought for a long moment. "I promise I'll never be cold and distant toward you. I'll never treat you the way my parents did me."

And then she added, "I don't care if you're a little girl or a boy. I'll love you." Secretly she yearned for a son—a tiny version of Tripp.

Honey Belle gathered her senses, because she couldn't let her heart go in the direction it wanted to go.

****

The next morning Aunt Tess drove Honey Belle to the vocational school. Honey Belle walked through the glass doors and couldn't deny her stomach was doing flip-flops. She rubbed her sweating hands down the sides of her jeans as she and her aunt walked across the tiled lobby.

"Aunt Tess, what if I'm not smart enough?"

Her aunt laughed a little. "You're smarter than you give yourself credit for, Honey Belle."

"And that's another thing, Aunt Tess."

"What is?"

"My name. I've never liked it. When I was thirteen, I asked Mama if I could change it. Of course, you know her answer." Judge Hartwell's sneering contempt of her name echoed inside her head—*Sounds like a fifty-dollar prostitute.*

"Takes money to change your name, and think of all the rigmarole you'd have to go through to change your driver's license and your Social Security card. Is it really that important to you?"

Honey Belle looked up, meeting kind eyes with crinkled lines of age and experience at the corners. "When you put it that way, I guess it sounds rather pathetic. Back in South Carolina my friends called me H.B."

"Then call yourself H.B. and others will, too."

"I can't avoid giving my *real* name when I fill out forms."

"Don't make things complicated. Simply fill them out, then in large bold letters write 'Prefer to be called H.B. Garrett.'"

Honey Belle ignored the impatience in her aunt's voice and followed her through a door marked Registrar's Office.

****

On the way home from registering for classes, Aunt Tess offered to treat them to lunch. They stopped at the Silver Bullet Diner.

"Why aren't you eating, Honey Belle?"

Honey Belle ignored the cheeseburger sitting on her plate. "I'm eating." She smiled and bit into the burger. She ate a bite, swallowing in a way that looked painful.

"Are you sick?"

"I thought pregnant women were supposed to have morning sickness, not afternoon sickness."

"Happens that way, sometimes."

Honey Belle scooted back her chair on the linoleum floor and stood up, feeling a little green and a whole lot wobbly. Perspiration beaded along her forehead and above her top lip.

"I'm going outside. I need some air."

Aunt Tess called for the waitress to put their food in to-go boxes. "I'll be back after I see to my niece."

The waitress nodded.

Honey Belle didn't go far, just to the edge of the building. She leaned against it, gasping deep breaths of air.

Her aunt followed. Honey Belle leaned into the cool hand touching her cheek as her aunt said, "You look a little pale."

"I'm fine now, Aunt Tess. Do you mind if we go home? I need to lie down."

The waitress stepped out the entrance door. "Here's your food. That'll be ten dollars."

Honey Belle watched her aunt rummage inside a uniform pocket. After handing the waitress two fives and accepting the bag of burgers, she placed her arm around her niece's waist. "Isn't your doctor's appointment tomorrow?"

Honey Belle didn't want to talk. She wanted to take a nap. "I don't mean to be a pest, Aunt Tess."

"Hush, you hear me. You're many things, and a pest isn't one of them."

She nodded and blinked away tears. "Remember when I asked why you'd never married?"

"Uh-huh."

Honey Belle drew in a wavering breath as she followed her aunt to the bright yellow Volkswagen Beatle. "You were a little evasive with your answer."

Tess opened the door as if impatient to be done with this conversation. "No more than you, niece, about the father of your baby."

"I need to know about your life, Aunt Tess. I see your career, the house you live in, your success." Honey Belle ducked her head as she settled on the car seat. Her aunt was standing at the door, shading her eyes from the sun with her hand. "I have so many doubts about raising this baby, about being a single parent." She stopped abruptly. "Never mind, Aunt Tess, your secrets are your own. Just like my secrets belong to me."

Honey Belle looked down and shuffled her feet to a more comfortable position on the little car's floorboard. She swiped her eyes with the heels of her hands, chasing away memories that threatened to spill over into tears.

Chapter Fifteen

Issues. Honey Belle had lots of issues to deal with. One part of her needed to share the threats Tripp's father had made if she didn't leave town, if she didn't get rid of the baby. Insecurities nagged at her, threatening to drown her in a whirlpool of self-doubt.

Reassurances. She needed reassuring that she was a good person, responsible and capable of loving and nurturing a child. What if she'd inherited her mother's mean-spiritedness, her inability to show love?

"Back all in the same day." Aunt Tess's drawl drew Honey Belle back to the present.

She nodded and blinked away the tears. "I've never cried this much in my entire life, Aunt Tess. What's wrong with me?"

Her aunt reached over and patted her niece's hand. "It's called hormones. Your body is trying to adjust to the changes it's going through. Add to that you're still grieving for the loss of your mama and daddy. Put it all together and that's a lot of emotions to deal with."

Honey Belle opened the door and climbed out of the car.

"Come on." Aunt Tess jiggled the sack from the restaurant. "We can pop these hamburgers in the microwave."

The thought of a reheated greasy hamburger caused a wave of nausea to sweep over Honey Belle. "I'd rather have a cup of your special hot chocolate."

She accepted the warm smile her aunt offered.

"Double Dutch with a generous splash of half-and-half. Guaranteed to make all your troubles seem trivial."

"If only that were true, Aunt Tess, the world would be a better place for all of us."

They walked through the back door and into the kitchen decorated with shelves of colorful jars of canned tomatoes, okra, and pickled peaches.

Honey Belle settled on a stool as her aunt melted chocolate in a double-boiler, then added the milk, a pinch of cayenne pepper, and a liberal pinch of cinnamon. Inhaling the savory aroma, she felt as if her aunt's house was the safest place in the world.

"You wanted to know if I'd ever married."

Absently thrumming her fingers on the counter, Honey Belle whispered, "What did you say?"

"You're a thousand miles away. Take the tray of cookies to the den. I'll follow with the hot chocolate."

Honey Belle set the tray of homemade pecan sandies on the coffee table and settled on the floor in front of the fire place, resting her back against the sofa while Aunt Tess poured two steaming cups of cocoa.

Tess sat down across from her niece. Honey Belle reached for a cookie. "It's your life, Aunt Tess. Really, you don't have to tell me."

Tess, too, reached for a cookie. "Post traumatic syndrome. And my confession comes with a condition."

Honey Belle wiped crumbs from the corners of her mouth and reached for a second cookie. Her voice reflected caution. "What is this post traumatic thing, and what is the condition?"

"When I finish telling you my story, you'll know what PTSD is and what caused it. Second, I'm not asking you to name names—just give me enough information to help me understand why you don't want the father of this baby in its life, or yours."

Honey Belle sipped her cocoa and set the cup down. "No pressure?"

Her aunt crossed her heart and hoped to die. "No pressure."

Honey Belle laughed. "Deal. You go first."

Her aunt's voice softened as she spoke. "I graduated nursing school a few months shy of my twenty-first birthday. I needed to get away...away from all the problems Delilah caused our mama, the endless screaming and arguments, the phone calls to the cops when my sister didn't come home at night. She was fourteen and more than Mama could handle. I'd had a bellyful of my sister's hateful shenanigans. I wanted to get as far away as possible, and I wanted to see the world, so I joined the Peace Corps.

"I was sent to Rwanda in Africa. The village consisted of a small but well-equipped hospital, a mission, and a school. The native people were wonderfully accepting of a white nurse with a southern drawl. The only other white women in the village were three nuns. Two were teachers, one was a nurse. Father Brendan O'Toole was fresh out of the seminary and, like me, on his first foreign assignment. Dr. Roger Kemp from the United Kingdom was the staff physician. He was thirty-five years old and reminded me of Clark Gable with his infectious smile and pencil-thin mustache.

"I don't remember when I fell in love with Roger. Maybe it was the time when we worked round the clock during a cholera outbreak. Roger was tireless, and I was proud to assist him. Our professionalism developed into a friendship, and from there into a full-blown, goo-goo-eyed love. Five months later, we said our vows in the chapel, with Father O'Toole officiating. Nine months later Roger Scott Kemp, Jr. was born. We called our beautiful baby boy Scotty."

Noticing the slight tremble in her aunt's voice,

Honey Belle lifted the teapot and refilled both their cups with hot chocolate. Eager to hear more of the story, she waited patiently until her aunt seemed satisfied the steaming liquid was cool enough to take a sip.

"About three months after Scotty's birth, a young native staggered into the compound. His wounds were so severe that, to this day, I don't know how he managed to survive long enough to get to us. Before he died, he said rebel warriors had destroyed his entire village."

An odd sense of trepidation raced up Honey Belle's middle. Wrapping her suddenly chilled hands around the warm cup, she sipped the sweet confection inside.

Her aunt's eyes looked like faucets that were about to be turned on. Honey Belle had had enough life experience to recognize raw emotional pain when she saw it. Only the crackling of the fire in the fireplace eased the tension of silence that hung over the room.

Honey Belle cleared her throat. She wished she'd never asked about her aunt's past. "It's too painful, Aunt Tess—these memories. I should have kept my curiosity to myself. I'm sorry."

"I'm sorry, too. Time hasn't healed the wounds in my heart. Maybe the telling of it will."

A visible tremor wracked Tess. Honey Belle didn't know if she wanted to hear the rest of the story. She sucked in a deep breath and blew out slowly.

Tess continued in a monotone. "Roger used the shortwave radio to notify the authorities in Tanzania. Officials in Tanzania said they were aware of sporadic attacks on villages, but they were short-manned and had notified officials in Brussels to send soldiers. We were advised to arm ourselves as best as possible. Roger then contacted the Peace

Corps officials. He was told to prepare to evacuate. Because we were more than five hundred miles away by Land Rovers, Roger requested a cargo plane. He wanted to evacuate the entire village. The Peace Corps said they'd do their best. We held out little hope for more than a bush plane.

"We armed ourselves with what little we had—a rifle, a handgun, spears—not much, I'm afraid. We were peacekeepers, teachers, healers, unprepared for what was about to happen.

"They came on us like a nightmare. Hutu rebels. We never heard them. One minute I was assisting Roger with an appendectomy, the next minute our ears were filled with gut-wrenching screams. Before we could react, rebels entered the operating room. The leader spoke English. He ordered us outside. When Roger protested the woman on the operating table would die if he didn't finish the operation, that horrid beast simply removed his pistol from its holster—"

Honey Belle shuddered. Her aunt's gaze was lost to memory.

"We were ushered outside. Women were screaming, children crying, and bewildered old men wailing. There was so much confusion. My immediate thoughts rushed to Scotty. He was with Sister Mary Clare and Bunni, my wet nurse. I fought my captors. My arms were twisted so tightly behind my back it felt as if they were being pulled from their sockets. And still I fought, I kicked, I used my head as a battering ram. Roger fought, too. I kept hearing him calling my name, saying he loved me, and to be brave. Before my head exploded with pain and darkness closed in around me, I saw Roger forced to his knees.

"It was morning when I finally opened my eyes. Even after I regained consciousness, the next hours had the unsteady presence of a dream. The compound yard was littered with bodies. Every male child had been murdered—"

It was painful for Honey Belle to think of what had happened to Tess's baby. She protectively cradled her hands around her middle. "And Scotty?"

"Him, too." The hurt came through in those two words.

"Aunt Tess, I—"

"Let me finish," she held up her hand. "I need to get it out. All of it."

Honey Belle watched as Tess raked trembling fingers through her short gray hair. "My baby looked like a broken doll lying there in the dirt." She shuddered and brushed away tears. "Roger and Father O'Toole hung on wooden crosses. The sisters lay spread-eagled on the ground, their hands and feet tied to stakes, their robes and dignity stripped from them. As my mind tried to absorb the horrors, it took several minutes before I realized that I, too, lay in the baking African sun, naked as the day I was born.

"I cried out to God asking him why he'd allowed this to happen. I cursed the Hutu devils for killing my child. I prayed for the plane to arrive, I prayed for safety, I prayed for maggots to eat the eyes of our enemy."

When Tess stopped speaking, Honey Belle assumed her aunt had finished the story, leaving the rest to imagination. She was wrong. Tess continued.

"If you even think you can picture how awful it was, you are wrong. The leader squatted next to me. He said his name was Ngoma. He called me *Nkento*. Woman. He said he wanted me to live so I could tell the world of his power and how the Hutu would rule Africa. As dry as my mouth was, I managed to create enough saliva to cover his ugly face with spittle.

"'You bastard,'" I screamed at him, "'You filthy murdering, bastard. I hope you rot in hell.'"

"He laughed a long, loud, barking hyena sound. In his language, Ngoma ordered his men to rouse Roger and Father O'Toole—by jabbing them with spears. Then turning to me, his eyes ferocious under his huge furrowed brow, he flung his hand toward the nuns, in disgust.

"For days, we were brutalized. Roger and Father O'Toole were forced to watch our degradation. I vowed I would live through the nightmare."

Tess seemed to concentrate on a fingernail as she clicked it back and forth. "There's a strange moment in time, after something horrible happens, when you know it's true but it seems like a fantasy.

"I don't even remember when the rebels left, or how many days I lay all alone with the dead in the baking sun. I awoke in a Tanzanian hospital. Roger's parents were sitting next to the bed. They had flown in from London."

Honey Belle stared into Tess's blue eyes. She wanted to wrap her arms around her aunt, to hold her as one would do to comfort an injured child. She whispered, "Roger?"

Tess spread her hands apart in a hopeless gesture. She closed her eyes and shook her head. "I needed a place to heal. Returning to South Carolina, to my mother's home with Delilah's problems, wasn't an option. Instead I went to England to live with Roger's parents, and to pretend Rwanda never happened. That Africa was a faraway place with make-believe people in history books. The tragedies that happened there were not mine." She sighed. "I stayed with Mr. & Mrs. Kemp for two years. Eventually, I couldn't stand the way people would duck their eyes and whisper about me, saying how tragic for having suffered such a loss.

"When I returned to the States, I worked in a few hospitals, but I couldn't stay rooted very long. Eventually, I made my way to Georgia."

Honey Belle reached for and accepted her aunt's outstretched hands. She was startled by Tess's next words. "For these many years, I've tried to heal myself by healing others."

"You're an attractive woman, Aunt Tess, why haven't you remarried?"

"The truth be known, I closed my heart and soul, vowing to never love again, nor allow anyone to love me. You've changed that, Honey Belle, you and your baby."

A honeycreeper sang from the bushes outside the window. It seemed impossible that an ordinary evening should proceed outside the house, when emotions inside the room with the glimmering fireplace were so raw and tangled.

"It's been thirty years and, though not as often, I still wake up in a cold sweat sometimes, with ghostly visions swirling inside my head. I work a great deal. It helps keep my mind in order. These days, my life is satisfying...

"As you said, Honey Belle, our secrets are our own. Now that you know mine, I'll not pressure you to tell me yours. All in your own time."

Emotions piled up as Honey Belle wrapped her arms around Tess and hugged her. Now she understood the shadows of pain she'd often noticed in her aunt's eyes. There were days when she looked like the loneliest person in the world. If a person didn't know better they'd think Tess never felt pain, had never been hurt. Honey Belle knew better. "You're a strong woman to have survived such a horrible ordeal, Aunt Tess. Mama always said the reason you stayed away was because you thought you were better than us. I have to say that a part of me believed her. She was wrong. Knowing how she was, if you'd told her, it wouldn't have made much difference. Mama had little feeling for other people's troubles."

A quick cramp in her stomach ended her thoughts. She drew in a breath and fought against the knife-sharp pain.

"You okay, Honey Belle?"

She nodded, because the pain had passed. "Yes, ma'am. I'm fine."

She met her aunt's serious gaze and felt the warmth of a smile such as she'd never known from her own mother.

She kissed her aunt's cheek. "I have lots to think about. Good night, Aunt Tess."

"Rest well."

Honey Belle climbed the stairs to her room. After listening to her aunt's tragic story, she wanted to be alone to figure out the next phase of her own life. And she didn't want to think about Tripp Hartwell the Third or his father.

Chapter Sixteen

"Not again." Honey Belle rolled out of bed and rushed to the bathroom. She sat on the edge of the bathtub, gulping deep breaths until the moment subsided. When the rolling nausea passed, she moistened a washcloth and pressed it to her face.

"I have peppermint tea."

She turned and Tess stood in the doorway, already dressed for work. Honey Belle looked down at her rumpled pajamas, inclined to return to bed and pull the covers over her head.

"I don't want tea. I want to die."

Tess laughed and headed for the stairs. "Peppermint will settle your stomach. Come downstairs. I'll brew you a pot, and there are saltine crackers in the pantry."

Honey Belle groaned. She used her foot to close the bathroom door as she took up a position next to the commode.

Her aunt's voice called upstairs. It wasn't a good thing, her aunt's insistence, not this morning.

"Give me another minute, Aunt Tess."

Honey Belle leaned toward the mirror over the sink. Wide eyes, bruised with shadows beneath them, stared back at her. She hadn't slept well. Visions of Tripp and Hutu warriors had swirled around in her dreams, leaving her with images she couldn't blink away.

She leaned against the sink, turned on the faucet, and splashed water over her face. She caught water inside her cupped hands to rinse the rancid taste from her mouth.

The soothing aroma of peppermint tea drifted to the upstairs hallway.

Honey Belle rinsed her mouth one more time and dried her face. She lifted her chin, opened the door, and stepped out of the bathroom. When she entered the kitchen, Tess pointed to the cup on the counter. Honey Belle picked it up and inhaled the minty fragrance.

"Go ahead, sip it. Guaranteed to settle your stomach."

Tess placed a poached egg on a plate and slathered a slice of toast with butter and homemade strawberry jam.

"If it does, I want two eggs and two slices of toast." Honey Belle sat down with the cup of tea and watched her aunt break an egg and gingerly slide it from the shell into a pot of boiling water.

It was just the two of them—and with baby, soon to be three. Honey Belle sipped her tea and wondered what the future held for her.

Her insides shook, and she felt cold and clammy as a wave of nausea swept through her again. Tess touched her arm. "Why don't you go back to bed?"

Honey Belle set the cup on the counter. She didn't argue.

****

That afternoon, Honey Belle pushed through the glass doors of the local vocational school. The queasiness in her stomach had nothing to do with morning sickness. Just a case of old-fashioned nerves, she told herself.

Doubt tugged at her as she walked down the carpeted corridor looking for classroom 4A. In the three years since she'd quit high school, she'd done nothing to better her education. Once, English had been her best subject. What if she didn't remember a noun from a verb, what if she couldn't write a proper sentence? What if she made a complete idiot of herself in front of the entire class? And then there was algebra. Math had always challenged her.

A war of words flittered inside her head. *I can't do this. Only cowards run away. Coward...coward...coward. Okay, then I'm a coward. I still can't do this.* She turned to leave the way she'd come, and someone said, "You look lost. May I help you?"

Honey Belle gave a resigned sigh. "I...umm...sure. I'm looking for Mrs. Keller. Room 4A."

Honey Belle towered over the diminutive, delicate woman with short gray hair curling around her face. She wore tan slacks with a matching tan cardigan. Her brown eyes twinkled when she smiled. "I'm Kathy Keller. My room is at the end of the hall. Follow me, Miss—"

"H.B. Garrett."

The woman glanced down at the clipboard in her hand. "Garrett, H.B. Oh, yes, here you are." She made a motion for Honey Belle to follow. "How far along are you?"

Honey Belle misunderstood the question. Heat raced up her neck to flush her cheeks. "Today is my first day. I-I quit school when I was sixteen. I'll work hard to get my GED. I'd really like to begin college in the fall."

"I have every confidence you'll do well, H.B., but I was referring to your pregnancy. When is your due date?"

Honey Belle flushed. She placed the notebook she carried in front of her belly as if to hide it. "Why, are pregnant students not allowed to take classes?"

A warm glint lit the teacher's face. "I didn't mean to upset you. Anyone who passes the entrance exam may attend. My concern is whether you'll complete course requirements before graduation."

"Oh, sorry. Between morning sickness and

116

hormones, I get a little snappy sometimes. I'm due the end of May."

Mrs. Keller pursed her lips and blew out a low whistle. "Graduation is the middle of May. Let's hope baby doesn't decide to arrive early."

"Come hell or high water, Mrs. Keller, I'll graduate. You'll see." Then, with a stab of guilt, she added, "Sorry, didn't mean to cuss."

Mrs. Keller rewarded her with a smile. "Since you're the first to arrive, you have your choice of desks."

Honey Belle listened to Mrs. Keller as she greeted other new arrivals. A charge of excitement filled her as she picked her way toward the front of the classroom. After sliding into a desk, she bent her head and whispered, "We'll do this together, baby. You'll never have reason to be ashamed of your mama. I promise."

She opened the notebook and removed paper and pencil. She was ready when Mrs. Keller stood in front of the room and said, "Welcome, class. Open your English books to page..."

****

All afternoon a storm had been building. The sky took on an ominous gray, and thunder sounded closer. A few scattered drops of icy rain struck the sidewalk. Honey Belle shivered against the chill. She tucked the blue canvas notebook and the English textbook beneath her zippered jacket to keep them from getting wet. Rain in January meant Valdosta was in for an exceptionally cold winter. She wished she had a pair of gloves to keep her hands warm, as she bent her head against the wind. Two miles to Aunt Tess's house wasn't far to walk. After all, she'd easily done the distance to Barrington Place to meet Tripp. But only on warm sultry days and nights.

Relief settled over her when a car horn beeped and a little yellow Volkswagen Beetle pulled alongside her. By now, the rain was falling in earnest. Dampness had plastered Honey Belle's hair to her head. She blinked to clear droplets of water from her eyelashes.

Her aunt shouted through the open door, "Get in, you're soaked."

Honey Belle scooted inside the car's warm interior and slammed the door against the downpour. She spoke through chattering teeth. "Geez, am I glad to see you."

"You are as bullheaded as your mama. Why didn't you just wait at the school? Didn't common sense tell you I'd come for you? Didn't you even think about catching your death and endangering the life of your baby?"

Tess's angry questions swirled inside Honey Belle's head like a volley of rifle fire. "Stop shouting, Aunt Tess, you're right on all counts. I didn't think."

Tess maneuvered the little car down the street. In minutes she pulled up the driveway to her house and parked under the carport. She said heavily, "I'll make dinner while you change into dry clothes."

Honey Belle felt the weight of responsibility as she entered the back porch. She kicked off her wet sneakers and removed her jacket to hang it across the clothesline Tess kept for drying nylon pantyhose. Gathering her schoolbooks, she followed her aunt into the warm and inviting kitchen. "Aunt Tess—" Honey Belle's face crumpled into a mass of emotional tears.

Tess opened her arms and Honey Belle walked into them, cherishing a moment she'd never shared with her own mother. "You must think I'm the stupidest person in the whole world."

Tess's voice was quiet. "Far from it, sweetie. Forgive me for overreacting."

"After I shower and change into something comfortable, I'll come down and help with supper."

"You've had a long day. Maybe you should lie down and rest. Later, you can tell me about your classes."

The storm struck overhead, and wind rattled the windows, closing out the rest of the world.

****

Two hours later, Honey Belle helped her aunt load the last dish in the dishwasher. "Aunt Tess, do babies come on time?"

"Give or take three weeks. It depends on how closely you calculated the date you conceived. Do you think you miscalculated?"

"Not really. My English instructor, Mrs. Keller, is concerned I might deliver before graduation. If that happens, I won't get my GED because I'll miss the final exams."

Tess dried her hands on a dishtowel. She filled the teapot with freshly brewed hot tea while Honey Belle set two cups on a tray along with a plate of homemade rice crispy squares.

Tess laughed. "Babies set their own time schedules, Honey Belle. All you can do is hope your little one won't be anxious to leave the nest."

Honey Belle followed Tess to the den. She set the tray on the coffee table in front of the fireplace, then nestled on the sofa, wedging herself comfortably against its overstuffed arm. She tucked a hand-crocheted afghan around her feet, and accepted the cup of tea handed to her.

She was the first to break the silence. "Aunt Tess," Honey Belle spoke over a clamoring heart.

"Hmm-uh?"

"Last night you shared with me a very painful part of your life. I think it's only fair that I tell you about my baby's father and why I don't want him in our lives." She held up a hand to quell the questions she saw building in Tess's eyes. "Mind you, I won't name names. When I finish, I think you'll understand why." Honey Belle set the cup aside and clenched her hands together.

Tess peered over the rim of her teacup. "I'm listening."

Honey Belle sucked in a large breath and exhaled slowly. "Okay, here goes. It all began this past May, on my nineteenth birthday, when a handsome young man driving a white BMW convertible drove up to the service window at the Burger Bin, where I worked—"

She spent the next hour explaining how she'd fabricated lies about where she lived. "He comes from an extremely wealthy family. There was no way I could ever let him know where I lived. I couldn't even begin to think about bringing him to the house, and I'm ashamed to say I didn't want him to meet Mama."

Honey Belle went on to describe the fancy restaurants and the romantic walks on the beach. "I didn't mean to fall in love. I knew I was playing with fire. Somehow it just happened."

She told about the night he'd asked her to marry him, and the plans they'd made to move close to the university he would attend. "It was a beautiful moonlit night, and when he proposed, it was the happiest moment of my entire life. He actually got down on his knees, right there in the sand."

She included details about deceiving him into thinking she also planned to attend college. And she fumbled with embarrassment when she simply stated, "I never intended to have sex, much less unprotected sex. I don't know what else to say other than...it happened."

She gave her aunt a quick look. Tess's eyebrows went up, yet she remained silent. She stared at Tess, searching for a hint of recrimination. When there was none, Honey Belle continued.

She explained about the photographs that had

been used to blackmail her into fleeing South Carolina. "His father is a powerful criminal court judge, Aunt Tess. I took the money he gave me, and that's when I called you. Except for naming names, you know the rest, because I'm here."

Tess looked at her. "If you tell me the names, I promise I'll never breathe a word."

Honey Belle licked her lips. Though the thought of saying Tripp's name pattered her heart, revealing the Judge's identity horrified her. "His father said if I was pregnant I should get rid of 'it.' He said he didn't want a bastard sullying their family's good name. He called me a whore. Believe me, I know this man's reputation." Honey Belle snapped her fingers to make a point. "Poof, just like that, he can ruin people's lives—make them disappear.

"Oh, no, Aunt Tess, the daddy of my baby will never know he exists because I'm afraid of what his father will do to my child if he finds out I didn't get an abortion."

With her heart racing and bile rising in her throat, it seemed to Honey Belle the room had suddenly grown cold. She pulled the afghan closer to her body to ward off the chill that threatened to set her teeth to chattering.

Tess blinked. "Merciful heavens, child, that judge sounds like a despicable man. I fully understand now why you wish to keep the names secret. I'm wondering, though, what you will do when your baby gets old enough to ask about its father?"

Biting her lip, Honey Belle considered the question. It was a fair one—one she didn't know how to answer. "I don't know, only that I'll cross that bridge when I come to it."

"Honey Belle has there ever been any question in your mind about not keeping this baby?"

"What do you mean, not keeping it?"

"You're young, single, an entire life ahead of you. There are families who'd love to adopt a child."

Honey Belle's stomach filled with butterflies. She responded in a low, unshakeable voice. "I want this baby with all my heart. I'm not giving it up."

Tapping her fingers against her lips, Tess's eyes narrowed and fixed on Honey Belle with an unnerving intensity.

"Aunt Tess—?"

Tess's breath escaped in one long sigh. "It doesn't matter who the baby's father is. One thing is for certain. I'll never have the opportunity to be a grandmother, but I can certainly be a doting great aunt. You and I will raise this child. We'll nurture it and give it more love than a kid could ever ask for. What do you think of that?"

Raising her palms to her cheeks, Honey Belle beamed through her tears. "Little boy or girl, I think my baby has a wonderful future. Thank you, Aunt Tess."

The hallway clock chimed eight. Honey Belle stood. She folded the afghan into a neat square and placed it on the sofa. "Mrs. Keller assigned us homework. I guess I'd better get it done."

Halfway up the stairs she turned to look at her aunt, who remained curled up in the recliner, staring at the smoldering embers in the fireplace. She knew Tess was thinking of Roger and baby Scotty.

Chapter Seventeen

Honey Belle padded down the stairs to the kitchen. She placed her school books on the table, then walked to the stove and turned on a gas burner. The note propped against a mug brought a smile to her face. *French toast in the oven. Will pick you up at 4 p.m.*

With the time change, the days grew dark earlier. Tess had insisted it was too dangerous for Honey Belle to walk home from school in the dark.

She switched on the small television Tess kept on the kitchen counter. Watching the syndicated news channel had become a morning routine Honey Belle enjoyed. The teakettle whistled, signaling the water inside was hot enough to steep a teabag. As she reached for it, a face on the television screen nearly stopped Honey Belle's heart. She didn't realize she had overfilled the mug until scalding water spilled from the counter and onto her foot. After screeching in pain and returning the kettle to the burner, Honey Belle turned the television's volume louder. The news commentator was reporting, "T. Harlan Hartwell, criminal court judge, has announced his candidacy for governor of South Carolina. Hartwell is known for his no-nonsense approach to crime."

As the image of Tripp's father flashed across the screen, it was as if the Judge were staring right at her. Honey Belle wrapped her hands protectively around her belly when he lifted his hand and pointed a finger, saying, "I promise to shake up the system and become South Carolina's top cop."

Motherly instincts she didn't know existed screamed a warning to protect her unborn child from this man. A trembling heat followed by a cold wave rippled through her. Last night she'd almost relented and revealed Tripp's name to Tess. Honey Belle tightened her lips. "The Judge is a dangerous man. And as much as I love your daddy, I don't trust what would happen if either one of them found out about you."

Switching off the television, she removed the plate of French toast from the oven and poured maple syrup over the eggy-fried bread, but her stomach rebelled. She settled for a cup of hot tea and saltine crackers.

Suddenly the kitchen seemed to close in on her. She needed fresh crisp air. Glancing at the clock, she gathered her books, walked out the back porch door and down the sidewalk toward the vocational school.

A brisk wind riffled her hair, and she pulled the hood of the jacket over her head. She enjoyed her morning walks to school, the scent of smoke from fireplaces. Somehow it made her troubles seem far away.

This year she looked forward to finding the next path to her future. With a child.

****

They got off the elevator on the fourth floor. A couple followed Honey Belle and her aunt out of the elevator. The man and woman looked happy as they entered the wide hall holding hands. The woman's belly was a large protruding mound.

She had an odd feeling, looking at the couple. Like a yearning. If she had to give a name to it—an ache in her heart.

Other than morning sickness and a positive litmus test, none of this seemed real to Honey Belle. But it was. She was glad Tess was with her.

"Relax." Tess walked with Honey Belle to the

reception counter.

"Easy for you to say." She signed in, walked to a chair, and picked up a magazine.

Thirty minutes later she followed a nurse through the doors to the exam room. Feeling like a frightened child, she looked over her shoulder at Tess, who offered a smile and gave a little shooing motion with her hands.

She loved her aunt, but with all her heart she wished Tripp was with her to share this experience. She undressed and slipped on the gown, front side open, as the nurse had instructed.

She sat down on the examining table and waited for the doctor. And waited. Her back ached from sitting up straight. She checked her watch. What was taking so long?

She groaned. "Five more minutes and I'm out of here."

She closed her eyes and tried to dig up the remnants of what she'd felt months ago, before fleeing South Carolina. She'd been seeking a new beginning, trying to find favor from a spiteful mother who constantly belittled her, giving all her energy to work, and also taking care of an ailing father.

Now she faced a completely different set of problems. She didn't want her baby to grow up feeling as if it were a problem.

She wouldn't let that happen.

"Good morning, Ms. Garrett. Are you ready for your ultrasound?"

Honey Belle put on a big smile and nodded.

"Down the hall, second door on the left. I'll be there in a few minutes. And we'll take a picture as a souvenir for baby's scrapbook."

Honey Belle hadn't thought of keeping a memory book. The idea appealed to her. She'd ask Tess if they could stop at the mall before going home.

Honey Belle hopped down from the bed. "What about activity?"

"With moderation, as long as you don't do anything dangerous or strenuous. Are you referring to any specific activity?"

"I'm taking classes at the vocational school. It's a two-mile walk."

"Walking will strengthen your abdominal muscles, which will make the delivery easier. It will also make it easier to get your figure back after the baby is born."

"What about morning sickness? Mine seems to last all day."

The doctor offered a warm smile. "It happens that way sometimes. By the time I see you next month, you should have a healthy appetite and no sickness."

Honey Belle nodded. She walked down the hall. Alone.

She wished Tess had come with her. Doing this by herself shouldn't hurt. She wished Tripp was with her. Instead, she walked into the darkened room feeling desolate. The technician said, "Lie on your back. The lotion I use is a little cold."

"Can I watch?" Honey Belle lifted her head and watched the screen as the technician moved the scope over her belly.

A few minutes later she saw the beating heart of her baby. Her own heart matched the rapid pulsations of the image on the screen.

Doctor Daniel entered the darkened room. "A healthy heart."

"Is it a boy or a girl?"

The doctor leaned closer and pointed. "This shadow makes it difficult to tell. You'll have to wait for the big reveal in about three and half months."

The technician rubbed the lotion from Honey

Belle's belly and handed her a picture of the ultrasound. "Here's your baby's first picture."

Honey Belle took the black-and-white photo. Her fingers trembled as she held it up and looked at a little blob that looked really like nothing—except for a beating heart on a screen that proved a new life was growing inside her. She couldn't wait to show Tess. She wished her parents were alive so she could show them. She didn't want to think about Tripp or his father.

When she walked back to the waiting room, Tess was there. Smiling. Honey Belle held up the picture.

"Boy or girl?"

"My question exactly, Aunt Tess." Honey Belle held the photograph toward the light and pointed. "Dr. Daniel says I'll have to wait until my little surprise package arrives to find out."

Honey Belle's face suddenly transformed to surprise, and her hands flew upward to clutch her stomach. "Oh."

Tess moved to her niece's side quickly. "What's the matter?"

"The baby kicked really hard." She massaged the swell of her abdomen, grinned sheepishly after a long moment, then captured Tess's hand in hers. "Give me your hand."

Tess frowned as if concentrating. She shook her head indicating she felt nothing. "Oh...oh, there it is, no more than a slight pressure against my fingertips."

She lifted her eyes to Honey Belle and smiled. "Isn't it wonderful to feel him move inside you?"

"It's a bit scary to think I'm responsible for this little creature growing inside of me. Aunt Tess, I've seen what happens to a child whose only mistake in life is to be born in the wrong place at the wrong time. What if I'm not mother material?" She blinked fast to chase away the tears before they built up on her lashes.

Tess used fingers to lift Honey Belle's chin. "Look me directly in the eyes, Honey Belle, and heed my words. You are...not...your mother. Do you understand?"

She looked at the compassion in her aunt's eyes and wondered why her mother had been the exact opposite—like an evil twin born years later. "I do understand, Aunt Tess. You may need to remind me every once in awhile."

Outside in the cold, walking to the car, Honey Belle felt invigorated. She noticed it all, every sound, the way the sun rays filtered through a hole in the darkening clouds overhead. Her senses had come alive.

She thought about the shock of seeing Judge Hartwell's face on the news, and the anxiety it had caused her. She thought about the sleepless nights she'd experienced since coming to live with her aunt, the short temper during the daytime. Even yesterday she had doubted her future. The tension was gone now, every bit of it, replaced by the image of her baby's beating heart, and she was glad of her new place in life.

She wrapped her arms around Tess and hugged her tight.

"My goodness, what's this for?"

Honey Belle laughed. "I'm starved."

"You hugged me because you're starved?"

"I hugged you because everything suddenly seems to have righted itself in my universe."

"In that case, let's celebrate. What would you like to eat?"

"Fried chicken, a mountain of mashed potatoes swimming in gravy, and pecan pie."

Tess cocked an eyebrow. "Are you sure your stomach can handle all that grease?"

"Maybe...maybe not, but right now I'm hungry

enough to eat a whole chicken—feathers and all."

Honey Belle opened the car door and slid in.

Life had been a lot simpler a year ago. What was ahead, that was a whole other matter.

Chapter Eighteen

Honey Belle awoke sweaty and breathless in her bed, her head full of unfamiliar images—long dark corridors, the sound of a baby crying, and herself, confused and frightened and unable to change any of it.

She sat upright, disoriented, but only for a minute or two. She knew why the baby dream had visited her tonight.

All day Saturday, with Tess pulling her once-a-month twelve-hour shift, Honey Belle had been at loose ends and with nothing to keep herself occupied. She decided to explore the attic. She had expected to find nothing of value, certainly nothing that would cause her heart to miss a beat. She was wrong. The attic had yielded a treasure trove of mementos.

She'd fingered the intricate carvings on the frame of a floor-length mirror, a chair with a broken rocker, an old seamstress dress form, and stacks of National Geographic magazines.

Nothing startling. Nothing dramatic.

Kneeling on the dusty floor, Honey Belle tested the lock on a steamer trunk that bore scars from its travels. Surprised when it opened, she hesitated, feeling like an intruder. Then, allowing curiosity to get the better of her, she carefully fingered the neatly stored contents.

The crushed remains of an orchid corsage, wrapped in tissue paper. A clutch of blue ribbons that Tess had won in various high school events. Letters bundled together with a red ribbon, addressed to Tess and postmarked from England, their faded ink revealing they were from Mr. and Mrs. Kemp, Roger's parents.

Recalling the emotions on her aunt's face the night she'd shared the painful events of Africa, Honey Belle decided the contents were too personal. She could not intrude on words meant only for her aunt.

She tried on several old hats and couldn't imagine women wearing such items. A lace-up corset caused her to grimace. She removed a shoebox, and when she set the lid aside, the contents yielded a little bit of surprise.

The box was filled with photographs, the white edges yellowed from age. Honey Belle lifted an old black-and-white of a man looking strong and handsome, with a charming smile. She turned the picture over and recognized Tess's neat penmanship where she had written the name—Roger. It was dated 1953.

There were other photographs. Some with Tess in her nurse's uniform, waving to someone off camera, others of her with three nuns, a few of native Africans, thatched huts, and several of Tess and Roger. They seemed so young. There were a few of Tess wearing maternity tops, and one especially poignant picture of Roger with his hand on Tess's protruding belly.

The sight of those photos brought no particular emotions. As she picked them up, her fingers brushed against something soft, and when she saw it, the smile on her face froze.

With the same care one would give to a newborn baby, Honey Belle lifted the half-finished, cross-stitched birth announcement. It was such a small thing—too small to be framed or hung on a nursery wall.

She ran her finger over the once cheery colors, now faded with age, and the patterns of childishly simple icons meant for a baby boy.

Seeing the announcement caused her heart to lurch as she recalled Tess's accounting of the Hutu rebels' attack on the village and the deaths of her husband and son. Soiled, fading, the fabric sat in Honey Belle's lap as a lasting reminder of Tess's sad memories. The name of her son still stood out plainly. ROGER SCOTT. Roger for his grandfather and Scott for his father.

Only the boy hadn't lived to carry the weighty, paternal pride of such an important name. He'd died, along with his father, on a scorching day in the African sun.

Now in the darkness of her bedroom, Honey Belle's hand fumbled for the bedside lamp. She squinted against the bright glare, shoving handfuls of tangled blonde hair out of her eyes so she could read the clock.

Her heart was no longer pounding, but with acrid bile in her throat and a bad case of heartburn, it would be impossible to get back to sleep.

She swung her legs over the side of the bed and trundled to the bathroom. Opening the medicine cabinet, she removed a bottle of antacids and popped two inside her mouth.

After rinsing her face, she returned to the bedroom and picked up the camera and the photo album Tess had bought her that afternoon at the mall.

She would do what Tess hadn't been able to bring herself to do. She would keep a scrapbook complete with pictures for her child.

A kernel of an idea wiggled its way into Honey Belle's thoughts. Perhaps it was the news report of Judge Hartwell announcing his candidacy for governor that spurred the notion. As she allowed the plan to grow, her enthusiasm grew with it. She didn't resist the smile tugging at the corners of her lips.

The day would come, she knew, when her child would ask questions about his father. Until that day arrived, she would collect newspaper articles, pictures, any written information about Tripp, and place all of it inside the scrapbook. The Hartwells were a prestigious family. One day, just as with his father, Tripp's face would grace the pages of newspapers and magazines.

And when the child, boy or girl, was old enough to completely understand, she would show him the copy of the check his grandfather had written to force her out of town. She would show the incriminating pictures and explain how Judge Hartwell had planned to use them against her.

Doubt crept in to replace enthusiasm. What if the scheme backfired? What if the child blamed her? Could she handle the rejection?

Her emotions broke and she swiped away tears with the back of her hand.

She placed the camera and album on the nightstand next to her bed. Closing her eyes, she willed herself to focus on an image of the one nearest her heart—the baby. What he would feel like in her arms. His sweet smell, the downy-softness of his hair, the whisper of his breath as she held him against her neck. Surely, there wasn't anything more heavenly?

As if responding to his mother's emotions, the baby moved in its warm nest. Honey Belle's hand went to her belly. She wondered if it was true that babies could hear from inside the womb. In a soft voice, she crooned, "Hush, little baby, don't say a word, Mama's gonna buy you a mockingbird—"

Chapter Nineteen

Sweat dribbled between Tripp Hartwell's shoulder blades as he stood alongside the station wagon packed with enough belongings to last him for the duration of his time at Harvard. Not even noon, and the August sun was relentless.

He kissed his mother on the cheek as she clung to him. "Don't cry, Mother. It isn't like you haven't seen me off to college before."

Mary Alice rested her hand on his chest. "You promise you'll be home for Christmas?"

He clasped her blue-veined fingers as he moved her toward his father. Tripp smiled. "Don't put the angel on top of the tree until I get home."

That small remark seemed to pacify her. "*La* sakes, I've almost forgotten. Will you bring your young lady with you?"

"What young lady, Mother?"

"The one whose family is related to sharecroppers from Tennessee."

Tripp had given up explaining to her that Honey Belle and her parents had never lived anywhere other than South Carolina. At the current rate of deterioration, he worried, the dementia might completely claim his mother's mind before she reached her next birthday.

With silent eyes he sought help from his father. Judge Hartwell's nod was barely noticeable. "Dry your tears, Mary Alice. It's time for our boy to get on down the road. After all, it's a long drive to Massachusetts."

Tripp felt the reluctance in his mother as he

handed her over to his father. The sorrow in her eyes cut straight to Tripp's heart. "You have the sandwiches Pearlie Mae made for you?"

"I do, Mother, and the thermos of iced tea, and the brownies." He patted his pocket. "And I have plenty of money for gas and lodging."

His father offered a smile. "Son, you've acted a bit stand-offish lately. I hope you still don't think I had something to do with the young lady and her family leaving town."

Tripp watched the expression on his father's face. Clearly, the Judge was being indulgent. Tripp spun on his heel, reaching for the door handle. His throat constricted with doubt, then anger. He thought of many things to say, but not in front of his mother.

He opened the car door and slid behind the steering wheel. "I'll call as soon as I get to the campus and settle in."

As he waved a final good-bye and pointed the station wagon down the long oak-shrouded drive to the highway, there was little doubt in his mind that his father had played a pivotal role in Honey Belle's sudden disappearance. Days after confronting the Judge, Tripp had telephoned Charlie Nichols, the detective who sometimes did investigative work for his uncles and their law firm.

He checked the speedometer, and for a while focused on the traffic. Settling into the smooth rhythm of driving, he mentally replayed the conversation with Detective Charlie Nichols.

"Charlie, this is Tripp Hartwell."

"How ya doing, kid? Hear you're off to that fancy lawyer school pretty soon."

Wanting to forego the small talk, Tripp pushed on. "Listen, Charlie, I'll come straight to why I called you."

"Okay. Shoot."

"Has my father ever mentioned a young lady by the name of Honey Belle Garrett?"

Silence.

"You there, Charlie?"

"Uh, yeah, I was trying to, uh, recall the name. Can't say I have any recollection."

"Think hard, Charlie. Honey Belle isn't a name you would likely forget."

"Sweet name, sure 'nuf. What's your interest in the little lady?"

"She's the girl I planned to marry. Now she's missing."

"Missing? You mean as in—kidnapped?"

Even now, recalling the conversation, Tripp's stomach clenched like a fist in the pit of his stomach.

"No, Charlie. I mean she and her parents have moved, and without telling me. She quit her job without notice. She didn't even tell her best friend she was leaving."

"Ah, well, there ya have it. Goes without saying, just can't put much stock in folks these days. Maybe she got cold feet and the only way she knew to break it off with you was to blow town."

Tripp could almost envision Charlie Nichols sitting at his desk, feet propped up and a glass of bourbon in one hand. The man had the appearance of an overstuffed turkey. Nonetheless, Tripp knew Charlie Nichols was a good detective and loyal to his father.

"What about Uncle Jake, Charlie? Maybe he asked, on my father's behalf?"

Silence.

"Charlie?"

"Listen, kid, like I said, I, uh...don't know nothing 'bout your girl. Now if you want me to do some nosing around, gimme her address and I'll see what I can find out."

"Never mind, Charlie. I've obviously hit a dead

end."

"Buck up, kid. Tons of beautiful dames where you're headed. All of 'em smart, and rich...uh...at least that's what I heard."

Tripp had wanted to pursue the conversation further, especially homing in on the word *rich*. Before he'd had time to respond, Charlie said, "Uh, listen, kid, I gotta go. A client just came in. Sorry I don't know nothing 'bout your girl."

"Thanks anyhow, Charlie."

"Yeah, sure, kid. Anytime."

The squealing of air brakes jerked Tripp back to the present. Through the windshield, he stared at gray smoke boiling from the rear tires of the semi-truck ahead of him. Skidding tires from other vehicles screeched against the pavement.

Tripp braked hard to keep from plowing into the rear of the truck. His knuckles whitened from his grip on the station wagon's steering wheel. His body tensed and then puddled with relief as the wagon stopped inches from giant red letters that had We Plant 'Em At Dirt Cheap Nurseries printed on the semi-trailer's double doors.

Seconds later, his heart slammed against his chest as the grinding crunch of metal against metal, coming somewhere from the line of cars behind his station wagon, reached his ears.

Tripp leaped from the station wagon and raced down the highway's right-of-way shoulder to the three-car pile-up. With reassurances from all parties that no one was seriously injured, he stifled a huge sigh, jammed his hands inside his pockets, and returned to his car.

While he waited for the tow trucks and the State Highway Patrol to arrive and clear the highway, he rolled down the window for some air and pulled one of Pearlie Mae's famous pecan-chicken-salad sandwiches from the sack and washed it down with sweet ice tea from the thermos.

The sandwich, the tea, and the summer heat worked together to produce a drug-like euphoria. Tripp fought to keep his eyes open. He glanced at his watch. With luck and barring no more accidents, he'd spend the night in Virginia.

He didn't remember leaning against the headrest or closing his eyes.

Honey Belle stood in his arms. The subtleness of her perfume aroused him. He savored the sweet taste of her lips, her body responding to his, she—

He reacted with a jerk at the roar of the semi's engine and the squeal of air releasing from the truck's hydraulics. Using the heels of his hands, he scrubbed the drowsiness from his eyes.

After inching through the traffic congestion and then crossing the state line into Virginia, he passed through a long corridor of rolling land. It was woodsy and wild and reminded him of the wonderful places his Uncle Carson had taken him camping. Tripp chuckled aloud. Carson Calhoun was the black sheep of his mother's family. He'd stayed true to his roots and preferred wearing bib overalls and plowing the dirt and planting the land to that of wearing a suit and tie and hobnobbing with the politicos on Capitol Hill. Yet Carson had taken a spoiled rich snob of a city boy to go tromping through the woods, searching for arrowheads, teaching him about the constellations. To Tripp it was like discovering a whole new world—like visiting the backside of the moon.

An hour later he pulled off the highway to gas up. He got out of the car and stretched his legs while the station attendant filled the gas tank, then cleaned the windshield.

Tripp leaned against the car and surveyed his surroundings. It was an interesting bit of irony to spot a sign that read Best Burgers In Town.

He paid the attendant. "Is it true what the sign says?"

The man answered with a toothy grin. "Yep. Everythin' they serve is good."

"What the hell...why not?" Tripp parked the station wagon in front of the red brick restaurant.

He took a seat by the window. A waiter brought a tall glass of water.

"Stranger in town?"

"Am I that obvious?"

"Small town like this, anybody new sticks out like a sore thumb. What'll you have?"

Tripp ordered a rare burger, fries, and cola. "Extra pickles, no onions." The waiter didn't bother to write down the order.

The meal came, and it looked delicious. A layer of glistening hamburger juice covered the top of the toasted bun.

The waiter set a fresh bottle of ketchup and mustard in front of Tripp. "You remind me of a hound dog who's lost his way home. 'Course, it's none of my business."

Tripp bit into the burger. As much as he'd like to talk about Honey Belle and his feelings of betrayal and bewilderment, he glanced around at the other diners. "If a fellow planned to spend the night in this town, where would you recommend?"

The waiter pulled at his chin as if thinking. "Well, if I was the fellow, I'd stay at the Dogwood Inn B&B. It's run by Mrs. Amelia Lee-Throckmorton, reputed to be the great niece, several times removed, of General Robert E. Lee. There's a little plaque in the front yard telling the history of the place."

Absently, Tripp watched the cola glass sweat a water ring around the place mat. He'd take a picture of the Inn and of Mrs. Amelia Lee-Throckmorton to send to his mother. She'd always fancied herself a distant relative of the famous Civil War general.

Thoughts of the camera reminded him he'd never taken a photo of Honey Belle. He quietly admonished himself. The only image he had to rely on was memory.

He inclined his head toward the window. "Where will I find the Dogwood House?"

Chapter Twenty

Tripp turned out the lamp. He lay staring up at the ceiling, his hands clasped behind his head. Thoughts of Honey Belle's disappearance remained foremost in his mind.

She had fascinated him from their very first meeting—the day she'd requested a ride in his convertible. There was more, too. He was charmed by the way she displayed her emotions with childlike ease. When she was sad, she cried, and when she was happy she laughed.

Their relationship had gone beyond friendship. He'd fallen in love, hopelessly enamored with her. It was heartbreaking to think Honey Belle had simply put on a good act and hadn't actually loved him at all.

He lay for hours trying to figure out what had changed between them. He'd asked her to marry him, and she had accepted. He'd flown to Massachusetts to take care of a registration glitch in his class schedule, and with the promise to return to South Carolina within the week. She'd promised to wait. He'd tried to telephone her to share the news about the apartment he'd rented within walking distance of the campus.

He rolled to his side. So many questions. Why had she lied about living on Barrington Street? Carla had answered that one—Honey Belle lived in the seediest section of Charleston.

In fact, according to Carla Biggers, Honey Belle was an uneducated high school dropout. Did any of that matter to him? No. Did it matter to his family?

Absolutely.

Was his father involved? The evidence was inconclusive.

"Time to give it a rest, Tripp, old boy. Put Honey Belle Garrett out of your mind and get on with the living." Tripp plumped the pillow under his head. His primary focus—law degree, first. Falling in love again—on hold, indefinitely.

And when Honey Belle's image began to fade, he closed his eyes.

****

Tripp was up at six and washed down his breakfast with two cups of coffee. He arrived in Massachusetts and drove straight to the apartment he had rented.

For the next two years, he concentrated on his law degree. During that time he dated a few women. He became serious with one, a political science major with chocolate brown eyes and hair the fiery red of a setting sun.

Although they dated and had good times together, he never came to feel about her the way he did Honey Belle.

But neither did he forget Kathryn Sutterfield. They would sometimes forego the frat parties and spend the entire evening and all day Saturday in bed, holding each other and making sensual erotic love until they were both fully satisfied.

He'd come close to proposing marriage. She was a perfect fit in every way. Beautiful and intelligent. The daughter of a United States senator.

The Christmas before graduation, he'd taken Kathryn to South Carolina to meet his parents.

Over a nightcap, the Judge said, "Senator Sutterfield could certainly advance your career, son." He gave a knowing wink.

"What are you suggesting, Father?"

"A holy union, of course."

"I like Kathryn. I don't love her."

Judge Hartwell pshawed. "You've got the monkey by the tail, son. You'll need a wife who will complement your career. Don't throw away the opportunity. As for love...well...you'll grow into it." He tossed back the bourbon, then grimaced at the liquor's bite. "In the meantime, your Uncle Jake is holding a place for you in the firm—not as partner, mind you. You'll have to work your tail off for that."

"I'm not ready to settle down, Father."

"You're almost twenty-five, son. Sowing wild oats is one thing; advancing your career is more important."

Tripp set his glass on the fireplace mantel. It'd been two years, and Honey Belle still owned his heart.

"Marriage shouldn't be considered a duty. Duty is no substitute for love." Neither was sex—no matter how good it was between him and Kathryn.

"Listen to me, son. Duty is everything, especially when it comes to making a good match to advance you up the ladder."

"Is that why you married mother—out of duty—because of her family name?" With a scowl, Tripp clenched his fists inside his pants pockets. "Good night, Father."

When he opened the door to his bedroom, Kathryn greeted him, wearing nothing but a smile. She patted the mattress as if extending an invitation.

He walked to the chair and gathered the silver negligee draped over the arm. "I'll not disrespect my mother. Not on Christmas Eve, and not in her house."

Kathryn swung her shapely legs over the side of the fourposter bed. She stood on tiptoes as she molded her body to Tripp's. "I find such old-fashioned virtue...charming. Darling, I—"

He stood arms akimbo while she continued in a pouty voice, "I'm sorry. Truly." She accepted the nightgown and slid it over her head, allowing it to freefall down her slender frame. "Don't be angry."

"I'm not."

"I love you, Tripp, but sometimes when you look at me I get the feeling you're seeing someone else. It's like you're waiting for her to pop up out of thin air. Who is she—someone from the university?" The indignant bite to her voice was evident.

"There's no one, Kathryn. Go to bed."

"I'm a woman, Tripp—I know these things."

He pinched the bridge of his nose between his thumb and forefinger as if to release the tension. "Tomorrow is Christmas. It has always been a special holiday for my mother. I'll not have her upset, so let's not argue."

She lifted his hand and placed it against the flat of her stomach. "Marry me, Tripp."

His gaze traveled down to her belly. He'd always been careful to use a condom. Still there was always that one percent chance. "How far along?"

She tossed her head, the magnificent mane of hair swirling around her face like a red cloud. The mischievous glitter in her brown eyes and the smirk tugging at the corner of her lips sent shock waves of relief through him. He knew that look.

"Don't look so worried, darling, there are no babies in our immediate future." She nibbled his bottom lip. "Fair warning, if you don't accept my proposal—" She left the threat open.

Tripp didn't like threats. He walked to the bedroom door and opened it. "Good night, Kathryn."

"It was a joke, Tripp. Can't you take a joke?"

He laughed harshly. "Which one—about being pregnant, the marriage proposal, or the warning?"

She danced around him, her fingers spider-walking up his arms. "I've always dreamed of a June wedding."

His mouth went taut. She stood on tiptoe and kissed him good-night.

****

Tripp enjoyed watching the childlike glow on his mother's face as she opened each of her Christmas presents. He cut his eyes away from his mother to focus on Kathryn. The color of her angora sweater turned her eyes mahogany; the neckline was cut square and exposed her throat and shoulders. When she bent over him to accept a gift decorated with a festive bow, a filigree locket on a long gold chain slipped into the mysterious shadow between her full breasts.

As if she felt his gaze, Kathryn drew back. A tiny telltale pulse beat in her throat.

He felt a bit bemused as a sensuous smile graced her perfect features. Today she wore her hair free, curling around her smooth shoulders. Her pouty lips were colored a frosty pink. He had the distinct feeling she was up to some mischief.

"Aren't you going to open it?" Tripp's mother inquired.

Kathryn's face flushed as if with amusement as she carefully removed the bow from the gold-wrapped oblong box. "It isn't the right size for an engagement ring."

Tripp knew she was teasing his mother. Kathryn lifted the box and shook it. "Hmm, it doesn't rattle. Perhaps it's a diamond necklace. What do you think, *Mother* Hartwell?"

Tripp narrowed his eyes. He didn't approve of Kathryn's title for his mother.

It was too late for him to regret his choice of Christmas gifts for Kathryn. She was teasing him, teasing his mother as she made a show of tipping up the lid and peeking inside the box.

His mother clapped her hands together. "Oh,

isn't this the most fun? Open it, dear...do, or I'll simply perish from curiosity."

At some point his father had joined them. Tripp accepted the cup of whiskey-laced eggnog. His father whispered, "She's a fine catch, son."

"Kathryn is self-centered and temperamental."

The Judge winked. "All the makings of a politician's wife."

Squeals of delight erupted from Kathryn. She dropped the gift box and held up two plane tickets. "This is the best pre-honeymoon gift a girl could possibly ask for." She extended two tickets to Paris for the Judge and Tripp's mother to see.

Her next words shocked Tripp into silence. "I officially declare June 21st as our wedding date."

The Judge bellowed. "This calls for a celebration. Pearlie Mae, we need more eggnog." Tripp wanted to shrug off the vigorous clap his father placed on his back.

Anger washed over Tripp like a riptide. His father said, "Go ahead, son. Don't be bashful, give my future daughter-in-law a kiss."

Tripp pulled Kathryn against his chest. He spoke in a low-toned voice, "You conniving little bitch. You know damn well those tickets are an early graduation present."

She mewed, "Look at the sparkle in your poor demented mother's eyes. Shall I tell her it was a joke?"

In a pretense of nuzzling Kathryn's neck, Tripp whispered through clenched teeth, "Don't even think of hurting my mother." He clasped Kathryn's hands until she grimaced against the painful grip.

The Judge cleared his throat, breaking the tension between Tripp and Kathryn. "Since this is Christmas and a day of celebration, and you kids have announced your future nuptials, now is as good as any to reveal my own surprise."

His father appeared nervous, unsure, his shoulders tense, his body rigid. "Senator Eugene Coppersmith is retiring due to illness. I've thrown my hat in the ring for his seat. Come January, I'll set up my campaign headquarters. I know I can depend on your support, son, and yours, too, Kathryn."

Tripp glanced to where his mother sat on a brocade stool next to the Christmas tree. Like a contented child, she laced and unlaced bright red and green ribbons through her opened fingers.

"What about Mother? It's stressful enough being the Governor's wife. How will she handle the added stress of being the perfect senator's wife?"

There was a certain strength and dignity about his mother when she looped her arm around Tripp's. "Why does everyone talk as if I'm not in the room?"

Tripp pinned a smile on his face. "You seemed preoccupied, Mother."

To his surprise, his mother's eyes twinkled. "The fog that covers my brain comes more often and seems to last a little longer before it decides to lift. I'm not worried, though. I'll always have you and Pearlie Mae to look after me. And your father will make a fine senator."

With a dreamlike air, Mary Alice loosened her hold on Tripp's arm. He thought her eyes pleaded with Kathryn as she lifted the young woman's hands into her own. "I won't always be here to look after my son. You'll take care of him for me?"

As the two women stared at each other, he knew by the expression on their faces that both were confused and unsure. His mother's smile wobbled.

The silence made him uncomfortable. His voice grew gentle as he lifted his mother's hands to his lips and kissed her knuckles. "You'll always be around to take care of me, Mother."

Her mood seemed to change. She bit her lip.

147

Tears clung to her lashes. She looked at her husband. "Harland, I'll do my best to never embarrass you."

Tripp was relieved when Kathryn loudly announced, "It's Christmas, and I propose a toast." She placed a crystal goblet in Mary Alice's hand. "Here's to Bah Humbugs, to good times, and to a bright and prosperous future for us all."

Mary Alice Hartwell raised her glass. She offered a salute to her son and husband and then to Kathryn. "In the words of Tiny Tim, may God Bless us one and all."

Tripp's father lifted his glass. "Hear...hear."

"Come on, Mother Hartwell, let's sing Christmas carols." Kathryn walked to the baby grand in the corner of the parlor decorated with twinkling lights and fresh pine boughs. Tripp offered her a smile of appreciation.

****

Outside, the evening skies had darkened like a shade coming down, and thousands of twinkling stars glittered in the inky sky. The air was cool—perfect for a Christmas evening.

Tripp was tired, but for some reason he was in no hurry to seek his lonely bed. Instead, he decided to go for a walk. A sense of loneliness gripped him and held him captive. The feeling wasn't all that new, but the intensity was. Like a thirst that couldn't be quenched with one draft, like a hunger that couldn't be sated with one taste, he longed to hold Honey Belle in his arms.

Little clouds of warm air escaped with each breath he blew out. He gazed up at the heavens. Orion the Hunter was visible. Tripp remembered the pleasure he'd felt over Honey Belle's excitement when he'd pointed out the constellations to her.

The week before Christmas he had driven to Shanty Groves and talked with a few neighbors, in hopes someone would remember Honey Belle and her family. Everyone he spoke to was new to the dilapidated neighborhood. None remembered a beautiful blonde girl with a name as sweet as her personality.

"Folks in Shanty Groves, they come and they go. Rent is cheap 'nuf. When folks ain't working and can't pay, the landlord kicks 'em out. Comin' and goin', that's the way of it. 'Course a young feller like yourself, driving a fancy sports car and all, wouldn't know 'bout hard times."

Tripp thanked the man whose calloused, gnarled hands had shown a lifetime of hard work. Then a sudden thought struck him, born of his subconscious suspicions. "Do you think anyone would remember seeing a black limousine parked in front of that house?" He pointed to the dwelling that looked as tired and worn as the man standing before him. To where Carla Biggers had driven him two years ago— to where Honey Belle had been too ashamed to bring him to meet her family.

The old gent guffawed. "Look around you, mister. You think anybody in their right mind would drive a limousine down here to Shanty Groves?"

Tripped opened his mouth. Closed it again. The old gent had made a valid point. Shrugging his shoulders, Tripp thanked the man for his time.

"Sorry, young fella. Wish I coulda hep'd you."

It seemed Honey Belle had dropped off the end of the earth. Tripp had lowered his eyes to a patch of sandspurs. He felt forlorn as hell when he returned to his car and drove back to town.

A brisk wind drew Tripp from his wistful thoughts. He shivered and pulled the collar of his jacket closer around his neck.

He looked up as a light in an upstairs bedroom winked on. The silhouette of a woman framed the window.

Kathryn.

Eventually, the light went out.

Only then did he make his way back to the house and up to his own room.

Chapter Twenty-One

Two months later, in February of 1966, at the age of twenty-five, Tripp passed the bar and received his *juris doctor* degree.

The plans for a wedding created a stir in the Hartwell and Sutterfield households. This wedding could mean family unity or political division. Tripp wondered which it would be. His father was a staunch Democrat and his soon-to-be father-in-law an even stauncher Republican.

His marriage, a gamble, was here. June 21st. The magical date Kathryn had announced on Christmas Day. The grim reminder ate at him, forcing him to admit he had hopes for this marriage. Except for the black-and-white picture of the life growing inside Kathryn's womb, he wasn't exactly sure what those hopes were—buried under a colorless outlook. He didn't love Kathryn, and she didn't love him. But he wanted her.

On the eve of his wedding, his father had been all doom and gloom. "I've had second thoughts, son. I'm afraid I've pushed you into marrying this little redhead for all the wrong reasons."

"A little late for that now, isn't it, Father?"

"You're not at the altar yet."

Tripp laughed a humorless sound. "All my life you've preached duty and honor. I'm duty-bound to marry Kathryn. If I leave her at the altar, where's the honor?" He almost wished he could bite back the words. Instead, he'd walked toward the church sanctuary, ignoring the heat rising under his collar.

The wedding rehearsal had proven awkward

and stiff. His mother wasn't feeling well and had retired to bed early. Pearlie Mae had baked Tripp's favorite, ham with a bourbon-glazed pecan sauce. As he cut into a slice, he felt like a death row inmate consuming his last meal.

How could anyone prepare to spend the rest of his life with an unloving wife? He wondered if someone had ever written a manual on how to survive marriage with a woman you didn't love.

He decided he didn't know anything of men and women, love and marriage, becoming a father or raising a child. With a scowl, he tried to shrug off his pre-wedding jitters.

On the morning of his wedding day, a small but persistent tapping on his bedroom door caused him to reluctantly open his eyes. He coughed to clear the rasp in his throat. "Who is it?"

The door opened and his mother peered around the edge. "May I come in?"

He scooted up against the pillows and motioned her forward. She wore gardening clothes and her slacks were damp and dirty from the knees down. "It's a little early, Mother. The ceremony isn't until two o'clock."

"A wedding should have lots of flowers. Look out the window." She offered her son a dreamy smile.

From where he stood, it looked as if his mother had cut every flower in her treasured garden. A wheelbarrow teemed with a variety of color—roses, daylilies, Queen Anne's lace, lilacs, Echinacea, periwinkles, and impatiens.

"They are lovely, Mother. I'll contact Horace at the flower shop to see if he has time to arrange them."

Unless the florist could arrange his mother's cuttings to fit with the calla lilies and pink miniature rosebuds Kathryn had ordered, he knew there would be hell to pay. Tension built behind his eyes.

Mary Alice reached up and kissed his cheek. His mother had always been there for him, especially during the times when his father was too wrapped up in the law to have time for a little boy. His father had showered him with everything—everything except father-and-son quality time.

"Tripp?"

"Yes, Mother?"

"Do you think the baby will be born before my mind fades completely into oblivion? I do desperately want to cradle a grandchild in my arms."

Tripp groaned inwardly. "There is no baby, Mother."

Their eyes met and she smiled. "I'm not so addle-patted, yet, that I don't recognize that special glow a woman wears when she's with child. Kathryn is glowing."

"Mother, there is no—"

As if turning a key in a lock, she lifted her fingers to her lips. "Tick-a-lock and throw away the key. It'll be our secret."

How could he resist? He hugged her. "She's eight weeks, Mother. Can you hang on for seven months?"

"As my great-granddaddy, Willard Calhoun, used to say when he'd imbibed a little too much of the corn whiskey, 'I'll do my damndest.'" She sighed heavily as she placed her hand on his chest. "Tripp, whatever happened to that young woman?"

"I'm not sure who you mean, Mother."

"Yes, you do. Her parents were the sharecroppers from Tennessee. I think she made you happy."

If he didn't know better, he'd think she was aware of his inner turmoil and the risk he was taking with his heart. "Her name was Honey Belle, and she went away."

"Be happy, son."

"I love you, Mother."

"And I you."

Be happy?

With his marriage a few hours away, seven months from becoming a new father, ready to begin his career as a junior attorney, being happy was a tall order. Could anything good come from a muddled beginning?

****

All was quiet. Tripp had contacted the florist, who assured him no one, not even Kathryn, would notice how he had blended Mary Alice's flowers with those Kathryn had chosen to decorate the church.

Tripp was running late. He still had time to dress and make it to the church on time. He checked his watch. It wouldn't do to keep the bride waiting. That would amount to a monumental mistake, and he'd made too many of those already.

He checked his watch again and took the stairs two at a time. At the bottom, his father grinned up at him.

"Let's get a move on. Don't want to be late for your own wedding." His father offered a wink as if approving of Tripp's long-tailed white tuxedo.

"Where's Mother?"

"She's in the limo with Pearlie Mae."

They drove to the historic church where generations of Calhouns and Hartwells had attended since before the Civil War. Tripp felt weak in the knees as he tried to picture Kathryn in her feminine glory.

At the church, ushers assisted Mary Alice and Pearlie Mae from the car and into the church.

Tripp swallowed hard. His great Uncle Carson Calhoun extended his hand. "Where's that little kid who used to follow me through the woods hunting arrowheads?"

Tripp lifted a brow. "Right now, he wishes he was still a little boy."

Carson Calhoun straightened his nephew's ascot. "Tripp's got the jitters bad, hasn't he, Harlan?"

Judge Hartwell agreed as he reached into his coat pocket. He pulled out a small box and removed a pendant. "This is my father's coat of arms from Scotland. He gave it to me the day I married your mother. Now I'm passing it on to you."

Tripp was more touched than he cared to admit when his father pinned the crest on the tuxedo's lapel. And he knew someday he would do the same for his son.

With a nod, Tripp murmured, "We should go in."

The three men followed the sidewalk to the east side of the church and entered through a door that led to the front of the church, where Tripp took his place before the altar, with his father as best man and his uncle as groomsman. As the pianist played the wedding march, Tripp struggled to quell the battle of emotions raging inside of him while everyone turned expectantly, all eyes on the bride as her father escorted her down the aisle. He placed her hand in Tripp's.

Moments later the reverend said, "Do you take this woman as your wife?"

The words shook Tripp. He stared at the bouquet of baby pink rosebuds tied with a deeper pink bow. He felt utterly indifferent at binding himself to this woman.

"Yes," he whispered, irrationally fighting down all his doubts, hoping he'd find a way to love this woman. Yes, maybe he and Kathryn could build a happy life together—for the sake of the child.

They exchanged traditional vows. He felt a moment of guilt over the words "love, honor, and cherish." Did he really mean to keep this promise? He would do what was expected. Theirs was a marriage of necessity, of convenience, the joining of two aristocratic families. The building of a political empire.

With a few brief words, he was tied to Kathryn.

The ritual went on.

They exchanged wedding bands—the physical ties that bound a man and woman together through sickness and sorrow, through hard times and good times. Or should. Tripp wasn't sure of anything. Not even his bride's loyalty. This was a marriage of convenience. Did the words "till death do us part" carry any weight, or were they meaningless, to be whisked away like dewdrops dying in the morning sun?

Tripp couldn't remember what they'd rehearsed. After he'd slipped the ring on her finger, he held her hand until the end, a small and delicately boned hand that had probably never washed a dish or pulled weeds from a flower garden.

It was time to kiss his bride. He had to admit she looked beautiful. Like an apparition he had conjured up, calm and filled with resolve, but he could feel the slight tremble in her icy hands. His eyes held hers for a long moment before dropping to her lips.

At that point, she lifted her face, parted her lips. She closed her eyes. She was a vision of beauty in her diamond tiara and white lace veil. He lifted the filmy material and gently took her mouth. There was hunger, as well. He felt it in her tremble.

Unsure of what to do next, he frowned as he released her. Though he and Kathryn had shared many intimate moments, he wasn't prepared for the effect she had on him. His mother's words of wisdom curled around his brain like a smoky whisper. *Marriage should start with friendship. Love will follow.*

The truth of the matter remained—were they

really friends, or simply in lust? Only time would provide the answer.

His eyes strayed to Kathryn's still-flat stomach. Until she'd shown him the picture of the sonogram, he'd thought she was pulling another of her not-so-funny jokes. Part of him felt possessive and protective. He was married. An admission he found difficult to accept.

When he'd kissed her, he wanted the earth to move under his feet. It didn't.

They turned, as one, to meet their wedding guests.

Tomorrow would take care of itself.

Chapter Twenty-Two

Tripp lifted the crystal picture frame from his desk. He pressed deep into the black leather chair and swiveled it toward the window as he looked at the image of himself and Kathryn standing in front of the Eiffel Tower.

Odd, he thought, how the adverse effects a simple gift could have on a man's life. Many changes had happened since Christmas, and not all of them happy.

For a moment he concentrated on the hustle and bustle of daily life taking place outside his office window. He leaned back and closed his eyes.

Paris in the springtime had been a romantic adventure—

His graduation gift to Kathryn. Looking back on it, he was certain he knew when Kathryn had conceived. It was the day they'd explored the Louvre, lunched inside the Eiffel Tower's cafe, consumed wine on a riverboat ride down the Seine, and then more wine in their hotel suite—and still more wine—until they were both deliriously drunk and totally uninhibited. No thoughts of birth control. Just wild drunken abandonment with no cares for the consequences.

The reality of those consequences came in May, the week before graduation with Kathryn's tearful announcement that she was pregnant.

As a wedding gift, the Hartwells had offered to buy a house in Charleston for Tripp and Kathryn. Not to be outdone, her parents wrote a check for a generous amount to furnish the two-story antebellum from stem to stern. With Paris still fresh in their minds, and a photo album filled with pictures to serve as a reminder of their holiday, much to Tripp's relief Kathryn had agreed to forfeit a honeymoon.

Six weeks later she no longer purred like a kitten when he came home from the office. Each day she grew more sullen and indifferent. He chalked her mood swings up to impending motherhood.

****

Tonight Tripp sat at his end of the dining table. A bottle of wine stood on the table, nearly finished.

"Tripp, we need to talk."

He looked at her. "Yes?"

"I hate South Carolina. I hate the heat and the bugs. I sit all day long and twiddle my thumbs. I have no friends, you work all the time, we never go out anymore..." She threw her napkin across the table. "Honestly, I don't know why I'm still here."

He drew a long breath, not trying to hide the weariness in his voice. "Because you're pregnant and because you are my wife."

To underscore his equanimity, he used his knife to cut another slice of meat.

She pushed back her chair. "Marriage was a mistake. Getting pregnant was a bigger mistake." Her pacing reminded him of a caged lioness, and then she pounced.

"You work for your uncles. Make them clear your schedule. Let's fly to Paris like we did in March."

Mentally Tripp was already leafing through his work calendar. "I'm second chair on the Bradshaw murder case. This is an opportunity to prove myself." He spread his hands wide. "With the trial only weeks away... I'm sorry, Kathryn. Now isn't a good time."

She snatched the bottle of wine and lifted it to

her lips. Tripp pushed from his seat and grabbed her wrist. "The doctor said moderate alcohol. You've had your one glass."

"To hell with the doctor. To hell with you." Her breath huffed out as if she'd been running.

By the way she avoided his gaze he suspected she had something else to say but had decided against it. A moment later, he sat alone at the dining table. The steak on his plate had lost its appeal.

Willing to negotiate, he rose from the chair and with hands shoved into his pockets, climbed the stairs to the bedroom.

"Kathryn." He spoke to her back.

"What?"

"We have enough evidence to put Everett Bradshaw away forever. I don't expect the trial to last more than a few weeks, at the most. When it's over, we'll celebrate the victory with a trip to wherever you choose."

Kathryn remained facing the window. He wrapped his arms around her waist and tried to hug her against his chest.

"Don't."

Tripp dropped his arms as she twisted around to face him. He'd heard that pregnancy caused some women to become temperamental. His uncle had advised him to agree with everything and with nothing at all.

Her arms hung at her sides. "I'm going home— to Illinois."

"For how long?"

"I was thinking of asking Daddy to find you a position as an aide on one of his committees. All your life you've lived in Podunk USA. You have no idea what it's like on Capitol Hill. I want that, Tripp, and I want it now."

He braced his legs apart with a direct challenge.

"Kathryn, we've discussed this. No favors. Everything in politics comes back to haunt you. I'll make my own way. When and if I decide to run for office, I don't want snarky reporters broadcasting it all over the news that my father-in-law paid the bill."

"Things aren't working out, Tripp. I've already bought my plane ticket."

"Just like that?" His gaze held hers, with no room for evasion.

"Why not?"

He conceded. "Perhaps a couple of weeks with your mother, some shopping trips, lunch with friends at the country club is exactly what you need. When you return home you'll feel better."

She looked at him as if weighing her reply. "I-I'm...not coming back."

His shoulders tensed. "For the baby's sake, don't you think our marriage deserves a chance?"

With a guttural sound that reminded Tripp of an animal's growl, Kathryn placed her hands on his chest and shoved with the force of a locomotive. The move caught him off guard and sent him sprawling. When the side of his head connected with the bed's footboard, he thought this must be how it felt to have a bomb go off inside your brain. He lay on the floor, black spots dancing before his eyes. Pain riveted down his neck.

Shaking away the dizziness, he was on his knees when Kathryn screamed. He stumbled from the bedroom.

The maid shrieked, "Mister Tripp, hurry! The Missus done had an accident."

Ignoring the violent throbbing and the goose-egg rising over his temple, Tripp rushed to Kathryn's crumpled body at the foot of the stairs. He placed fingers to the side of her neck, checking for a pulse. "Stay with her, Martha, while I call for an ambulance."

The maid wrung her hands as she fretted. "Lawsy me, Mister Tripp, Miz Kathryn come barreling down dem stairs like a nest of yellowjackets was after her. She was 'most to the bottom when she missed a step and flung her poor self to the floor. Oh, lawsy, she ain't gonna die, is she?"

His lips were tight. "If she rouses, keep her quiet and don't let her move." He prayed the fall hadn't hurt the baby.

****

Tripp accepted the cup of coffee his father handed him. The Judge said, "I spoke with Mrs. Sutterfield. The Senator is tied up in special session, but she's leaving on the first flight out."

For the umpteenth time, Tripp checked his watch. "Why hasn't the doctor come to speak to us?"

The Judge patted his son on the shoulder. "Try not to worry, son."

For two hours Tripp paced, sat, drank more coffee, and prayed. He'd finally settled in a chair, resting his throbbing head between his hands, when the doctor's voice interrupted his thoughts.

"Mr. Hartwell?"

Blood pounded inside Tripp's ears as he stood. "Yes?"

"Your wife is resting."

"The baby?"

"I'm sorry," the doctor said, and a heavy sadness filled Tripp's chest and his eyes closed, tears managing to slip between his lashes.

Chapter Twenty-Three

Two days later, Tripp sat in his office, his mind no longer on the impending trial. He stared at the letter in his hand and wondered what travesties he'd committed to cause the laws of nature to turn his once perfect life upside down.

All during his childhood his mother had told him things happened in threes. He'd never really believed her—until now.

Married less than two months, he'd mourned the death of a child and seen his wife pack her bags with the declaration that she was leaving. While Kathryn had agreed, for the sake of her father's political reputation, to not file for a divorce, she'd announced her move to Illinois was permanent.

This morning's mail had delivered circumstance number three.

A rap on the door caused Tripp to glance up from the letter in his hand. He motioned his Uncle Jake inside.

"You have the Bradshaw briefs ready?"

Tripp scrubbed a hand through his hair. He heaved a sigh. "Almost."

"I'm sorry about...everything."

"Yeah."

"I wish I could say life gets easier."

"Seems it's about to get a lot tougher." Tripp handed the letter to his uncle, the senior partner in the law firm.

Jake Hartwell released a low whistle. He read the letter aloud. "This is to inform you that the United States Selective Service Board has selected your lottery number. Your report date is..."

His uncle thumped the letter. "I can call in favors—pull a few strings."

Tripp's mind shuffled through a list of reasons why he should accept his uncle's offer. He frowned, trying to make sense of the irrational notion his brain was screaming at him.

"Mother has always been proud of the family's long military history. I think I'll add my name to the list."

"Vietnam is a long ways from South Carolina. Are you sure this is what you want to do?"

"I need a change, Uncle Jake. Southeast Asia is as good a place as any to start."

Five weeks later, Tripp Harlan Hartwell the Third found himself at South Carolina's Fort Jackson, in boot camp. And then, assigned to 1st Battalion 212th Aviation Regiment, he was transferred to Alabama's Fort Rucker, where he trained to fly Huey UH-1 helicopters.

****

Tripp admitted he was more than a little nervous about being summoned to the top brass's office. He drew a deep breath, blew it out slowly, then rapped on the office door.

"Enter."

Tripp stepped into the dimly lit room. He snapped to attention with a salute.

"At ease, Captain."

Though his stance was legs apart and hands behind his back, Tripp felt anything but relaxed. He waited, wondering if the document the post commander held was deployment orders.

Major Jankowski seemed to scowl as he lifted stern eyes to stare at him. Tripp noted the sarcasm as his superior officer spoke. "Captain Hartwell, what I have here is a letter from your father requesting I grant you special leave so that you may stand next to him when the votes are counted next week. Is he that sure he will win a second term for South Carolina governor's seat?"

Tripp swallowed the knot of agitation in his throat. And while he felt heat growing under his collar, he hoped his face remained stolid. "My father does place great confidence in the voting public, sir."

"What is your position on being granted early leave from aviation training, Captain Hartwell?"

"I wish no special favors, sir."

"I see."

Tripp was surprised that he was even engaging in this conversation with a member of the senior staff. He found himself annoyingly irritated that his father would use rank and position to wheedle special favors—especially without consulting him first.

"I can sign off on this with the condition you forfeit your two-week Christmas leave."

"May I speak freely, sir?"

The Major nodded his consent.

"I cannot gain the respect of the men assigned to my command if I allow my father to use his political position to get me particular favors. Christmas has always been a special time for my mother. She isn't in the best health, sir. Since I'll deploy in February, I'd like to make this holiday exceptional for her." In truth, Tripp wasn't sure how many Christmases he'd miss once he landed in Vietnam.

"Spoken like a true solider, Captain, a gentleman and a caring son. I'll notify your father his request is denied."

On the night of the election, Tripp sat in his quarters watching the returns on a small portable television. Cameramen focused on his father at the Judge's campaign headquarters. Among the throng of people, he spotted his Uncle Jake and searched for his mother but knew, of course, her state of mind

165

was much too fragile and his father didn't need the paparazzi homing in on her.

The moment the count was over and his father had been declared the official winner as a second-term governor of South Carolina, Tripp picked up the telephone and dialed.

"Congratulations, Father. I'm certain the people of South Carolina made the right choice."

"Damn right they did. Wish you were here sharing the victory. I should get that Major Jankowski busted down to buck private for not letting you leave the base."

Tripp chuckled. "I'll be home December twenty-third. In time to help Mother put the angel on the tree. How is she?"

He heard the hesitancy in his father's voice. "We'll discuss it later, son."

"Reporters?"

"Like bees after honey."

"I understand. Tell Mother I'll be home in a few weeks."

****

The crisp December night invigorated Tripp as he switched off the engine of the BMW. He lifted the box, wrapped in red foil paper and sporting a large green bow, from the passenger seat. A picture of him in his uniform would delight his mother.

The sound of sirens caught his attention. His heart lurched as he watched the red bubble lights flashing up the driveway. He tossed the package back to the seat and sprinted toward the front door of the house.

Once inside, he shouted, "Father? Pearlie Mae?"

The maid came to the top of the stairs. She held the apron to the corner of her eye. "Oh, Mr. Tripp, praise be, you're home."

"Who is it, Pearlie Mae?" A ball of white heat seared Tripp's stomach. Sprinting up the stairs, he wrapped Pearlie Mae in his arms as she wept.

"It's your dear mama. I called the Judge, but he ain't got here yet."

"How bad is she?"

"Barely hanging on by a thread."

"And you called the ambulance?"

"I was too scared not to, Mr. Tripp. Did I do right?" She wiped her eyes again.

"You've always taken care of us, Pearlie Mae. I don't know what we'd do without you." He gave her shoulder a reassuring squeeze. "Go let the emergency team in."

A table lamp cast a shadowy light over his mother's face. She reminded him of a small child lying there in the massive fourposter bed that had once belonged to her mother. It pierced his heart to see how much she'd withered in the few months he'd been at training camp.

He wasn't familiar with death. Yet he knew by the ashen pallor masking his mother's face there was no need to check her pulse. Somehow it seemed appropriate that the woman he loved most in the world should die in the same bed in which she'd been born.

On Christmas Day, instead of helping his mother place the angel on top of the festively decorated tree, he laid the delicate ornament to rest between her hands. He leaned into the casket and placed a kiss on her cheek. "I wish you could have hung on a little longer, Mother."

Chapter Twenty-Four

Sounds from the creatures of the night reverberated through LZ-Albany's moonlit encampment. Tripp stepped to the doorway of his quarters and flicked the spent cigarette. Unease crept over him. It was quiet. Too damned quiet.

A voice said, "Eerie, ain't it, Cap'n?"

Tripp squinted through the dark. "That you, Private Wilson?"

"Yah, sir. Good night for them VC vermin to creep up on us."

"We've doubled the guards, and the dogs are out. All the same, stay alert, Private."

"Yah, sir, Cap'n."

Even though it was February, the night air was thick with heat that seemed to boil down daily from the sun and swell up from the earth in a shroud of humidity.

Sweat moistened Tripp's face and saturated his underarms. He propped a shoulder against the door frame. His thoughts drifted to the unopened packet that lay on his desk.

"Begging your pardon, Cap'n, don't mean to break any protocol 'tween ranks, but I'm bustin' at the seams to tell somebody."

"Speak freely, Private Wilson."

"My wife sent me a picture of our new baby boy. Duane Wilson, Jr. Sure wish I coulda been there to witness his birth." The sentry went quiet for a moment. "Sometimes I'm afraid I might never get back home to Mississippi."

"How old are you, Private?"

"Nineteen, sir. Be twenty next week."

Having reached his twenty-eighth birthday, Tripp felt like an old man compared to Private Wilson's youth. He understood the lad's homesickness. He, too, longed for home, the lemony tang aroma of South Carolina's magnolias, sweet iced tea, and Pearlie Mae's home cooking. He allowed his dreams of home and family to dissolve in the hot night air.

"Thoughts like that will get you killed, Private. Keep the picture of your wife and son close and you'll be okay."

"Yah, sir. Thank you, Cap'n."

Turning, Tripp stepped away from the door and returned to his desk. He picked up the large brown envelope and crossed the small space. He tossed the thick package on the cot, unstrapped his service revolver, and tucked it behind his pillow. Sitting on the edge of the small bed, he tugged off his brogans and set them within easy reach. The bed springs squeaked as he propped against the wall, his right knee crooked to a comfortable position.

Mail from the States was rare. An occasional note from his father with newspaper clippings regaling his position as governor, sporadic notes from his Uncle Jake, and Christmas cards from Pearlie Mae that arrived long after the holiday had come and gone. Three years and never any letters from Kathryn—not even a greeting card. Until now.

From the postmark, it had taken six months for the envelope to arrive. He slid his finger under the flap, reached in, withdrew a packet of paper-clipped documents.

Tripp felt his middle drop to somewhere below his knees. Why did he feel so disappointed? Why was he even surprised? It wasn't as if he and Kathryn had spent much time together as husband and wife. Six weeks, to be exact. Other than sex, there had been no real connection between them. Their marriage had all been the creation of Kathryn's overly fanciful desire for a fairy tale wedding.

He closed his eyes, feeling dejected and pitiful. He felt older than the majestic oaks that lined the driveway up to the antebellum home that had survived the Civil War and still stood strong back in South Carolina.

His first inclination was to rip the divorce papers into shreds. Kathryn's letter explained how she hated Dear John letters, but she had met her true love. She hoped sending the divorce papers wouldn't unduly upset Tripp.

Upset him? Hell. His mood turned black. His stress level peaked. He felt angry, reckless even. It'd serve her right if he didn't sign the damned papers. Who was to know any different than that the documents had never reached him? Plei Me was a remote Vietnamese outpost, after all.

His stomach soured as he tromped from the cot to the table that served as his desk. Flipping through the maze of legal documents and decoding the finer implications gave him no satisfaction. Not tonight. Tonight his mind was pricked by anger. He gripped the pen and scrawled his signature on each line marked with an X.

"How generous of you, dear Kathryn, to included a return envelope," he muttered aloud as he jammed the signed documents inside the large, brown, self-addressed, stamped package. He licked the glue and sealed it shut by slamming his fist down on the flap.

****

The rains came, hot and humid weather with monsoon-like downpours. Tripp recorded in his journal: *June, 1969, VC sappers have attacked our camp every night for a month. Our lines are holding. The Hueys are the main target. The VC's objective— to keep our birds grounded so we can't give air support to our guys pinned down on some Godforsaken hill. Every night, Hanoi Hanna announces over the radio that a regiment of NVA troops are going to annihilate our camp. Hasn't happened, yet. Several of the men are sick from the heat. Private Duane Wilson, KIA. I hate writing letters to the families of these boys dying for a meaningless cause.*

He scrubbed the heels of his palms against his eyes. Three years ago when he had enlisted in the Army he'd felt a sense of adventure. Now, three years seemed like a lifetime. When he'd arrived in Nam, he knew he'd have to always be on guard. The watchword was—*Be alert or be dead.*

****

Four months later, dawn came with a crispness that gave new life to the wet misery of the soldiers, and it brought the news that during the night a battalion of infantry had crossed into the La Drang Valley, seventeen kilometers from Plei Me.

Tripp dodged mud puddles as he sprinted across the encampment yard in response to the summons from Major Armstead.

He stepped inside the office. "You sent for me, sir?" Tripp snapped off a salute.

"We have a situation, Captain." Tripp listened intently while the major outlined the details. "Four hundred fifty men from Black Horse Company are pinned down here." He pointed to the location on a large wall map. "Last word is they're surrounded by two thousand NVA and taking on heavy casualties."

"My squad is ready, sir. We'll give fire support so the medevac teams can get in and out." Tripp's muscles jumped. An eagerness was upon him like a pit viper uncoiled from sleep and ready to strike.

An awkward silence descended the quarters.

Major Armstead scowled. "Enemy fire around the LZ is too heavy. Major Blessing is refusing to

171

allow his medical evacuation helicopters to fly into the landing zone."

Tripp's gut clenched. "Give me a pilot of my choice, sir. There's no way in hell we can let our guys die without giving it our best to get them out."

"You're volunteering, knowing the dire consequences?"

"I am, sir."

"You'll be unarmed. Go in light and tight, get in, and get the hell out fast." Major Armstead snapped to and saluted Tripp. "Can't expect a man to do what I wouldn't myself. I'll ride shotgun."

Tripp's lips lifted in a half-smile as he returned the salute. "Can't think of a better man to have guarding my tail, sir."

"Good luck to us both, Captain Hartwell."

"How soon do we leave, Major?"

"Soon as your bird is ready."

Tripp shook hands with his superior officer. "She's ready now, sir. Saddle up. Time to lock and load."

Tripp and his commander had volunteered to fly the unarmed, lightly armored UH-1 Huey in support of the embattled troops. The terrain over La Drang Valley was deceiving. Ringed by sparse scrub brush, with occasional trees ranging upward to a hundred feet, the landing zone was covered with hazel-colored, willowy elephant grass as high as five feet.

To the west and northeast, the area was inundated with thick jungle growth, and a dry creek bed ran along the western edge of the valley.

Tripp spoke through his mouthpiece. "Looks like a bunch of sun-baked termite hills, sir."

The major responded, "From my view, some look as tall as a man."

Tripp blinked. He adjusted his goggles. "Is it my imagination, Major, or are those termite hills moving?"

"Hellfire and damnation. Go in low, Captain. Let's see if I can pop a few tops with this M67."

Tripp flew a total of fourteen trips to the battlefield, bringing water and ammunition and taking out wounded soldiers. Regretting that he couldn't get them all out, he watched American soldiers die around him.

By the time he grounded his bullet-riddled Huey, Tripp had been wounded four times by enemy fire. Major Armstead, KIA.

Airlifted to a nearby MASH unit, and in guarded condition, Tripp imagined he saw Honey Belle watching over him. He tried to reach out and touch her. He thought he spoke her name.

He was sent home from Vietnam, and a year later he was separated from the United States Army with an honorable discharge.

During a ceremony with full military honors, his father, Governor T. Harlan Hartwell, pinned the Medal of Honor and the Distinguished Flying Cross on Tripp's uniform.

"You're a hero, son."

Tripp closed his eyes and heard the womp-womp-womping of a Huey's giant chopper blades inside his head. He could still smell the acrid smoke from mortar rounds. "No, Father, the real heroes are the men who didn't make it home."

Inside the war zone, Tripp had experienced the roar of battle and adrenaline and fear and hope all rolled into one. A prosthetic leg was his permanent reminder that getting home had been the longest journey of his life.

Chapter Twenty-Five

Washington, D.C.
1980

Honey Belle lurched up from the bed, her heart racing from the images of the nightmare echoing in her mind. Although the temperature inside the hotel room was comfortable, she was coated in sweat. Her nightgown clung to her like an extra layer of skin.

She swallowed, trying to bring her rational mind into focus. But her dream had been so vivid, the leering face of Judge Hartwell so clear as he'd shown her picture after picture of herself reaching for an empty cradle. Her skin felt pricked by shards of glass, and anxiety pierced her heart. Perhaps it was the Judge's image, jabbing a finger in the air, and his voice, mean and low, that awakened her. *No bastard babies to taint the Hartwell bloodlines. Forbidden...hear me...forbidden!*

With her heart in her throat, she kicked off the sheet. She turned and was on the edge of the bed. She scooted back to keep from falling off. It took her a full minute to collect her wits, to remember she was in a hotel room in Washington, D.C. and today was Monday—the day she intended to seek an appointment with Senator Tripp Hartwell. The day she had dreaded for seventeen years.

She stumbled to the bathroom and bathed her face in cold water. But afterward she stopped to stare out at the morning, memories of walks on the beach with Tripp bringing tears to her eyes... Honey Belle drew in a deep breath. This time she didn't feel the sting of tears. She was done crying.

She remembered waking up weeks ago, when her son had proudly shown her the letter stating he'd been selected by Georgia's state representative to serve as a page to Congress. That one letter had brought back to the forefront of her mind the mistake of falling in love with a rich and powerful man's son. That one letter had unraveled her world.

****

Honey Belle glanced out the window of the yellow cab. The view of the city did nothing to lift her spirits. The driver hit the brakes at a traffic light, lurching her forward.

The traffic light turned green, and the cab moved again toward the Hart Senate Building. The cabbie maneuvered close to the curb, and she paid the fare. Midmorning heat was rising from the sidewalks in shimmering waves. Perspiration beading on her upper lip, she stood for a moment admiring the nine-story structure before pushing through the senate building's glass doors and stepping into the atrium. There was no need to check the information board for Senator Hartwell's office number. A simple phone call had given her that information. She stepped into the elevator and pushed the second floor button. There didn't seem to be enough room in the elevator's car to breathe. No matter what, she swore she wouldn't give an inch. Not when it came to protecting her son.

She second-guessed her decision to confront Tripp. There were two senators for each of the fifty states. With that many politicians and their staff, plus the house representatives, sixteen-year-old Jack Tripp Garrett would simply be another young page, and certainly not one significant enough to warrant the attention of a popular senator from South Carolina. If anyone questioned Jack's middle name, it could be construed as a coincidence. After all, Tripp was a common name in the South, wasn't it? Perhaps she should turn around, go back to the hotel, and stay there. She would wait for Jack's nightly telephone call, tell him how much she loved him, to enjoy his summer in D.C., and that she was flying home on the next flight to Atlanta. Yes, that seemed like a good plan. No one would be the wiser about Jack's parentage. She had always allowed her son to believe his father had died in the war, had brushed off details when he'd come home from school filled with questions as to why he didn't have a daddy to play fly ball with him or to take him fishing and camping. She feared, if the truth came out that Jack was illegitimate, he would hate her. Hate her for not telling him who his father was. How could she tell him why she'd kept his birth a secret without condemning herself?

Her pep talk had helped. She'd made her decision, until the elevator doors opened and the little voice in her head chided, "Coward...coward." She'd heard it before, that hateful little reminder. "Okay, so I'm not the most courageous person in the world. Give me a break."

An impeccably dressed man holding a briefcase said, "I beg your pardon, miss?"

She winced at the fact she'd spoken aloud. "Bad habit..." She gave an eloquent shrug. "Talking to myself." She swallowed more emotions than she could explain.

In a split second before the elevator doors closed, she called out, "Senator Hartwell's office?"

The man hurried his answer. "Down the hall. Last door on the left."

There was no time to thank him.

She was more nervous than she'd thought she would be, and found herself mentally rehearsing exactly what she wanted to say. This sort of rote memorization had served her well during college and graduate school.

She took a moment to stare down the long hall and felt as if she were walking to her doom. Tucking a wayward strand of hair behind her ear, she sucked in a steadying breath. What would she say to him after all these years? *Hello, Senator Hartwell, remember me?*

No, that wouldn't do. She tried again. *Hi, Tripp, I was in town, and thought for old times' sake—*

She quickly dismissed that one.

The more she walked, the longer the hall seemed to be. She could hear her breath, felt the pressure of the carpet under her high heels, until she reached the last door on the left.

She took a step toward the closed door, placed her hand on the doorknob, and hesitated. What if he didn't remember her? What if he did remember her? Which was worse? Both, she decided.

Outside the building the air had been stifling, but inside it was air conditioned, so why was she perspiring? She stood frozen in place.

A man's voice said, "Excuse me, miss, I have an appointment with the senator. Do you mind?"

She hesitated for the barest second. "Oh, certainly, I was just going in."

She turned the knob and swung the door open, stepping inside ahead of the man. The office had an air of formality. Behind a dark cherrywood desk sat a woman in her mid-fifties. Honey Belle guessed she was Tripp's secretary or—what did they call them these days? Ah, yes, administrative assistant. A further glance around the room showed a set of comfortable leather chairs against a wall. Black-and-white framed photographs of the Capitol building, Lincoln Memorial, and Presidents John F. Kennedy and Lyndon B. Johnson decorated the wall.

The secretary looked up. Her glance seemed to bounce off Honey Belle as she acknowledged the gentleman, her voice pleasant, yet all business. "Good morning, Senator Clarksdale. He's expecting you."

As the senator opened the door, Honey Belle craned her neck hoping to catch a glimpse of the man she longed to see, yet at the same time dreading the encounter.

Before the door closed she heard Senator Clarksdale say, "We need to talk, Senator."

Honey Belle's heart fluttered as she stepped forward. She couldn't help but wonder about the woman's expression toward her. Not friendly. Indifferent, Honey Belle decided.

She felt a little unnerved as the woman seemed to scrutinize her. "If you are here to see the senator, he isn't taking any appointments."

For a long moment, Honey Belle held the secretary's gaze. The woman removed her glasses, plucked a tissue from a box on the corner of her desk and began wiping them.

Honey Belle glanced at the gold nameplate on the desk. "Oh, I see, Mrs. Evans. Is he not taking appointments for today, only, or for the rest of the week?"

The secretary put her glasses back on again, scowling softly. "The rest of the week. He's quite busy."

"Five minutes is all I need. Just five minutes."

The woman harrumphed. "That's what they all say."

Honey Belle searched her mind for a logical argument. Right now she felt taut and insecure. "I'm certain everyone also says their business with Senator Hartwell is important. The truth is my business with him is...urgent."

"Yes, of course, it is." The secretary's voice sounded droll. As if she'd heard *that* excuse a thousand times before.

****

Meanwhile, in that very same office, Tripp stared at the other side of that same closed door, praying that someone would enter and save him from Senator Clarksdale's tiresome laments about the way the Arms Committee was shaping up. The man was a proverbial worrywart.

"Listen, Tripp, I don't have the same clout as you carry. All I know is that if we don't have all the i's dotted and t's crossed, the President will veto this bill and send it back to the House. We can't risk even the smallest delay."

Tripp reached down to rub away the phantom pains he still felt in his missing limb. He stood stiffly and walked around the desk. Clapping Clarksdale on the shoulder, he reassured him. "You worry too much, Jim. Rest assured this bill will pass. The future of our service men and women and the future safety of our country depend on it."

When it came to protecting his country, he acted with utter assurance that his decisions would not be countermanded. He reached for the cane resting at the corner of his desk. His leg hurt like the dickens...no, not his leg...it wasn't there anymore...the prosthesis.

He gripped the brass knob and pulled the office door open. "Keep me abreast of any changes, Jim. We don't have much time before we go into session."

The senator nodded. It wasn't until Clarksdale stepped aside and moved toward the exit door that Honey Belle came into view. Squaring his shoulders and wincing at the pain where the artificial leg fitted above his knee, Tripp stared at the woman, her golden brow pinched with concern. Her face searched his as if looking for some kind of answer. He thought she looked tense and frightened.

"Mrs. Evans, what time am I to meet with the new group of junior congressional pages tomorrow?"

He observed the younger woman's heightened color at his words. Some inner reflex caused him to speak to her.

"Excuse me. Have we met?"

She spoke, a slight quake to her voice. "A very long time ago. I-I know how busy you are, Senator Hartwell, but it's imperative I speak to you...in private."

The secretary stood as if Honey Belle had overstepped boundaries. "Senator, may I remind you that—"

Tripp sent the woman a scowl as if reminding her that he was still capable of making decisions. He turned toward the opened door to his office. With a sweeping motion of his free hand he invited Honey Belle in. "I can spare a few minutes."

****

Honey Belle straightened. Her heart went out to him. She knew from past television reports and newspaper accounts of his heroic actions in Vietnam and how he'd lost his leg, and even after all these years she knew him well enough to see the pain he hid so well from others.

Neither of them moved as they stared at each other. His muscles seemed frozen, and, for a second, she was certain he didn't recognize her. Suddenly, she felt guilty showing up this way, without warning, unannounced. She had thought it would be easier, somehow. That she would know what to say. She didn't. Everything she had in her head to say seemed inappropriate. Thoughts of the summer they had shared together in South Carolina came back to her, and, as she stared at him, she noticed how little he had changed since the last time she'd seen him.

She tried not to be unsettled by this tall, powerful man. He towered over her, his stare drilling into her. His eyes seemed to capture her from hair to high-heeled shoes. Clearing her throat, she tried to appear businesslike.

"Have I changed so much that you don't recognize me, Tripp?" This wasn't at all the way she had rehearsed the scene in her head. She didn't blink an eye—afraid any reaction might betray her uncertainty.

"Look, miss, I don't have time for twenty questions. I meet a lot of people, if—"

She wanted him to remember, to remember her, to remember—what? That seventeen years ago she had walked away from him? That she hadn't had the courage to stand up to his father and fight for her position in the life of the man she loved. That for sixteen years she had raised the son he never knew existed. She should never have left Tripp. So much guilt, for so many mistakes. She had no one to blame but herself.

She lifted her eyes to his. "Seventeen years ago, in Charleston, South Carolina, I asked you to take me for a ride in your shiny white BMW."

The silence of the office closed in around her. Every feminine instinct screamed a warning that he would deny knowing her.

He shook his head as if flummoxed. "Honey Belle Garrett?"

When his frowning gaze swept over her, she felt completely inadequate. Something she hadn't felt for a long time. The force of his scowl was like a windstorm scorching her skin.

"Why are you here?"

She wanted to reach out to him. To touch him. Instead, she kept her hands clenched around the handle of the briefcase that held the condemning evidence Judge Hartwell had threatened to use against her. "There's an important reason for leaving my home in Georgia and coming to D.C., Tripp. Believe me I would rather have stayed in Valdosta and completely out of your life, forever."

She watched the muscle in his jaw work as he motioned toward a chair. "Please, sit."

Glancing around the space, her laughter was more of a nervous twitter. "Maybe I've watched too many spy movies, but is it possible your office is...bugged?"

Her question seemed to shock him out of his surprised stupor. Hooking the cane on the corner of the desk, he lowered himself to the plush black office chair, the steel in his voice evident. "Anything is possible, Miss Garrett. Obviously you aren't here for old times' sake. I'll ask again, what is the purpose of your visit?"

She drew in a deep breath, the tension leaving her. He was going to hate her guts. Here wasn't the place to reveal her secret.

"I have something of extreme importance to tell you. Because of who you are and your political position, your office may not be private enough."

Tripp leaned forward, and the chair squeaked loudly. "All right, out of curiosity, I'll play your little game. Meet me at the Lincoln Memorial in an hour."

"There are a lot of steps. How will I find you?"

His voice was laced with condemnation. "One hour."

When he looked down at the papers on his desk, Honey Belle knew she had been dismissed.

Chapter Twenty-Six

The image of Honey Belle's ethereal beauty rose up in Tripp's mind like a specter to haunt him. He stared at the closed door long after she had left his office, then leaned back in the chair and closed his eyes. Oh, how he had loved her, from the first moment she had slapped his face when he'd suggested he drive her to the beach to watch the submarine races.

He had fully intended to take advantage of the young woman who had bared the fullness of her breast as she had leaned out the Burger Bin's drive-through window to hand him his order of fries and a hamburger with double pickles, hold the onions.

A rich college kid used to getting his way, the slap and her refusal to accept his apology had won his heart.

Now a familiar grief constricted in his chest like a vise. It had been seventeen years since he had stood on the steps of the house located on Barrington Street only to find out that Honey Belle and her parents had never lived in the antebellum home with the wide wraparound veranda. She had stolen his heart, she had lied to him, and then like a wisp of wind she had disappeared.

To his utter amazement, her features had grown more beautiful than he remembered. Sighing, he welcomed the anger, the feeling of betrayal that twisted hot in his gut.

The intercom's buzz caused him to jump. Pressing the answer button, he ground out his response more forcefully than he intended. "What is it?"

"Shall I order in lunch for you, Senator?"

"Not today, Mrs. Evans. I'm going out."

"But Senator, you haven't fully dictated the changes in the documents for the Arms Committee."

He wanted to say, *Screw the schedule*. He didn't. "Notify the answering service, Mrs. Evans, that we're closing the office—" he glanced at his watch— "until two o'clock. We all deserve a break once in awhile, including you."

After a long moment, he removed his jacket, draped it over the back of his chair, loosened the knot on his black tie, and grabbed his cane.

Outside, he walked down the sidewalk, the soles of his shoes cushioned his steps. It felt good to be out, to feel the heat against his back. He rolled the sleeves of his white shirt up to his elbows.

He had always paid attention to details. Especially when he'd begun his law practice, and even more so while stationed in Vietnam, and now as a United States senator. Little things, obscure things, and it had become a habit.

And now a little detail bothered him. Honey Belle's out-of-the-blue visit.

Detail.

Something significant. Something important.

But what was it?

He stopped at Roscoe's Dog and Suds stand and ordered two hot dogs, extra relish, hold the onions.

"That be all for you today, Senator?"

"Two waters. Extra ice."

"You got it. Man, it's hot enough to melt Antarctica."

Tripp chuckled as he accepted the sack and paid the vendor. "Let's hope not, Bernie." There was a joke. Bernie Lebowitz had bought the hot dog stand ten years ago and had never changed the name.

Moments later, with the aid of the cane, he

limped up the steps to the top of the Lincoln Memorial. Early, he stationed himself in the shade next to the massive statue, where he could see the comings and goings down below.

Removing a hot dog from the sack and savoring a man-sized bite, he realized he'd forgotten how good simple food tasted.

****

Honey Belle felt the heat on her face as she looked up. Squinting through her sunglasses, she scanned the steps. Her heart dropped. Tripp was nowhere in sight.

She glanced at her watch. On time, she'd wait a half hour. If he didn't show, she'd leave and never look back.

And then she spotted him, standing far enough out of the shadows to be seen. She wondered how long he'd been there watching her. The thought sent a shiver down her spine—one she quickly rejected.

By the time she reached the top of the steps, she was glad she walked every day. She had to admit climbing steps in high heels wasn't as easy as walking two miles wearing sneakers. She drew a long, lung-refreshing breath and blew it out.

Tripp was clearly upset. She could tell by the scowl on his face. She opened her mouth, but before she could greet him he blurted out, "I took the liberty of bringing lunch. I hope you like hot dogs."

Surprised, she didn't know how to respond. In truth, she was certain the butterflies in her stomach would refuse anything she put in it. "Thank you. I had a large breakfast." She wiped a hand across her brow. "Do you have anything cold to drink in that bag?"

They were both stalling for time, and she knew it. She accepted the Styrofoam cup, removed the lid. The water cooled her parched throat.

She worried her bottom lip, wishing he wasn't so

damned handsome. "Do you mind if we sit?"

Without waiting for his answer, she sat on the top step relishing the coolness of the shade. She balanced the briefcase on her knees.

She looked up at Tripp, who was still standing. His eyes seemed involved in some sort of inner search for understanding as to why she was here. She patted the place next to her. "I promise not to bite."

He snapped his head around as he joined her. His face softened as soon as his eyes met hers. She wanted to hold on to that gaze. She clicked the clasps on the briefcase and opened it. She spoke no words as she handed Tripp a photograph.

She wondered what he was thinking as he studied the image. He frowned. "A picture of me in my senior year of high school. I don't remember giving you this. How did you get it?"

The day was crisp and hot, bright with sun, blue as only a summer sky in Washington, D.C. can be. And suddenly, sitting on the top step in shade cast by the massive stone statue of Abraham Lincoln, Honey Belle felt confined.

She scooted a little ways from him to better see his face. This was it. The moment of truth. Her heart thrummed inside her ears. She didn't know whether she was speaking aloud. "It isn't you, Tripp. His name is Jack Tripp Garrett. JT, for short. He's my son...our son."

****

He had a son.

Son.

The word whispered through Tripp and stole inside his heart.

His son.

His.

Tripp's heart turned over in his chest as he continued to stare at the image he'd mistaken for his own.

Confusion and rage coursed through him in equal measure. He didn't know whether to sweep Honey Belle into his arms or strangle her with his tie.

Questions fired off inside his head like mortar rounds. He glowered at her, secretly admiring the red blush on her cheeks. He blurted out, "Is that why you slunk out of South Carolina? Because you were pregnant? Because you didn't trust my love for you?"

He raked a hand through his hair. "My god, Honey Belle, can you imagine what I felt when I went to the house on Barrington Street and found out you'd lied to me? I loved you."

"I'm sorry." Her voice was husky.

The sun had reached its peak and was already inching toward the horizon. Tripp stared out across the expanse at the Washington Monument. "Why have you waited all these years to tell me I have a son?" His mouth twisted. "And don't tell me it's complicated."

She closed her eyes and sighed. "JT is an exceptional young man. He excels in everything—academics, sports, and politics. When he received the letter stating he'd been tapped to serve as a congressional junior page, it was the happiest day of his life, and it felt like a death sentence to me. There is no way for either you or me to come out a winner in this.

"You've seen the photograph. Even you mistook it for yourself. I've never stopped loving you, Tripp, but I love my son more. JT was so excited about the appointment that I couldn't take his joy away by denying him the opportunity."

Honey Belle spread her hands wide as if desperate. "D.C. is a place of scandal. My greatest fear is what will happen if you and he are seen together. There's bound to be questions, speculation from reporters, other members of the House and Senate. My son thinks his father died in the war. I never told him any different."

Anger flashed in his gut, but he suppressed it. "You keep referring to him as *your* son. He's *mine*, too."

Honey Belle's sharp intake of breath revealed her acknowledgement of his fury. Staring back at him, she drew in a deep breath and slowly released it. "Yelling at me won't solve the problem."

Her announcement that he had son had come as a shock. He managed a tight-lipped reply. "Yes, of course, you are right."

He glanced at his watch as he stood. "I have to get back to the office." His eyes darkened. "You owe me an explanation. I want to know all of it right down to the last detail."

Honey Belle clenched her hands around the briefcase handle. She stood, too, almost matching Tripp's height. "On two conditions—one, that you make certain JT is protected from scandal, and two, when I tell you the circumstances of keeping my...our son's birth a secret, that you will listen, without comment, until I'm finished."

"You are in no position to dictate terms, Honey Belle." He used his cane as balance to help him maneuver down the steps. Halfway down, he turned and looked at her delicate features, the stubborn tilt of her chin, and he searched for the right words. "The President has called a special session of the Arms Committee. I head the committee and will no doubt be sequestered until all committee members are certain the wording in the bill cannot be challenged by the opposing body." He offered a sardonic smile. "We could be tied up for weeks, or at least until summer is over and the junior pages have left D.C."

Honey Belle placed a hand to her heart. "Thank

you, Tripp."

He raised an eyebrow. "I'll be in contact. You still owe me an explanation, and no lies, Honey Belle. I despise liars."

He was close enough to see her blink back the tears. "Should I stay in D.C. or return home?"

He gave her a measured look then shrugged. "Earlier you said you were from Georgia. Valdosta, I believe. I'll contact you."

"You won't try to see JT, will you? I mean, you know what would happen?"

"I didn't get to where I am today by making stupid decisions, Honey Belle." Yeah, he already knew the temptation was there to seek out young Jack Tripp Garrett. He also knew reporters were vampires seeking their next victim to bleed dry. For the sake of his son, he would go MIA to avoid a scandal.

But by no means did he intend to let Honey Belle Garrett off the hook.

****

In heavy silence, Honey Belle strolled down the boulevard. The air had cooled. Dark clouds billowed with the promise of rain.

She knew the way back to her hotel and decided the walk would help clear her head. Too much had happened today. She wrestled with her conscience. All she had ever wanted was to protect her son. To love him the way her mother and father had never loved her. Until JT had received the letter announcing his appointment as a congressional junior page, life had been uncomplicated, peaceful, and filled with happiness.

She greeted the doorman at the hotel and rode the elevator up to her room. Her stomach growled, reminding her that except for a cup of coffee she hadn't eaten all day.

Kicking off her shoes, she padded to the

telephone and ordered room service. Tomato soup and a grilled cheese sandwich.

Her mind floated back to Tripp as she lifted the scrapbook from the briefcase. She had intended to show him the book filled with newspaper clippings showcasing his life, and to explain about his father. The opportunity hadn't presented itself.

Aimlessly turning the pages, her eyes settled on the article about Tripp's marriage to Kathryn and the loss of their child. Honey Belle wiped a tear from her cheek.

The poor man. He'd lost his mother, a wife, a child, and his leg. He'd suffered, probably more than anyone knew. Her imagination painted a dark and brooding picture of Tripp's life.

All she knew of him lay between the pages of a scrapbook. Seventeen years of memories. She'd probably never know his deepest secrets. He certainly wasn't about to share his life with her. In fact, she doubted she'd ever see him again. The one fact she knew for certain about Tripp was his honesty. He was the most trusted senator in Washington, D.C. If he said he would protect the identity of their son, she knew he would live up to his promise.

Leaning back against the pillow, she allowed herself to create a new picture of Tripp. Not the angry man she'd confronted today. One who was selfless in his protection of others, one who would forgive her and rekindle their love.

She wondered if he too suffered from loneliness. Yes, she had JT and Aunt Tess, and her students. For all practical purposes, she led a full and satisfying life. There was one void that needed filling. The love she had walked away from seventeen years ago.

The telephone startled her out of her reverie. Her heart pattered. She hoped it was Tripp. "Hello?"

"Hi, Mom, just calling to say 'good-night' and I love you."

Honey Belle swallowed the lump that threatened to keep her from speaking. "Tomorrow is a big day. Are you still excited?"

"You know it. Listen, Mom, I know you're concerned about all those articles you read about, well, you know...the guy who molested one of the pages. That was last year. I don't want you to worry. Nothing like that will happen to me. I won't let it. Why don't you and Aunt Tess take a vacation? Do something fun."

She smiled. "I take it you don't want me making a fuss over you tomorrow. Anyhow, my plane leaves in the morning."

"I'm sorry I couldn't spend time seeing the sights with you, Mom. Truly, I am."

"What did I ever do to deserve a son like you?" It was a question she had often asked herself. "Learn as much as you can about politics, Jack Tripp Garrett, but don't forget to enjoy yourself. I'll see you in August."

It was difficult for her to say good-bye. She cradled the receiver and went to answer the room-service announcement at the door. Sighing, Honey Belle pushed away all thoughts of Tripp from her mind.

When the truth came out, she hoped JT would forgive her.

Chapter Twenty-Seven

Honey Belle set the food tray out in the hallway and retreated into her hotel room, making sure the door was closed and locked. She rubbed her eyes, stretched, and yawned. She hadn't slept well the night before, and the stress of today's meeting with Tripp had left her exhausted. She shed the housecoat and climbed into bed.

She didn't remember shutting her eyes or falling asleep. She saw herself in a swirling fog of darkness. A man wearing a mask approached her. Though she couldn't see his face, there was a familiarity about him. He warned her it wasn't safe for a woman to be on the streets at night and alone. He asked if he could escort her someplace. She felt safe with this man. Because of his mask, could she trust him?

He grasped her hand and lifted it to his lips. Her body flamed, and she ached for more of his touch. His tongue caressed the inner harbor between her thumb and forefinger. Desire rushed through her and she felt faint. The flash of longing pulsated with such power it frightened her. She pulled her hand away. "I have to go." And she turned and ran, allowing the swirling fog to engulf her.

She came to a door and knocked. No one answered. She balled her fist and rapped against the wooden frame until the sound echoed in her ears.

She knocked again.

She pleaded, "Please, let me in."

Knock. Knock. Louder.

Stirring in her sleep, she wondered why someone didn't answer the door.

Knock. Knock.

Honey Belle sat up. Her heart raced. The knocking was real. Someone was actually rapping on her hotel room door. She looked at the clock. One-thirty in the morning. She quelled the panic in the pit of her stomach. Had something happened to JT? Was it her son? Had he changed his mind about staying in D.C.?

Knock. Knock.

Scooting out of bed, she ran on tiptoes across the carpeted room and pressed her eye against the peephole. The last person she expected to see stood in the hall. He turned to walk away. Releasing the security chain, she opened the door.

"Tripp, what are you doing here?"

He pushed in past her. "Shut the door."

Puzzled at his mysterious late-night visit, she obeyed. "Do you know what time it is? What's wrong?"

Tripp handed her a paper sack. "Coffee."

"Uh, thanks, I think. Are you going to tell me why you're here?"

"You were right this afternoon when you asked if my office was bugged. Capitol Hill has eyes and ears everywhere. That's the reason I waited until those eyes and ears went to sleep." He lifted the lid off the cup he held and sipped.

"Excuse me for asking an irrational question, but what about when you get ready to leave? Won't there be eyes and ears?"

He warmed her with a smile. "I'm not staying that long. I've thought about it all afternoon, Honey Belle. I need to know why you ran out on me."

Disarmed by his smile, she relaxed her guard. "Okay. You have to promise you won't interrupt, that you'll hear me out all the way through."

He settled in a chair, stretched out his legs and crossed his ankles. He gave what sounded like a resigned sigh. "On my word of honor."

Honey Belle was conscious of his undivided attention. She hid her pleasure. The feeling came from deep inside, a warm tide that felt like it couldn't be emptied.

She pulled the other chair around to face him, then gathered the scrapbook and large brown envelope from the briefcase and held them in her lap. Her voice even, she began. "The day after you left for Massachusetts, a sleek black limousine parked in front of the home I shared with my parents in Shanty Groves. A man dressed in a black uniform asked if I was Honey Belle Garrett. He said Judge Hartwell wished to speak with me. I very naively thought your father had come to congratulate me on our engagement. I was excited, but disappointed because another part of me thought you must have asked him to take me shopping for an engagement ring."

The entire time she talked, she watched Tripp's face. It was obvious that over the years he had learned to mask his emotions.

Mask? A portion of her dream came to her. Was Tripp the masked man in her dream?

She continued her story. Refraining from referring to the Judge as Tripp's father, she called him the Judge. "The Judge said he wanted me out of town, that I wasn't good enough for you. He offered me a large sum of money. I told him you and I loved each other, and no amount of money could force me to leave you."

She clutched the envelope of incriminating pictures. "That's when he showed me pictures, shameful pictures. I explained the people were my father and mother and my cousin Bubba. He laughed and said you wouldn't know the difference. That trash was trash. It wasn't until he threatened my family, saying he'd fix it so my father couldn't get medical treatment at any hospital, and that he'd see to it my mother and I lost our jobs, and he'd have us kicked out of our house... I couldn't allow him to hurt my parents.

"I tried one more bluff. I snatched the pictures from him and ripped them to shreds. I shall never forget the sound of his laugh when he reached inside his briefcase and pulled out another pack of these." She handed Tripp the envelope. When he hesitated, she said, "Where we lived was a dump. Mama and Daddy, well, they were who they were, and I didn't know any different. As bad as the pictures look, they really are all innocent."

She watched Tripp's frown as he flipped through the stack of black-and-whites. "Part of me wants to believe you, Honey Belle. The other part knows my father wouldn't stoop to blackmail. Threats, maybe. Blackmail, no, I'll never believe it."

She saw the white outline of anger around his pressed lips. A muscle ticked under his right eye. And he rubbed his leg. The prosthetic leg...as if it ached.

She closed her eyes because she didn't want to know, didn't want to recognize the accusation she saw in his eyes or to look too deep into his heart.

She reached inside the briefcase and removed a folded sheet of paper. "I wasn't smart back in those days. Yet somehow I knew the time might come when I would need to defend myself. I made a copy of this."

She reluctantly handed him the photocopy of the personal check, written in Judge Hartwell's own hand and with his signature, in the amount of ten thousand dollars. She didn't tell Tripp that his father had equated her to a fifty-dollar whore.

"Fearing a bank might ask questions if I tried to cash the check, the Judge also gave me five hundred dollars in cash. He wanted us out of town the next day. We packed up our few belongings, boarded a Greyhound bus, and went to live with my mother's sister in Valdosta, Georgia."

Tripp's jaw worked as he looked at the reproduction. Honey Belle held her breath, waiting for him to speak.

He threw her an irritated glance and enunciated clearly. "Did you know you were pregnant when I left for Massachusetts?"

Honey Belle hugged her knees close to her body. "No, I honestly didn't. All those nights we spent together on the beach, getting pregnant never entered my mind."

"When you found out, why didn't you tell me?"

An ache had grown behind her eyes, and she rubbed her temple. "Oh, Tripp, back then I was young and dumb. What did I know? Nothing. The Judge...he...he said if I was pregnant to get rid of it, that he'd have no bastard baby tainting the Hartwell's pure bloodlines or ruining your chances at a political career. I kept my pregnancy a secret, and I've kept my son a secret all these years, because I was afraid of what your father might do if he found out about JT."

Tripp shot out of the chair as if he'd been fired from a cannon. The copy of the check fluttered to the floor.

Honey Belle got up and put her hand on his shoulder. He was clearly upset and, she could tell, about to get very angry.

****

Tripp frowned. He, of all people, knew about the walls people built up to protect their hearts. It was evident Honey Belle had ramparts around hers a mile high.

By the square of her shoulders, and the tilt of her chin, she seemed strong, resilient, and yet there was a vulnerability about her eyes that elicited compassion, even empathy. It was as if she'd seen many lows and was valiantly prepared to face more. He hoped he was that prepared to face the final outcome.

Old thoughts crammed his head. The long-ago conversation with Charlie Nichols, the detective his father sometimes used for cases. He'd often wondered about the detective's hesitancy when answering those questions. It was too late, now, but he should have listened to his gut instinct and hired his own detective.

"I know why you lied about where you lived, Honey Belle. When I returned home and found you had never lived on Barrington Street, I went to the Burger Bin to see Carla. She couldn't tell me where you'd gone, but she laid it on pretty thick about why you had left. Me, a college kid born with a silver spoon in his mouth, and you, a high school dropout born on the wrong side of the tracks. An imperfect match doomed to disaster from the very beginning. Carla advised me to forget about you and get on with my career.

"Later, I drove out to Shanty Groves. I was determined to find you. By that time, the house you'd lived in was a crumbling shell and no one remembered your family."

Tripp studied Honey Belle for a long moment. He was overcome by the sudden urge to unclasp her hands and gently loosen her shoulders so she didn't appear so...so knotted up.

Something shifted inside Tripp, and he felt the familiar coldness envelop him like steely armor. He gritted his teeth. He needed to confront his father.

She stared up at him, wide-eyed. "What's done is done, Tripp. We can't go back and change any of it. I know you don't want to believe the Judge's role in this. It was difficult for me to tell you. Honestly."

"We'll work through this, Honey Belle. We *will*. I

promise."

She reached up and brushed his hair away from his forehead. He felt her fingers tremble against his skin. His body seemed to pull toward hers. More than anything in this world, he wanted to give in to that pull and kiss her.

The time wasn't right.

He had a son, and he wanted to know the boy. Before he could do that, he had to confront his own father.

He rubbed his thumb over her fingers. "Go back to Valdosta, Honey Belle. Let me work this out with my father in my own way."

Tears rolled down her cheeks. "I can't go through this again, Tripp. He will only deny it. The question is—will you believe him? Frankly, I don't care, as long as I don't lose my son."

Tripp leaned close, touching her cheek. "He's my son, too, remember? And it's my job to protect his mother. Good night, Honey Belle. I'll contact you when the time is right."

And then he was gone.

Honey Belle sighed. She pressed against the closed door and strained to hear the rhythmic thump of the cane and the footsteps in the hall.

****

A son.

The news filled Tripp with a myriad of emotions.

Elation.

He reveled at the idea of having a son. Nearing forty, he had feared his days of being a father were over. What woman wanted to make love to a one-legged gimp? He tossed that emotion aside. Pity parties weren't his style.

Anger.

Definitely. But at whom? His father or Honey Belle? Honey Belle's explanation sounded plausible. Part of him believed her story. His father? The same gnawing question he'd felt years ago had returned. Oh, yeah, his father had denied a role in Honey Belle's disappearance. Who to believe—that was the enigma.

Frustration.

As much as he desired to hop the first plane to South Carolina to confront his father, Tripp's first obligation was making certain the wording of the bill regarding the arms regulations for the military had no holes the opposing members could punch through.

He slowed his pace a little. Maybe this wasn't the hornet's nest he wanted to walk into. It was times like this he missed the counsel of his mother and Pearlie Mae. Both gone.

Honey Belle's face floated before his eyes, standing in the middle of the hotel room, her arms wrapped around herself, hugging her middle tight, she'd looked angry, sad, and about a dozen other female emotions he didn't have a name for. He didn't like seeing her that way, hurt. She seemed as fragile as an eggshell.

He shook his head, chasing off memories that would more than likely spell trouble. He would keep his promise to Honey Belle and not make contact with young Jack Tripp Garrett. At least, not yet.

Chapter Twenty-Eight

Tripp leaned over, planting both palms on the conference table. "Well, ladies and gentlemen, it's been a long eight weeks. A few subtle details, and we'll have a bill that neither the House nor the Senate can afford to shoot down."

Senator Eleanor Whipple lamented, "And then we can go home. Hopefully, we can wrap this up by the end of the week. I'd like to spend time with my twins before school starts."

Minutes later, Tripp and the committee members bent to the silent task of rereading sections from the lofty pyramid of documents.

Intent on the page he was reading, the voice bending to whisper in his ear startled him. "My apologies for interrupting, Senator Hartwell, but you have an urgent phone call."

Tripp looked at the fretful expression on his secretary's face. "Who is it?"

"It's your uncle. He says it's about your father."

Tripp pushed back his chair and excused himself. Moments later he returned to the meeting room. "My father is seriously ill. Senators Clarksdale and Whipple will fill my stead."

His eyes shifted around the table as he bid the committee members good luck.

****

A few hours later, Tripp landed at Charleston's airport and collected a rental car for the drive to the hospital. Usually a cautious driver, he changed lanes frequently and bore down on the accelerator when the lights turned yellow, feeling the weight of every passing moment.

When he arrived, the scene in the hospital reminded him of the time when Kathryn had fallen down the stairs and miscarried their baby. It was as if nothing had changed. The same ammonia and antiseptic odors filled the air, the same fluorescent lights in the same fiberboard dropped ceilings, and more people than the waiting room had chairs.

Jake Hartwell looked every bit the lawyer in his navy blue suit and shiny black shoes. At the age of seventy, he was still a robust man. Tripp reached out to grip his uncle's hand in a hearty shake. "How is he, Uncle Jake?"

"Dr. Chapman is running tests. He thinks the fall may have triggered a stroke."

"Not down the stairs?"

"No. It appears Harlan was trying to change a light bulb in the bathroom, fell off the stepladder, and hit his head on the tub. He was barely conscious when the nurse heard the crash and ran upstairs to investigate. She called the ambulance. I called you."

"Waiting is the worst part, Uncle Jake. Brings back painful memories of another time when the waiting seemed to last forever."

"Kathryn?"

Tripp nodded. "Father is eighty-one. Even with a certified nursing assistant with him night and day, he has no business rambling around inside that big old house all by himself."

"Are you suggesting an assisted living facility?"

"Yes."

"I don't disagree. Convincing my brother is a horse of another color. Let's see what Dr. Chapman tells us about Harlan's condition."

Tripp hadn't finished his coffee when a nurse entered the waiting room and called for a Tripp Hartwell.

He stood. "That would be me."

"Dr. Chapman wanted me to let you know he'd be out shortly."

Tripp thanked the nurse and sat back down.

Thirty minutes passed and the nurse emerged again. "Your father is a little disoriented. His vital signs are good. He's been moved to a room. Dr. Chapman said he'd talk to you when you arrived there."

Tripp felt his uncle's eyes drift toward him. "You go on. The two of us might wear Harlan out."

The nurse shook her head. "If you're Jake, then Mr. Hartwell wants to see you *and* his son, together. He insisted. Room 402."

****

"The news isn't good, Senator Hartwell. As I suspected, the fall triggered a mild stroke. However, that isn't my major concern. The x-ray shows a large mass on the temporal lobe. I've sent the reports to a neurosurgeon for a second opinion. All indications suggest a malignancy."

For a moment, Tripp stood without speaking. "What does that mean in terms of time, Dr. Chapman?"

The doctor patted him on the shoulder. "I can't tell you that until I hear from the neurosurgeon. I'll let you know as soon as I get his report."

Tripp and his uncle traded handshakes with the doctor. As he entered the room, Tripp thought his father looked small in the bed, his face paper white. Tripp pulled a chair close to the bed and sat. His uncle did the same.

"Hello, Father."

"Hello, son," the Judge said shakily.

"Uncle Jake said you fell off a ladder."

"Got a little dizzy and lost my balance."

His father's eyes had grown curiously misty. He said, "Jake, I want you to bear witness to what I have to say to my son."

Jake Hartwell said, "Your will is in place, Harlan. Did you want to add a codicil?"

The elder man waved his hand in the air as if popping invisible bubbles. "Hell, no. I've got a confession to make. Somebody ought to hear it besides Tripp."

The heart machine beat steadily, soothing in its monotony. His curiosity piqued, Tripp had no idea what deep dark secret his father harbored. "What do you have to confess, Father?"

A coughing spasm caused pain to constrict the Judge's face. Tripp poured a glass of water. While his uncle assisted in lifting the Judge to a sitting position, Tripp held the glass so his father could drink. Water dribbled down the wrinkled chin to stain the white sheet. As if exhausted by the mere act of swallowing a few sips, Harlan Hartwell leaned back on the pillow and closed his eyes. Tripp exchanged glances with his uncle, and waited.

Harlan rolled his head to the side of the pillow. His eyes snapped open. "I've known about the brain tumor for quite some time. It was confirmed at the Mayo Clinic. I told that idiot Chapman." Harlan's laugh was short and unpleasant. "I told him to send for the medical records. Young upstart. Thinks he knows more than me, the retired governor of South Carolina. What does he think I am, stupid?"

Tripp tried to calm his father. "Dr. Chapman is doing what any good doctor would do. He's covering all the bases. Why didn't you tell me or Uncle Jake about the tumor?"

"I don't want to talk about it. I have other things on my mind."

Not wishing to agitate his father, Tripp smiled. "All right, Father. Uncle Jake and I are listening."

Tripp saw pain mirrored in his father's eyes, saw infinite sadness dwelling there. The small black clock on the wall told him it was almost three-thirty.

Tired from his flight and the drive through Charleston, Tripp felt impatient. He wanted to pace around the room, to stretch his long legs. Instead, he remained seated.

The Judge coughed, cleared his throat. "When I met your mother, she was so beautiful, so warm and loving. I knew the moment I laid eyes on her she was the woman I would wed. The cruelest thing your mother ever did in her entire life was to die and leave me alone."

Tripp envisioned his mother in her old gardening clothes and floppy hat, wearing a smile that could brighten the dreariest day. He, too, missed her.

His father's voice broke through Tripp's musing.

"Kathryn was a mistake. I should never have insisted you marry the girl. She was shallow, selfish, and greedy. Not at all like my Mary Alice." Harlan's eyes closed and he seemed to drift off. His eyes looked wide and startled when he opened them.

"My fault for your unhappiness...all my fault. My fault you went off to war. I could have used my power to keep you home. My fault you lost your leg. All of it...my fault."

"You're not making sense, Father. I chose to join the Army. Vietnam happened without your help. As for my leg, I was a casualty of war. It's over and done. In the past. What does this have to do with Mother, Kathryn, and a confession?"

As his father toyed with the edge of the blanket, the mist continued to cloud the Judge's eyes. "That girl, Honey Belle Garrett—you remember her?"

Tripp laced his fingers together in a tight grip. His stomach clenched. "What about her?"

"There's no easy way to say this, son. I paid her to leave South Carolina. Oh, she tried to get feisty, but I had Charlie Nichols take pictures of her. When I showed them to her, I said you would believe whatever I told you. I misused my power. I did it because I was afraid she'd ruin your chances at a successful political career."

Oh, God, he thought, if he'd ever had any doubts about Honey Belle's confession—Tripp shook his head, eager to leave the hospital, and his father. "Did you tell her to abort the child if she was pregnant? The truth, Father."

"I...well... I didn't want the Hartwell-Calhoun bloodlines tainted. That girl was white trash from the seediest section of Charleston. I did it for you. But I need to make my peace before I die."

"Oh, I get it. Confession is good for the soul. Is that it, Father?"

Tripp felt as if he'd stepped into the hottest depths of hell. In spite of the hospital room's frigid temperature, sweat trickled between his shoulder blades. Fingers of fire gripped his stomach. Bile burned the back of his throat. As much as he wanted to hate the shriveled shell his father had become, instead he pitied him. He fought to keep his voice calm. "I found out eight weeks ago that I have a son. His name is Jack Tripp Garrett. He is sixteen years old, and he served as a congressional junior page this term. His mother kept him a secret because she was afraid you would make good on your threat to harm the child. I refrained from meeting the boy to protect his mother's privacy." Tripp rubbed his brow as he paced about the room in agitation. "All these years, because of your self-righteous spitefulness, you denied me the right to know *my son*, and my son the right to know his father...and a grandfather." He stopped pacing to stand at the edge of the hospital bed. "I should hate you. If you weren't a sick old man, maybe I would."

Judge Hartwell blinked fast as if to hold back the tears. "I can never make amends for what I've done. Your mother, God rest her soul, always wanted a grandchild. In a sense, I denied her, too." He struggled to prop up on his elbows. "I've changed my mind, Jake. Write this down and let me sign it. Add a codicil to my will stating that a trust fund in the amount of one million dollars be set aside for Tripp's son...m-my grandson."

Tripp felt his chest constrict. He couldn't breathe. *His son.* The words sounded so foreign to him, he couldn't grasp the true meaning.

"Tripp, do you suppose I could meet my grandson before I die?"

Tripp's heart slammed against his chest. "JT doesn't know about me, or you, Father. I think the odds are impossible that either of us will ever know him."

****

Honey Belle felt like a trapped rabbit. Trapped in a lie by omission. Moving her gaze from each passenger to the next exiting the gangway at the Albany airport, she searched until she spotted JT waving at her.

After the initial hugs and loading his luggage inside the car, Honey Belle still wrestled with how to tell her son about the father he'd never known. "So, did serving as a junior page and hobnobbing with politicians help you to decide if you'd like to major in political science when you go to college?" She knew it was a lame way to begin a conversation. Still, with a hundred-and-ten-mile drive to Valdosta, she had plenty of time to get to the dreaded topic.

"Being in D.C. was a cool experience. I mean, like, man, it was really rad. You know? But that scene's not for me."

Honey Belle laughed at the typical teenage lingo. She decided to do a little fishing. "Did you meet any particular congressman who impressed you?"

"They were all pretty cool, some more than

others. I didn't get to meet my original mentor. Senator Tripp Hartwell. He was in a special session the entire summer. I really wanted to meet him, especially since he's a war hero and we both have the same name, Tripp. Pretty cool, huh? I heard he was a real stand-up guy. Say, Mom, did you deliberately name me after such a famous person?"

She loved the way her son prattled on and, without knowing, had opened the door for her big reveal. Sidestepping the question, she asked, "Are you hungry?"

"You know it. I could go for a bacon cheeseburger, extra pickles, hold the onions."

Hold the onions. A laugh escaped her. She knew another Tripp who loved hamburgers with extra pickles, hold the onions. She wondered if taste buds were genetic.

An hour later she removed the scrapbook from the briefcase on the back seat, slammed the car door, and slid behind the steering wheel. Her pulse raced out of control. Was she so conditioned to accept the worst out of life that she feared her son would reject her once she told him the truth about his parentage? She frowned, hating to admit it was true. Life had dealt Honey Belle her share of blows, but that was no excuse for hiding the truth. Was it?

"JT, earlier you asked if I'd deliberately named you after a famous person. The truth is I knew Tripp Hartwell long before he was a senator." She held the thick blue album toward her son. "I created this scrapbook while I was pregnant with you. I knew one day you would want to know about...about—"

Honey Belle held her breath. She couldn't bring herself to finish the sentence. She tried to remain cool and calm.

"What is it, Mom? I can tell by the look on your face something has upset you."

Her voice was husky when she spoke. "I never

expected to choose a Hardee's parking lot on the outskirts of Albany, Georgia, to make my grand confession. I hope when I finish, you won't judge me too harshly."

"Am I the reason you're upset? Did I do something wrong?"

She did her best to smile. "No...never. I just need you to understand there are times when people don't always use good judgment in the decisions they make. I also want you to know that you are the best thing that has ever happened to me, and that I've always loved you and always will."

"Oh, man, Mom, you're freaking me out. Please don't tell me you've got cancer. You're not gonna die, are you?"

Honey Belle reached out and cradled JT's cheeks in her hands. "No. I'm not sick, and I don't mean to frighten you."

"I'm sixteen, Mom. Whatever it is you're afraid to tell me, I can handle it. Okay?"

She drew a deep breath and slowly exhaled. "Okay. Here goes. I lived with my parents in Charleston, South Carolina. I met Tripp Harlan Hartwell the Third on my nineteenth birthday. He was twenty-two years old, drove a fancy white BMW convertible, and he was everything I wasn't. He was on his way to Harvard Law School, and I was a high school dropout flipping hamburgers."

She spent the next two hours explaining about her life, Tripp's marriage proposal, his father's threats, the blackmail money, and the reason for keeping her pregnancy a secret.

"One evening, when you were six years old, you and I and Aunt Tess were watching the news. On the television screen names were listed of the soldiers in Vietnam who were missing in action. You asked if your daddy had been killed in the war and was that the reason he didn't live with us. I always intended to tell you the truth. At that moment, when you looked up at me with such sorrow in your big wide eyes, it was easier to simply say yes.

"The years slipped away, and now you're on the cusp of becoming an adult." She shrugged her shoulders. "I guess I thought I could keep from you forever the fact that Senator Tripp Hartwell is your father."

The way JT looked at her, his silence, the two bright red spots on his cheeks, Honey Belle steeled herself for an outburst. "I get it now. This is the reason you didn't want me to go to D.C. Not because of the articles you read about some House Representative molesting a couple of junior pages, no. It was because you were afraid I'd meet Senator Hartwell, and we'd both figure out the truth."

A jolt of sick numbness surged through Honey Belle. "I started to tell you so many times."

His reply was stony. "Yeah, right. So, let's choose a fast-food parking lot to tell poor JT a sordid story. Does your conscience feel better, Mom?"

Honey Belle's gasp turned to anger. "How could you even think such a thing? You know I'm not that kind of person. I took no pleasure in this. It's been tearing me apart all these years."

He smacked his fist into the palm of his hand. "Yeah, like finding out I'm the bastard son of a rich senator is supposed to make me feel better? Big whoop, Mom."

"That's unfair." Tears streamed down Honey Belle's face.

JT pivoted toward the door handle. The scrapbook slid from his lap to the floorboard. The door swung open and he propelled out of the car.

She hated the frantic tone in her voice. "Where are you going?"

"I don't know. Away...from you."

"JT!"

Honey Belle swung her door open. She raced around the front of the car, banging her knee on the corner of the front bumper. She grimaced in pain. She lunged to grab her son's arm as he headed toward the highway.

"JT, I've...I've messed up. I know this. Please, honey, get back in the car. You don't have to talk to me. You can hate me, if that will make you feel better. Just, please, running away isn't the answer."

She tried to form a prayer, but the words in her mind were all jumbled up. "I deserve your anger, JT."

He looked at her. The emotional turmoil in his young face twisted her heart. "All this time, Mom, you let me believe I was the son of a war hero. What will my friends think when they find out I'm really an illegitimate bastard?"

That question jarred Honey Belle to the core. Her eyes held her son's. She hoped he saw the understanding and compassion. "First of all, you are not a bastard. You are *my* son. Secondly, your father *is* a war hero. Even you said he's a great man. As for your friends, nothing has changed...not really. You are still the same person you were when you were born...the same as eight weeks ago...the same person as five minutes ago. Who's to tell your friends? Certainly not me."

JT nodded. "Yes, but—"

Honey Belle risked wrapping her arms around him and holding him tight. "Right now you feel like the weight of the world is on your shoulders. Well, guess what, kiddo, I understand. More than you know."

JT blurted out, "I don't know if I can deal with this."

Honey Belle held him at arms' length, still afraid to relinquish her hold. "Remember when you were a little boy and had nightmares, and when you broke your arm, and when your puppy got run over, who was there to soothe away the fear and the hurt?"

JT looked at his mother as if a light had dawned in his numb brain. "You, Mom. You and Aunt Tess. But...but this is different."

"We all make mistakes. Mine was running away instead of trusting the man I loved would care for me no matter what side of the railroad tracks I was born on. Everyone deserves a second chance, JT. One day you may find you'll need a second chance, too." She brushed a hand over his hair. "Okay if we go home now?"

He looked down at the purpling bruise on his mother's knee. "I'm sorry I made you hurt yourself, Mom."

Honey Belle let out a breath of relief. "C'mon, kiddo. Let's go."

She waited for him to shut the car door before she turned the ignition key. With a deep sigh, she suppressed a smile when JT reached down, picked up the scrapbook from the floorboard, and opened it.

Chapter Twenty-Nine

Whenever he came back to Charleston, Tripp experienced a feeling of excitement. No matter how long he had been absent, be it months on end, a week, or merely a few days, he returned with a sense of well being inside, the knowledge he was coming home.

Tonight was no exception.

His anticipation started the moment he nosed the rental car between the massive twin oaks that marked the entrance to his family's house.

Tripp drove slowly. Peering out the window at the azaleas, he couldn't help thinking of his mother and how much she had loved her flowers.

Seventeen years ago he had been only twenty-three, so long ago, and yet it might have been yesterday, the memory was so clear in his mind of the evening he had told his parents about Honey Belle and his intention of marrying her.

Casting his mind back now, he pictured her as she had been then—tall, skinny, legs like a young colt. Yet pretty, in a fresh sort of way. She had been full of life and vitality. He had taken to her at once. And so he had experienced an extraordinary relationship with a vivacious young woman, a relationship that had lasted all of one summer.

You meet thousands of people, and then you meet just one, he thought, and your life is changed forever.

He straightened in his seat as the house came into view. One lone window was lit. He had barely braked when bright light flooded the front porch.

Moments later Blanch Milford, his father's nurse, opened the door. "Welcome home, Senator. How is your father?"

Tripp gave her the shortened version of his father's condition. "He's resting. We anticipate the doctor will keep him in the hospital a few more days."

"Until then, will you need my services?"

"Starting tomorrow, take the week off, Mrs. Milford. Feel free to remain in your quarters until we know more about my father's long-term prognosis."

"Very well, Senator. I wasn't sure if you had taken time to eat. I baked a ham and made potato salad for you. Oh, and there's grilled peaches topped with fresh mint. It was one of your father's favorites. Now, if you don't mind, I'll excuse myself."

Tripp went into the kitchen, removed a glass from the cabinet, and added ice. Inside the walk-in pantry, he found a bottle of Stolichnaya Cristal and filled the glass with a good measure of his father's favorite vodka.

Once he'd made his drink, he went to the parlor, glancing around as he strolled to the large fireplace. The weather was too hot for a fire. The room had been his mother's favorite, its blue carpet, blue velvet sofas, and tub chairs covered in blue floral and cream linen giving it a homey, comforting feeling. This was further enhanced by blue brocade curtains at the leaded windows, the polished mahogany paneled walls, and the blue shades on the wall sconces. It was a slightly masculine room.

Facing the empty corner next to the fireplace, he envisioned the brightly decorated blue spruce with barely enough room to place the Christmas angel on top without it touching the high ceiling.

He had wanted to add to his memories. He'd wanted to watch his child and his wife place an angel on top of the tree as had he and his mother. Yet Kathryn had hated this room. Garishly boring, she had called it.

Thanks to his father's malevolent interference, Tripp had missed the opportunity to form those traditions with young Jack Tripp Garrett.

His musings were interrupted when his uncle entered and walked rapidly to the bar. "Got another one of those?"

"Kitchen. Hungry?" Tripp explained about the ham and the potato salad.

"Beats the hell out of hospital cafeteria food."

Settled at the kitchen table, Jake said, "Guess my brother's confession comes as a shock to both of us. Before I honor the codicil, are you one hundred percent certain this boy sprang from your loins?"

"Give me a second and I'll let you answer your own question." Tripp placed his half-eaten sandwich on his plate and sprinted to the parlor. He lifted the suit jacket where he'd draped it over one of the tub chairs and in two shakes was back in the kitchen.

He laid the photograph in front of his uncle. "You tell me, Uncle Jake."

Jake Hartwell stared at the image that could have passed for his nephew's twin—if he'd had one. He wiped his hand on the linen napkin across his lap. As if picking up a piece of evidence, he held the picture at one corner with his thumb and forefinger. He turned the picture over. "Jack Tripp Garrett, Valdosta High School, 1980."

Tripp saw the calculator working in his uncle's brain as he did the math. "The boy was born in 1964."

"May 24th, to be exact."

Jake Hartwell lifted an eyebrow. "Your birthday."

Tripp nodded.

"What are your intentions?"

Tripp let out a small sigh. Taking his glass with him, he rose and walked to the bank of windows overlooking the garden. He stood staring out at the view for a few minutes.

Finally, when he swung around, he said, "I'm going to do what I should have done seventeen years ago. There's no excuse why I didn't search hard enough for her, Uncle Jake. I lost Honey Belle once. I'm not going to lose her again. I only hope she'll have me."

"The boy is sixteen. Young men that age tend to be protective of their mothers and resentful of intruders. You might want to treat this as if you were walking through a mine field."

Tripp turned up the glass and swallowed the last of the vodka. "Honor the codicil, Uncle Jake. My father owes his grandson that much."

****

The insistent ringing of the telephone awakened Honey Belle with a start. As she jumped up to answer it, she realized she had fallen asleep on the sofa.

"Hello?"

"May I speak with Honey Belle Garrett?"

She blinked against the sleep-haze film covering her eyes. Glancing at her watch, she saw it was six o'clock. No one called this early on a Saturday morning.

It surprised her that she had spent the entire night on the couch without waking up once. She must have been extremely tired. On the other hand, the big overstuffed sofa was as comfortable as her bed upstairs.

She coughed to clear the rasp from her throat. "Who is this?"

"It's...Tripp Hartwell. Honey Belle?"

"Do you realize what time it is?" Idiot, stupid thing to say, she berated herself. "Why are you calling?"

"I'm here in Valdosta. I'd like to see JT, and you. It's important."

Afraid she was still asleep and dreaming, Honey Belle gripped the phone.

Tripp broke the silence. "I know it's early. I thought telephoning was better than showing up on your doorstep. How about it—may I come to your house?"

Deeply torn, Honey Belle set her concerns aside. "Yes, of course. I'll make breakfast. Do you need directions?"

His chuckle filtered through the phone lines. "There are certain advantages to knowing the Secret Service. Is eight-thirty too soon?"

She closed her eyes. Behind her lids she could see his face. She remembered what had gone through her mind that day on the steps at the Lincoln Memorial as she had stared back at him, held in the grip of his mesmeric gaze.

Such a beautiful face for a man, she had thought, such a sensitive mouth, and those extraordinary eyes...such a lovely blue, like bits of sky, she had thought then.

Breakfast was the least thing on her mind when she asked, "How do you like your eggs?"

****

"Bogus, Mom. Senator Hartwell is coming here, to our house? Why?"

"I should think it's pretty obvious, JT. He wants to know his son. Are you okay with that?"

"It's weird. I mean, after reading all the articles and stuff about him in the scrapbook... Sure, I guess it's okay."

"You won't be rude?"

"You mean like putting a garter snake in his coat pocket?"

Honey Belle joined her son in raucous laughter

at her son's childish Halloween prank when he disapproved of the man who had come to pick her up for a date. "Poor Mr. Ridley. You scared him bald-headed."

JT managed to contain his laughter. "He was already bald."

She sobered. "I don't think Tripp Hartwell is the type who scares easily."

Her son's knitted brow brought the usual motherly concerns. "Okay, kiddo, spit it. What's on your mind?"

"Nothing."

"Hey, we don't play those games, remember?"

"Do you think he really tried to find you? I mean really seriously."

Honey Belle moved between the gas stove and the countertop next to the sink, washing pots and spoons as she dirtied them.

"It's a fair question. The senator is an honest man. If he says he did, then all we can do is believe he's telling the truth."

"He asked you to marry him once—do you think he will again?"

Startled, Honey Belle gaped at him. "No, absolutely not."

JT said, "What if he did ask you?"

"This is silly." She wiped her hands on the apron tied around her waist, then cupped JT's cheeks. "He's coming to see *you*, not me."

"But would you say, yes, if he did?" JT pressed.

"I honestly don't know."

"Why?"

"Why don't I know? Is that what you mean?"

"Yes."

Honey Belle lifted her shoulders in a small shrug. "I just don't, is all. It would be a big step for me to take, it would mean rearranging my life completely...and yours. Besides, aren't you jumping to an awful lot of conclusions?"

"So what. Ever since you told me about you and the senator, when you were young, and what his old man did to keep you apart, I've given it a lot of thought. If the senator asks, I think you *should* marry him."

"I'm not discussing this any further, JT." She pointed a finger at him. "This subject is no longer open for discussion. Hear me? Closed."

She could feel her close ties to JT stretching. In nine months he would graduate high school and then go off to college. As much as she refused to admit it, he didn't need her as much these days, and with Tripp entering their lives her maternal instincts were all mixed up. She felt as if she were losing control of her life.

JT snapped his fingers in front of Honey Belle's face. "Mom, you zoned out. If you're worried about me pulling a blind side on the senator, don't." He crossed his heart and said, "Scout's honor." He reached around her to sneak a strip of bacon.

She playfully cuffed his shoulder. "Go set the table."

Lately, Tripp was seldom out of her thoughts. Frowning at that admission, she dropped a spoonful of butter into the grits and gave a vigorous stir.

Marriage. Where had JT come up with such an idea? Somehow she couldn't get their discussion out of her head. It would mean leaving Georgia, her job, and all she'd grown to love.

Right now she wished Tess were here to lend moral support, instead of off attending a nurse's retreat in North Carolina.

Chapter Thirty

Tripp needed to see Honey Belle. The sky looked low and bruised. Black thunderheads gathered against the darkening sky. Dense and full-bellied, they threatened the type of summer storm common in the south—intense rain for twenty minutes, then bright clear skies.

He turned into the driveway.

Instead of getting out immediately, he cut the motor and stared at the two-story white house surrounded by tall pine trees and low, neatly trimmed boxwood shrubs. The house and yard looked peaceful and serene. Like a picture on a postcard.

He stepped out of the Lincoln Town Car, unsure of his next step, except that it had to be taken. Waiting for the ideal moment was no longer an option.

It felt good to wear comfortable faded jeans and a golfing shirt—regular clothes. Despite his position in life, he liked to think of himself as a regular guy.

How did one converse with a sixteen-year-old? He tried to recall what he was like at the age of sixteen. What was it Honey Belle had said? Oh, yes. JT excelled in sports. Tripp couldn't remember the last time he'd actually watched a football game on television.

He'd faced a lot of fear in his life—Vietnam, the loss of his leg. Today was no exception. He actually feared the reaction he'd receive from his sixteen-year-old son.

He found Honey Belle waiting when he got to

the house. Apparently, she was anxious to get this meeting over with. She looked pale, carved out of ice. She greeted him with just about the same level of warmth.

****

Honey Belle couldn't deny the thought of seeing Tripp again left an aching emptiness in her heart. Watching him get out of the car and cross over the sidewalk, she wanted him to go away, she wanted him to stay. In all honesty, she didn't know what she wanted but suspected it was about six-foot-two, chisel- featured, fair haired, blue-eyed, tanned. So quick and sprightly and energetic. Full of good humor, tall tales, laughter, and life. No wonder she had fallen in love with him instantly, the first day she had set eyes on him.

So long ago now.

In his faded blue jeans and a pale blue golfing shirt, he cut a crisp stride up the walk. Even with his prosthetic leg, she'd never seen him take an awkward step. Something was wrong. He stopped in the shade of the magnolia tree. His eyes shadowed with determination.

He appeared nervous—unsure—his shoulders tense—his body stiff. Apparently this wasn't easy for him either, which brought some comfort. And he didn't look any happier than she felt.

This morning, he'd said they had to talk. What if he tried to take JT away from her? No, JT was old enough to make his own decisions. Like all sixteen-year-olds, he wanted a car, a dune buggy, a telephone in his room, his own personal television. All the toys every kid desired. In her heart, she trusted her son wasn't so shallow that he would cave in to the lure of money and expensive gifts.

Until this moment, she'd hoped for a reprieve. There was none. No masked man wearing a black cape, riding up on his magnificent black stallion to rescue her. There was only Tripp, and he didn't look any happier than she felt. Where was Zorro when she needed him?

She opened the front door and took a step toward Tripp. "What's so important that you'd leave D.C. and come to Georgia?"

"My father is seriously ill."

As much as she wanted to feel compassion for the Judge, her heart wouldn't allow it.

A crescendo of thunder rolled across the sky. Fat drops of rain splattered the sidewalk, forcing Tripp up the steps and onto the porch.

She drew a breath as he stepped closer. She didn't have the words to respond regarding his father's illness. How could she?

After a second or two of reflection, she opened the screened door. "Please come in. Breakfast is ready. I hope you're hungry."

Tripp followed as she led the way down the hall and to the kitchen at the rear of the house.

"I'm starving, but you didn't have to go to all this trouble, you know."

"It's no problem. With Aunt Tess and JT and me going in different directions during the week, Saturday and Sunday is our family time for a sit-down breakfast."

"Speaking of JT, does he know? About me, I mean?"

Slowly, in an indifferent tone, she said, "Yes."

"And?"

I think you should marry him, Mom. Her mind raced over the unexpected declaration her son had made. She closed her eyes. Behind her lids she recalled the uncertainty she'd read in the face that reminded her so much of his father.

She flinched when Tripp touched her shoulder.

"Honey Belle?

She gave him a measured look. "If you were

221

sixteen and this type of bombshell was dropped on you, how would you feel?"

"Point taken. Does he hate me?"

"JT feels betrayed. By me, mostly."

Honey Belle looked at him, then away as she fought the emotions that threatened to crumple her face. Tucking her hands inside the pockets of her apron, she invited Tripp to sit at the dining table.

****

His chest constricted. He couldn't breathe. JT stood at the second-story bedroom window gazing down at the man who walked up the sidewalk toward the front porch. Tripp Harlan Hartwell, war hero and senator, was his father.

His father. The words echoed inside his head. They sounded so foreign to JT he couldn't grasp the meaning. All his life he'd secretly envied his friends whose dads had coached little league or invited him on camping trips. Yeah, sure, there were times he'd longed for a father and had even conjured up images. Never in his wildest dreams did he imagine he was the illegitimate son of a United States Senator.

JT stood there, his head resting against the window sill, staring out the window, his mind awash with emotions he didn't know how to handle.

He wondered if the senator would sit him down and feed him a line of sorrowful garbage about being a long-lost father, stepping up to the bat, doing the right thing. Sure, he'd told his mom to marry the guy. Did he really mean it? For sixteen years he'd never had to share his mother with anyone. Punching his fist against the wall, JT didn't know how he felt.

His mother's voice filtered up the stairs. "JT, breakfast is ready, and Senator Hartwell is here."

Slowly, he walked across the room and opened the door. Smiling at his once childish prank, he wondered if the senator was afraid of snakes.

****

Tripp's heart did a funny little lurch when JT entered the kitchen. He looked at the boy in front of him. Tall, broad of shoulder, hair the color of beach sand, and eyes that were clearly sizing him up, wary.

Offering his hand, he watched a slight hesitation before JT accepted. Good, Tripp thought, a firm handshake. In fact, the boy tightened his grip and matched Tripp's stare. *He's letting me know I'm treading on his territory.* The trait appealed to Tripp.

"Just so you know, Senator, you hurt my mom and I'll knock your block off." JT lifted his chin, his blue eyes unwavering.

Honey Belle gasped. "Jack Tripp Garrett, you apologize this instant."

Tripp wanted to laugh out loud. Instead, he smiled. "No apology necessary. I respect any man who stands up for his mother."

Honey Belle picked up the coffee pot. "Well, okay then. Let's eat before the grits get too stiff to soak up the egg yolks."

Rather than sitting in stony silence, or suffering through meaningless small talk, Tripp filled his plate with grits, two eggs, bacon, and a biscuit. "I haven't had a good southern breakfast since my mother passed away."

Silence followed on the heels of polite requests to pass the strawberry preserves or for more coffee, until JT blurted out, "Why are you here, Senator?"

"JT, I swear, where are your manners?"

"It's a fair question, Honey Belle." Tripp could feel the boy's anger coming in waves. "If I were wearing your shoes, JT, I'm not sure how I'd react. This is new territory for both of us. Right now we're treading water—not knowing which way to swim. It isn't every day a man learns he has a son, much less a sixteen-year-old son. If you think I'm here to change your life or take your mother away from you—that's the least thing on my mind."

"Same question—why are you here?"

"Several reasons, good ones, I hope. Are you willing to listen and give me a fair chance?"

JT nodded.

"First, my father is an old man. A few days ago, he confessed to his duplicity. What he did to your mother was reprehensible. I'll make no excuses for him." Tripp drew in a sigh and blew it out. "The thing is, JT, he'd like to meet his only grandchild."

Tripp watched JT weighing the question before giving an answer. Without glancing at Honey Belle, Tripp felt her tension.

"I'm not sure I want to meet him. I mean, I don't owe him anything."

"No, you don't. My father is dying. Oh, I know you might see this as a pitiful excuse for my asking you to go see an old man who did a grave injustice to your mother...and to me. The thing is, JT, a man's character is determined by the maturity of his decisions."

JT loaded his fork with eggs and grits. Then as if he'd lost his appetite, he set the fork aside. "You said there were other reasons for coming here."

Tripp was impressed by his son's directness. "Through circumstances beyond my control, I've been denied the right to know you. I missed your birth, I've missed out on your first words, first steps. I see by the trophies you're an excellent athlete. I've missed your games, missed sitting beside your mother in the bleachers, cheering for you. You're sixteen. I can't make up for the lost years, but if you'll give me the opportunity, I'd like to get to know you. Maybe we can eventually become friends."

"And my mom, what are your intentions toward her?"

This time Tripp laughed out loud. "JT, my

mother—your grandmother—would have spoiled you rotten. You have her directness. In fact, I see much of her in your facial expressions. She was also a master gardener. Do you like gardening?"

Not to be shut out of the conversation, Honey Belle said, "I've always wondered where JT inherited his green thumb. Aunt Tess and I are pitiful when it comes to growing flowers and vegetables. Not JT. Even as a little boy, he loved digging in the dirt and making things grow."

"Mom...that's embarrassing."

She smiled, cut her eyes at the man sitting across the table from her son. "He even likes cheeseburgers, extra pickles, hold the onions."

"Man, Mom, you're killing me, telling all this personal stuff."

"No kidding. You like cheeseburgers, extra pickles, hold the onions?" Tripp beamed.

"Yeah, so?"

"Tell him, Honey Belle."

When she blushed, Tripp had the urge to kiss her petal-pink lips. She was incredibly beautiful, watching him. He felt his loins stir. Shifting in his chair, he reached for his cup, grimacing at the cold coffee's bitter taste.

"Your father, that is to say, the Senator—" her hands fluttered as if she was confused about what to call him in front of her son. "Anyhow, I suppose you still order your hamburgers the same as when we first met."

"Exactly the same."

An awkward moment passed as if no one at the table knew what to say next. Tripp's mood took a nose dive. This was tougher than he'd expected. He braced his wrists against the table.

"My last reason for being here is your mother. When I was wounded in Vietnam and half out of my mind with delirium in a field hospital, more dead

Loretta C. Rogers

than alive, I thought I saw your mother smiling down at me." Tripp hesitated. What could he say to win over his son without sounding maudlin? "Look, JT, in all these years I've never stopped loving your mother. I didn't know why she'd left South Carolina. Then, to be honest, when I found out she'd lied about where she lived, I was hurt, even angry. Things happened. I married, joined the Army, immersed myself in politics. Until a few days ago, I thought your mom was lost to me forever, and I didn't know I had a son. All this may sound like pathetic excuses to you. Unless I miss my guess, you're a judicious young man. The truth is, JT, I'd like your permission to date your mom."

There. He'd laid it on the line—all his reasons for coming to Valdosta. The ball was in his son's court. As much as he wanted to reach out and clasp Honey Belle's slender, delicate hands, Tripp refrained from touching her.

His senses on edge, a drip from the kitchen faucet seemed to crescendo in his ears. Tripp worked to quell his impatience as he watched the turmoil in his son's young face. The very act of wrestling with a grown-up decision was written in the creases of his forehead, the taut muscles in his neck, the stiffness in his shoulders.

Always one to tackle a problem head-on, Tripp worried he'd asked too much too soon.

****

JT scooted the chair from the table. He stood. "The Three Musketeers, you, me and Aunt Tess. That's what you used to call us. Remember?"

Honey Belle smiled and nodded.

His face sobered as he continued. "I'm not sure I want that to change." He shrugged his shoulders forward. "Aunt Tess is getting older, I'm going off to college... Kids my age don't usually worry about stuff like this, but I don't want you to be alone one day."

Honey Belle stared at her son, touched by his words. Then her brow drew together in a furrow. "You're worrying about my old age, is that it, JT?"

Laughing, he shook his head. "Well, you *are* thirty-five."

"I'm not exactly in my dotage yet," she shot back, laughing with him.

JT's face sobered as he continued. He met Tripp's gaze, gave him a piercing look. "When I was little, I used to hear my mother crying...sobbing as if her heart was breaking. I would stand outside the door and listen, hurting for her, wondering if I was the reason for her sadness. But I didn't dare go in, even though I wanted to comfort her."

"You could have," Honey Belle's voice was soft, touched by his words.

"I once asked you why you cried at night, when I was a little bit older. Do you remember?"

"Yes, vaguely."

"Do you remember what you said?"

Honey Belle shook her head.

"You told me you cried because you'd lost someone you'd loved very much. When I asked you who, you wouldn't answer me, you just turned away. Then, that time we saw the soldiers' names on the TV screen, I figured you were crying for my father."

He looked into her face. His own had a loving expression on it. Slowly, he said, "It hurt my heart to hear you crying. I wanted to help you and I didn't know how. For as long as I can remember, it's worried me that you cried that way."

Honey Belle, wiped the tears only to have more spill from her eyes. "Oh, JT."

"Senator, I guess it was you she was crying for. Maybe you can make up for...everyone that hurt her."

Tripp swallowed the lump that threatened to choke him. "We'll do it together, son."

Chapter Thirty-One

Tripp felt as if he'd won some, lost some. Who was keeping score? Not him. With a mutual cessation of hostilities and the white flag from all sides, JT had agreed to visit his grandfather.

In the time following that visit, the Judge had begun to lose his bitter edge toward Honey Belle. He'd fooled science and the doctors by living months longer than the original prognosis. Insisting on attending his grandson's high school graduation, he had proclaimed JT's valedictorian speech as nothing less than brilliant.

And then after dinner he'd dropped the bombshell.

Honey Belle walked to the porch, where the Judge sat in his wheelchair. "Would you like a glass of tea, Judge?"

"I've never been one to bandy with words. My motto is say what you have to say. Girl, do you love my son?" the Judge fixed her with a look.

"Well, I..." Honey Belle had found it difficult to stand her ground with her old nemesis, but she straightened her spine and stood tall. "As a matter of fact, I do."

His voice had lost some of its timbre. Nonetheless, he bellowed. "Tripp, you and JT get yourselves out here."

Honey Belle clenched her hands.

Tripp pushed through the screened door. "What's wrong, Father?"

"Nothing. I'm righting another wrong. This girl says she loves you."

"My name is Honey Belle, Judge Hartwell. I'll thank you not to call me 'girl.'"

Shrugging his shoulder as if ignoring her plaint, he said, "My days are numbered. I want my grandson to carry the Hartwell name. Why haven't you proposed to this girl...er...Honey Belle?"

JT cut his eyes toward her. "Mom, I don't want to change my name."

"Of course you do." The Judge banged his hand on the arm of the wheelchair. "Tripp Hartwell the Fourth has a nice ring to it."

"No, sir. Father, if my son agrees, the name on the adoption papers will read Jack Tripp Garrett Hartwell."

"So be it. Now, do I have to propose to Honey Belle for you?"

Tripp looked at his son. After a year of getting to know each other, their bond, while tenuous, seemed to grow stronger each day. "JT?"

JT smiled and with a nod gave his approval.

Tripp reached out and drew Honey Belle forward. He felt the slight resistance. His mouth slowly lowered over hers, gently stealing her breath away. When he lifted his head, he said, "Honey Belle Garrett, will you do me the honor of becoming my wife and making me the happiest man in the world?"

"On two conditions, Senator Hartwell."

Tripp cut his eyes toward JT. They both shrugged their shoulders. He warily answered, "Only two?"

"Yes. First, no lengthy engagement. I've waited long enough."

With a twitch of his lips, Tripp raised an eyebrow. "Your wish is my command. And condition number two?"

Honey Belle's eyes were serious. "No reporters or television cameras, no Washington, D.C. sensationalism, no expensive wedding dress, no towering cake, and a guest list limited to family. And a simple ceremony where my son—our son—walks me down the aisle, with Aunt Tess as matron of honor."

Tripp's lips lifted into a small smile. "I have a request of my own."

Placing her hands on her hips, she cast him a lofty look. "And it is?"

"If you don't mind traveling to Charleston, I'd like to hold the wedding in my mother's garden. I think she'd be pleased."

Sudden tears filled Honey Belle's eyes. "That's a perfectly beautiful idea."

Tripp gave her cheek a lingering caress. He mouthed softly, "I love you."

The Judge made a small, satisfied grunt. "This is an auspicious day and deserves a beverage stronger than sweet tea."

Honey Belle offered her future father-in-law a warm smile. "We have a bottle of sangria. Will that do?"

****

Two weeks later, on the second Saturday in June, Honey Belle stared into the mirror and saw a stranger, a woman in a delicate white dress. Today was her wedding day.

A bride.

She stood in the middle of the room, thinking how welcoming it was, struck by its warmth and charm. It was of medium size, with mauve walls, tastefully decorated. A dark red-and-blue Oriental rug in front of the fireplace. A canopied bed. Between the two tall windows, an antique desk facing out toward the back garden with its arched bridge over a koi pond.

It was a lovely summer day. The sky was cerulean blue, clear and cloudless, filled with sunshine, and the foliage in the garden was spectacular. The massive oak trees were a riotous mass of green.

"We couldn't have asked for a better day," Tess said, glancing out the window, looking down at the garden. "It's perfect for a wedding."

Joining her aunt at the window, Honey Belle said, "Thank you for being here with me these past two weeks, and for doing so much to help with the wedding."

"You are more than my niece, you're the daughter I've never had. And, JT, well, what can I say—he stole my heart the day I helped bring him into this world. Lending a hand with the wedding is nothing compared to your happiness and knowing my nephew's future is secure." Tess gently dabbed a tear from Honey Belle's cheek. "Why are you crying? You'll ruin your make-up."

"This—" Honey Belle spread her arms wide— "all of this...Tripp, the wedding...this old magnificent house. It's like a fairy tale come true. I'm afraid I'll wake up and discover it's all a dream."

The painful pinch to the fleshy part of Honey Belle's arm brought a resounding, "Ouch! Why did you do that?"

Tess leaned into Honey Belle and kissed her on the cheek. "To prove a point. None of this is a dream, because you are obviously wide awake."

Honey Belle was silent.

Tess looked at her niece. "Spit it out. What else is on your mind?"

Honey Belle glanced out the window again, her face thoughtful when she finally turned toward her aunt. "Not so long ago, JT expressed concern because he didn't want me to be alone when he went away to college. Oh, Aunt Tess, South Carolina is a long way from Georgia. I wish I didn't have to live so far from you."

Tess said, "As it turns out, I'm not going to be so

far away after all."

"*Oh?*"

"Umm-huh. The senator is not only a prize catch, he's also quite astute. Suspecting you'd feel this way, he made me an offer I couldn't refuse."

Honey Belle shook her head. "Don't keep me in suspense. Tell me what conspiracy the two of you have cooked up behind my back."

"At sixty-six, I'm no spring chicken, though I've still got a lot of spark left in me. With my nursing experience and with a recommendation from the senator, I am now a part-time nursing instructor at The Citadel."

Honey Belle gasped her delight. "That's wonderful! But what about your house?"

"Put it up for sale as soon I knew the teaching position was secured." Tess pointed to a building at the edge of the property. "That's the old horse stable. For years it's been used for storage. The senator hired a contractor to completely renovate it into a cottage. He told the contractor to work with me on the design."

Choked up, unable to speak, Honey Belle placed her hands against her heart.

A loud rap against the closed bedroom door released Honey Belle from her emotions. JT called, "Mom...are you ready?"

****

Dressed in a gray tuxedo, Tripp waited inside the gazebo. His Uncle Jake, serving as best man, stood next to him.

His father and assorted aunts, uncles, and cousins, all sworn to secrecy, were the only guests. His Uncle Jake would make the official announcement of the wedding after Tripp and Honey Belle's plane left for a honeymoon at an undisclosed destination.

Tripp's eyes met his father's, and he smiled.

With his failing health, the Judge had charged his brother, Jake, with the duties of best man.

"Nervous?"

Tripp glanced at his uncle. He refused to admit to pre-wedding jitters. Hell, when he analyzed it, what did he know about love and marriage, and all the rest? His personal experiences hadn't given him much reason to trust the "weaker" sex. As a result, he'd held his emotions in check for years, never allowing himself a close relationship with any woman.

"Shaking like a leaf, Uncle Jake."

His uncle grinned and gave Tripp an encouraging pat on the back.

Tripp watched Tess rush up the path leading to the gazebo and take her position. Breathless, the spritely woman smiled up at Tripp. "She's ready."

Tripp nodded to the pianist. At the first chords of the wedding march, the guests stood and turned expectantly toward the bride. Tripp watched as his son, tall and handsome, escorted his mother along the path leading to the koi pond.

His soul stood still.

Whatever doubts he'd had melted away.

****

The melodic notes of the Wedding March, mixing with the trilling of birds in the sunshine, carried the weight of the song—a pledge of fidelity and a promise for tomorrow.

A path wound its way to the koi pond. Standing at the top of the arched bridge, with her arm linked through her son's, Honey Belle saw Tripp—tall and straight, his hair streaked with gold, his eyes blue but unwavering. A sense of peace flowed over her. Until this moment, she'd questioned her decision to marry Tripp. Now she felt grounded. This was where she belonged. With this man.

The center of all eyes, she drew a deep breath

and began to walk forward in time to the music.

At the gazebo, she took her place in front of the altar.

The minister said, "Who gives this woman in marriage?"

Her heart swelled with love when JT placed her hand in Tripp's and then placed his own over theirs. "I do, sir. I give my mother and father to each other."

Honey Belle felt Tripp's strong grasp and lowered her eyes, afraid to reveal how he moved her. She beseeched her thumping heart to be still, but her heart wasn't listening.

The minister spoke. "Do you take this man as your husband?"

She clutched the flowers Tripp had gathered that morning from his mother's garden. Tess had fashioned them into a bouquet, tied with a white ribbon. Honey Belle's emotions felt as scattered as the scudding clouds in the sky.

She had dreamed of this moment, longed for it, planned for it. She allowed the clouds to carry away any doubts she had about binding herself to Tripp Harlan Hartwell the Third.

"Yes." The word came strong and with assurance.

She listened as Tripp promised to love, honor, and cherish her for the rest of his days. He steadied her hand as he slipped the Scottish Thistle and Celtic Knot wedding band on her finger.

Repeating her vows of devotion through sickness and sorrow, she eased the Scottish Rite Eagle ring over Tripp's knuckle and saw the tenderness in his eyes as his gaze drifted over her.

The reverend pronounced them husband and wife. "You may kiss the bride."

Tripp took her mouth gently. She felt the hunger in his kiss...and trembled.

Chapter Thirty-Two

Tripp pressed the door to his bedroom shut and secured the lock. "Do you think we fooled them?"

Honey Belle stood in the middle of the dimly lit room. She suppressed a tremble. "It's a well conceived plan. I have every confidence that JT and Aunt Tess pulled it off without a hitch. Everyone will think we're off to our honeymoon."

With his father's failing health, Honey Belle had worried the Judge might not live until she and Tripp returned from a month-long romantic retreat.

"Our son was very smart to suggest he and Tess take our place in the limousine. With the darkened windows, no one will know the difference. And all the time we'll be right here."

With an audible sigh, Honey Belle placed Tripp's hands around her waist. "How long do you think before someone finds out?"

He drew Honey Belle to his chest. "I told my secretary I was taking a hiatus in Australia, and I'd phone in for updates. With my father at the care center, I don't have to worry about being away in case of an emergency."

She sighed. "Do you suppose JT and Aunt Tess will enjoy trekking around Australia? It's a little out of the ordinary for a seventeen-year-old and his elderly aunt to travel together."

With the drapes drawn, the room was dark. Tripp released Honey Belle long enough to switch on a lamp. "You raised our son right, Honey Belle. JT loves and respects Tess. I'll stake my life they come back with dozens of stories about their adventures, and photographs to match."

"You don't think any of your family members will alert the press about us, do you?"

"You know the old saying, 'There's always one bad apple in the barrel.' If the press finds out, we'll handle it together."

He bent his head to claim her mouth. "Enough talk. Let's begin our own adventure."

Honey Belle teased, "Where are we going, Senator Hartwell?"

"To the island of love and exploration, Mrs. Hartwell." He kissed her until she had no resistance left. And when he reached for the zipper on the back of her dress, she let him.

"Tripp," she whispered, "I haven't...not since...you."

He slipped the dress off her shoulders. "You mean...never once? Not since the last time we made love at Folley Beach?"

She loved him so much her heart almost ached with happiness. "Uh-huh."

She wanted to lose herself in him, to feel the touch of his hands, the taste of his mouth, the heat generated by their bodies. Just thinking about his hands caressing her again took her breath away. Her nipples began to tingle, and she felt an exotic warmth between her legs.

Moments later, the sheets on the bed felt cold against her naked skin, but not for long.

Tripp's heart banged against his chest. Caught up in the emotions of the day, he suddenly felt inadequate and uncertain.

She patted the edge of the bed. "I thought it was the bride who was supposed to be nervous. Aren't you going to undress? Or shall I do it for you?"

She watched as a war of emotions played across his face. "What is it... Is it me?"

When he didn't answer, she said, "Tripp, please,

whatever it is that's bothering you, let's talk about it."

The edge of the mattress sagged when he sat down. "My prosthetic leg is so much a part of me... If making love to a one-legged man repulses you, I'll understand. I should have discussed this with you long before asking you to marry me."

He raked a hand through his hair. "I'm sorry. If you'd like to file for an annulment, I'll not resist."

She sat up, the sheet dropping away to reveal her breast as she took his hands and laced her fingers through his. Her voice was soft and gentle. "I don't know much about your first wife, only what I heard on the television and in the papers, but she must have hurt you terribly for you to think I'd reject you for any reason. I love you, Tripp...your heart, your soul, your gentleness, the relationship you've built with our son.

"I've always known about your leg. All the media outlets were filled with your heroic deeds in Vietnam, and the loss of your leg. I wanted so much to hold you, to let you know how much I ached for you. I'm the one who was a coward. Trust me when I say I've never thought of you as anything other than the man I want to grow old and gray with. Please, let me see you—all of you."

For Tripp, her words were a gift from God. Still hesitant, he slipped off his shoes. He removed his shirt, his slacks. He watched Honey Belle's face, searching for the slightest repulsion. He detected no uneasiness, no roll of emotion when he unbuckled the straps, removed the artificial limb and then the protective stocking to reveal the stump that dangled below his knee. He didn't turn to look at her just then. For some reason he couldn't.

Honey Belle surprised him when she squeezed his hand, let go, and moved closer. She draped his arm around her and laid her head against his shoulder. He could smell her, soft, like orange blossoms, and warm. In that quiet moment, thunder rumbled in the distance. Their eyes met and Tripp's senses reeled. He felt his loins stir.

There was tightness in his voice, and Honey Belle could hear his pain. "Are you sure, Honey Belle?"

She leaned in and felt the heat between them, felt his body tremble with the same anticipation she had felt the first time they were together so many years ago.

Lightning cut across the sky, and the thunder rolled, vibrating the old house. It felt right to be here. Everything felt right. The brewing storm made it even more perfect. And then rain pelted against the windowpanes, as if God had sent the rain to wash away years of hurt, doubt, and loneliness.

Honey Belle lifted her head and looked at him with hazy eyes, and Tripp kissed her softly on the lips. When she kissed him back, the years of separation dissolved into passion.

She took his hand and led it to her breasts, and a whimper rose in her throat as he gently touched them, and she was suddenly short of breath as he lowered his head and kissed between them and slowly sampled one and then the other.

Their bodies came together almost in slow motion, both of them trembling with the memory of what they had once shared, what they were about to share.

****

He was struck by her beauty, and the way her hair shimmered in the light. Her skin was soft and beautiful in the lamp's glow. Her hands on his back beckoned him.

He lowered her to the bed. She arched as he rolled atop her in one fluid movement, and then he was on all fours above her, his knees astride her hips.

She lifted her head and kissed his chest, his shoulders, ran her hands through his hair as he held himself above her, his arm muscles straining from the exertion. With a tempting little frown she pulled him closer. He kissed every inch of her body, listening as she made soft whimpering sounds. And when they finally joined as one, she cried aloud, her fingers pressed hard into his shoulders.

****

She buried her face in his neck and felt him deep inside her, felt his strength and gentleness, felt the hurt ebb from his soul. She moved rhythmically against him, allowing him to take her wherever he wanted, to the place where they were meant to be.

She opened her eyes and watched him, marveling at his beauty as he moved above her. She saw his body glisten with sweat and tasted the saltiness of it with her tongue. Their bodies reflected everything given, everything taken, and she was rewarded with a sensation she'd forgotten existed. It went on and on, the ebb and flow, and she struggled to catch her breath while she trembled beneath him. But the moment it was over another wave overtook her, and she rode the crests one right after another, until her body was exhausted, yet unwilling to stop the pleasure between them.

****

They spent the day in each other's arms, alternately making love and, when exhausted, napping. Sometimes Tripp would wake up and look at her, her body soft and radiant, and feel as if everything was suddenly right in his world.

Then, when they were ready, they would join together while he whispered endearments between kisses as they wrapped their arms around each other. They went on throughout the evening making up for the years they were apart.

Once when he was watching her in the moments before daybreak, her eyes fluttered open and she smiled and reached up to touch his face. He gently placed his fingers on her lips to keep her from speaking. It was as if she knew what he was thinking, and for a long moment neither of them spoke.

He fought to swallow the lump in his throat. When he was finally able to speak, he whispered, "You are the answer to every prayer I've offered. I never want to live without you again. I love you, Honey Belle, more than you can ever imagine. I always have and always will."

He looked at her and found her eyes filled with unshed tears. For him. She smiled through the moisture, and he knew that somehow she understood all he was feeling.

"Oh, Tripp, I know it sounds like a cliché, but you really do make my heart sing." She pulled him toward her, needing him again.

The feelings inside him rolled like ocean waves.

Their bodies sated with passion, Honey Belle took a shower, then Tripp. When he came out and found her asleep, he set his crutches aside and climbed into bed beside her and drew her close to his body, her curves molding perfectly to his.

A black cloud enveloped Tripp, threatening to obliterate the hours of happiness he'd shared with his new wife as thoughts of Kathryn slipped in. He pushed the memories aside.

Honey Belle's eyes fluttered open as if she knew he was watching her. Her voice was heavy with sleep. "You're wonderful..." Her voice trailed off into slumber.

Honey Belle's words struck a deep chord in his heart. And while sleep overtook him, he thought about their future together and all the ways he planned to make her happy.

Chapter Thirty-Three

An off-key whistling drifted to Honey's Belle's ears. She had slept late, catching up on some much-needed rest. She shifted to a more comfortable position against the pillow. As much as she wanted to close her eyes and drift back to sleep, savory aromas of bacon and coffee drifted up to the bedroom, tantalizing her nose. Sitting up, she stretched and yawned. A man in the kitchen cooking breakfast, while she slept away the morning, was a fantasy come true.

Showered and dressed in tan khaki shorts, yellow T-shirt, and bare feet, and in high spirits, Honey Belle bounded downstairs to the kitchen. Tripp stood facing the stove. She slid her arms around his waist. The smell of his cologne, his clean hair, and his body overwhelmed her.

The heat of that body drew her closer. "I never knew a man could look so sexy while scrambling eggs."

Tripp moved the frying pan from the burner and switched off the stove. He turned in Honey Belle's arms. "And you, Mrs. Hartwell, look good enough to eat."

Honey Belle stared deeply into his smoky-blue eyes. Very slowly, taking her time, never breaking eye contact, she raised her mouth to his. She parted her lips slightly and their breaths mingled. He tightened his hold around her waist and pressed his mouth hard against hers. She tasted the tip of his tongue.

Lightheaded and unsteady, she was glad he held

her, because at that moment she knew she swayed on her feet.

As their tongues met and tasted one another, she felt as if the earth had shifted on its axis. She heard his sharply indrawn breath, felt the heat emanating from his body. When they finally parted, breathless and panting, nothing seeming the same as it had a moment before.

Honey Belle lifted a hand to Tripp's cheek. "Wow."

"Wow," he repeated.

Her eyes met his and her breath seized in her chest. A fire burned in his eyes, and its heat focused on her. His mouth claimed hers with a passion that stole the breath from her throat and weakened her knees.

She clung to him, surrendering to an igniting desire so intense, she quivered. "Th-the eggs are getting cold."

He groaned deep inside his throat. His lips nipped the column of her neck. "Forget about the eggs. I'm hungry for something else."

She did not answer for a moment or two. She simply returned his penetrating gaze. Unexpected tears welled in her eyes. She swallowed hard, trying to push them back. She could not. Slowly they rolled down her cheeks. "You make me feel complete, whole."

Tripp lifted his hand and wiped the tears away with his fingertips. As he kissed her cheeks and her eyes, he said against her damp face, "I've always loved you, Honey Belle. From now on there will be only happiness in our lives. I'm going to make sure of that."

His words melted Honey Belle's heart.

"When I was a little girl, I used to pull the petals off wild daisies, praying the last petal would say he loved me. Only I didn't know until I met you who *he* was."

She tucked her arm through his, and together they moved toward the stairs and their second-story bedroom. They had the rest of their lives together. Eternity.

Thank you for purchasing
this Wild Rose Press publication.
For other wonderful stories of romance,
please visit our on-line bookstore at
www.thewildrosepress.com.

For questions or more information
contact us at
info@thewildrosepress.com.

The Wild Rose Press
www.TheWildRosePress.com

To visit with authors of The Wild Rose Press
join our yahoo loop at
http://groups.yahoo.com/group/thewildrosepress/